D0567377

HOOD WINKED

the spy who didn't die

*'Tis strange,— but true; for truth
is always strange; stranger than fiction…*

Lord Byron's famous poem
Don Juan, canto 14

Lowell Green

Lowell Green

2010

**Spruce Ridge
Publishing**

ISBN 978-0-9813149-0-7
Printed and bound in Canada

Publisher's note: This book is a work of fiction but contains numerous facts that are identified as such. Most of the characters are historical figures, but some of the events characters, places and incidents either are the product of the author's imagination or are used fictitiously and any resemblance to actual person living or dead is entirely coincidental.

This book was written, published, edited and printed in Canada without the aid of government grants of any nature.

Design and pre-press W. E. O'Keefe
Author photo Couvrette/Ottawa

Library and Archives Canada Cataloguing in Publication

Green, Lowell, 1936-
    Hoodwinked : the spy who didn't die / Lowell Green.

ISBN 978-0-9813149-0-7

    1. Gouzenko, Igor--Fiction. I. Title.

PS8563.R41663H66 2009   C813'.54   C2009-905459-0

This book is dedicated to my three grandchildren,
Samantha, Peyton and Rowan,
who are already developing a love of reading.
May your questions never cease.

Author's Note

SEPARATING FACT FROM FICTION is never easy, especially since there are frequently several versions of "facts."

What I have done here, to the best of my ability and through the use of footnotes, is to identify the facts of which we can be reasonably certain. The rest of the story—well—you decide!

Although this book is a work of fiction, it contains many historical facts. Nazi Germany's genocidal plans for the Soviet Union during WWII and the atrocities in Minsk are well documented.

Documentation concerning the Cold War that followed is much more difficult to verify. Some of the stories we have come to believe may be true. Others may not. That, after all, is the nature of espionage!

Many mysteries remain unsolved concerning the spy world that surrounded atom bomb secrets and the Manhattan Project, not the least of which is the following very puzzling fact.

For 57 years, from 1893 when he was an 18-year-old student at the University of Toronto, until two days prior to his death in 1950, William Lyon Mackenzie King faithfully kept a very detailed daily diary of virtually every aspect of his life, including the time he spent as Canadian Prime Minister from 1921 to 1930, and again from 1935 to 1948. It is an incredible 30,000 pages.

On display now at Library and Archives Canada, the unedited King diaries reveal fascinating and often intimate details including his conversations with his dead mother. Incredibly, for all those 57 years, King did not miss a single day's entry—except for one glaring exception: two entire months—November and December 1945 are mysteriously missing! *

It was during those two months that the Cold War was launched with the reported defection of Igor Gouzenko in Ottawa. There has never been a plausible explanation for those missing pages. At least not until now!

Lowell Green, October 2009
Ottawa, Canada

FACT: Mackenzie King's diaries can be viewed at Library and Archives Canada or at « www.CollectionsCanada.gc.ca », all 30,000 pages—except for those two missing months! The strangely missing entries are mentioned in one of the most definitive books available concerning the "Gouzenko Affair." The book, entitled *How the Cold War Began: The Gouzenko Affair and the Hunt for Soviet Spies* is authored by American journalist Amy Knight and published November 2008 by McClelland & Stewart.

The Call

CAUTION DICTATES that I not reveal my name until I can be assured that my family's lives are not at risk for what is revealed in this account. I will identify myself simply as "N."

When you do what I do as long as I have, you develop a kind of sixth sense to sniff out nutcase phone calls. This caller doesn't sound whacko, but I have to admit his story is about as off-the-wall wild as anything I'd ever heard. Crazy I mean, and yet! And yet! Check the facts as I have, do the research, and you will be astonished to learn that many of the events he relates here are a matter of recorded history. The more I dig into his claims, the more I come to realize that this man at the other end of the phone is either the world's best actor or, just maybe, he is telling the truth!

"I can't meet you," he says, "I'm not even in your country. And by the way, do not try to trace this call; far smarter people than you or I have made sure you can't." The voice sounds tired, too old for stupid games, very serious, quite formal, with just a hint of an accent. Hungarian I think, maybe Czech, and something else I just can't quite place. You can tell almost immediately that he is educated, cultured and well-read.

"You're going to get some tape recordings in a few days," he says, "listen carefully to them please. They tell what I think you will find to be a shocking and fascinating story. You'll probably find it hard to believe, but if you listen to them all, I think you will agree this is a story the world needs to hear."

Before I can say anything, he adds hurriedly, "I know, I know you're wondering why I'm sending the tapes to you and listen, I don't blame you if you think I'm just a crazy old man, but give me a moment and let me explain.

"I've been reading your column and blog on the Internet for a long time now here in my safe little hideaway and am convinced you've got enough guts and I hope enough curiosity to at least listen to what I've got to say and then tell the world about the lies you've all been fed."

He's got me intrigued so I let him continue.

"I've got to be honest with you, it's my wife who has finally convinced me it's time to set the record straight. 'Stop watching all those stupid old black and white movies,' she nags me, 'and instead of reading all those books, why don't you *write* one? Your story is far more interesting than anything I see on the shelves around here.'

"She's probably got a good idea, but let's be perfectly frank, the calendar says I don't have enough time to write a book. Over the years I've jotted down a few notes and kept a few records and my memory, thank heavens, is still very good, so I have this idea that I'll tell you my story, complete with all my "dirty laundry," and hopefully you will finish the job for me."

Experience has taught me that the best question is often silence so I pause for several seconds. There's a long sigh and he continues. "She's right you know, I've let the lies go unchallenged far too long." There's another brief pause. "If you do what I hope and pray that you do—compare my story with the known facts—you can't conclude anything other than what I am about to tell you is the truth, the absolute truth: Every word of it."

I'm about to ask him his name when he hangs up!

I never talk to him again. A series of recorded tapes arrives three days later, carefully boxed and delivered by hand to the security desk at my office building.

I take them home and hole up there for a few days, unable to stop listening. His "Western" expressions puzzle me at first and make me suspicious, but when I learn he's spent much of his life in the West and is a great fan of old Hollywood movies it all makes sense. When I finish, I am absolutely gobsmacked! And I know what I must do.

Here, with my occasional comments, and a few slight revisions to grammar and tense for clarification, is the story they tell.

Signed, "N"
October, 2009

Photograph of Dumbarton Oaks mansion, 3101 R Street NW,
Georgetown, Washington, DC, USA

I Am Alive!

MY NAME IS IGOR GOUZENKO. You believe I am dead. The history books certainly say so. They report I died near Toronto in 1982, just as they claim it was I who triggered the Cold War by defecting from the Soviet Embassy in Ottawa on September 5, 1945, bringing with me a long list of the names and secrets of Soviet spies operating in the US and Canada. Wrong! Dead wrong! While I cannot say at the age of 89 I am very much alive, I am nonetheless, as they say, still kicking, albeit with a few more aches and pains than I'd like.

As for the defection part, don't feel badly if you believe it because at least for a while even that doddering old fool of a prime minister you had, Mackenzie King, and "the buck stops here" guy, American President Harry Truman, bought that one. How do you Canadians say it? Hook, line and sinker!

Actually, I now know that at some time fairly early in my ordeal, Truman was told of what they were doing to me, but in the fall of 1945 and spring of 1946, the President of the United States had a few things on his mind more important than the fate of one poor bugger from the Soviet Union.

And by the way, one of the facts you might start checking into is this: For 57 years Mackenzie King faithfully kept a very detailed daily diary, which included such personal matters as his conversations with his dead mother. That entire diary is in your National Archives today, complete except for one very curious thing. Two entire months are missing. Two months missing from 57 years of daily record keeping! What do you suppose those months might be? Check it out. Missing are November and December 1945.

Why is that time period so important? I'll tell you why. Because during those two months in 1945, Prime Minister Mackenzie King's government, along with the FBI and others, including perhaps the dreaded Soviet Secret Police were hunting me down like a dog so they could kill me. I'll bet no history book you ever read told you that. Impossible, you say. Really! Well just listen to what I have to say. Listen to all of it. Then and only then can you make an informed decision. And if what I am about to tell you is not true, then the question remains. Why are those mysterious two months missing from King's dairy?

Those who chronicle are correct with some facts. It is true I was born on January 13, 1919, in the small town of Rahachow, about 30 kilometres from Minsk in what is now Belarus but was then the Byelorussian Soviet Socialist Republic, part of the Soviet Union.

As for the rest of it, well let me set the record straight.

None of what I am about to tell you would have happened, certainly not to me, if they hadn't killed that poor wee fellow. That little boy. And we have no one but that rotten pervert Klaus Fuchs to thank for that. Oh I know, everyone today claims that skinny piece of dog dirt only sold out his country because of his political beliefs. The little bastard wanted to save the world from the terrible Americans is what some believe even today, but I know better.

There was nothing noble about Klaus Fuchs, believe me. He showed Stalin how to make an atomic bomb and handed over all the other secrets of the Manhattan Project to the Soviets only because it was Moscow supplying him with little boys. Good old Fuchs had a voracious appetite for three things: booze, cigarettes and boys. When it came to the latter, the more tender the years the better. Hell, he would have sold his mother to the devil for a ten-year-old! *

I know a lot about what really happened in those grim days and not just what J. Edgar Hoover and the FBI wanted you to know, but I admit I don't know who killed that poor little boy, or why. I suppose his parents must have learned what was going on and threatened to turn Fuchs in to MI5 or the FBI or expose him to the newspapers for the pervert he was. I'm pretty certain Anatoli Yakovlev had a hand in it. He was the Soviet vice-consul in New York City at the time and he controlled Fuchs. From what I know of the delightful Mr. Yakovlev, he would gladly have set fire to the Vatican, rather than have the guy feeding him all the A-bomb secrets be tumbled by some snot-nosed kid. Yakovlev was a true acolyte of Stalin.**

---

* **FACT:** Klaus Fuchs passed secrets concerning both the atom and hydrogen bombs to the Soviets. He was convicted of espionage in January 1950, and sentenced to 14 years in jail—the maximum penalty for passing military secrets to a friendly nation. Prior to the "Gouzenko Affair," the Soviet Union was considered a friendly nation.

** **FACT:** Yakovlev was indeed the Soviet vice-consul in 1945 and history records show that he "controlled" Klaus Fuchs.

And then, of course, there's the role played in all of this by that uptight, snotty "superspy" Alger Hiss, the great "fixer" at Dumbarton Oaks and the Yalta Conference.* Wait until I tell you about him! I should have killed him when I had the chance!

Sad to say, I don't remember the murdered boy's name, but I do recall he was from Manassas, Virginia, and they found him, believe it or not, at the Civil War Battlefield Memorial Park in nearby Fredericksburg. It was made to look like he had tripped and whacked his head on one of those old cannons that rim the park, but I know different. It was murder pure and simple.

I may have forgotten the boy's name, but as for the rest of it— it's like it was yesterday.

---

* **FACT:** The Dumbarton Oaks Conference was held from August 21 to October 7, 1944, in a mansion in Georgetown, Washington, DC. The conference involving China, the Soviet Union, the United States, and the United Kingdom formulated proposals for a world organization that became the basis for the United Nations. Many of the issues raised there were resolved later during the Yalta Conference held in February 1945 attended by US President Franklin Roosevelt, Prime Minister Winston Churchill of Britain, and Premier Joseph Stalin of the USSR. In addition to deciding to divide Germany into three zones of occupation after the war, it was announced at Yalta that a "conference of United Nations" would be held in San Francisco in April 1945. Alger Hiss, a senior member of the US State Department, helped organize and set the agenda for both conferences and was later revealed to be a Soviet spy.

Irish Eyes

I WAS A RIDICULOUSLY EASY TARGET. I was young—only 24 when I arrived in Canada in 1943—in a strange country with strange customs. All of my family murdered and I so lonely I would sometimes lie on my bed at night and cry, if you can imagine a grown man crying. I didn't know a soul in dull, drab, dark and gloomy Ottawa. My social life was pretty well restricted to the odd feeble grunt from a fellow worker at the Soviet Embassy. I missed my family, especially my mother, terribly. Thank heavens for my night course in the English language at the University of Ottawa. Otherwise, I think I might have gone mad with boredom and homesickness.

My instructions were to befriend one of the professors at the university who was involved in some of the work underway at the nuclear laboratories at Chalk River; in other words to do some spying. But I was a miserable failure at this, unable to interest the professor in even having a coffee with me. I suspect he had been warned.*

"You were easy pickings for a sharp little cookie like Patsy Regan," one of Hoover's men told me later.

She was something, that's for sure, almost worth what she cost me. Tiny, not much more I wouldn't think than, how does that song go…*five foot two, eyes of blue?* Except she had green eyes. Irish eyes that, yes indeed, did smile, most of the time they looked at me anyway. Long black hair that she always seemed to get fanned out on the pillow as she lay beneath me. Small but perfectly shaped breasts whose nipples she loved me to nibble on. Altogether a package which would have, I am sure, incited Gandhi to trade in his toga for a suit and tie. Of course, I now know they were paying her for doing a job, but even today I kind of think it wasn't all work for her.

Sex? Oh my goodness, we'd sometimes go at it four or five times a night. In all my life I never have run across anyone quite like her. "Please!" she would say at each thrust. "Please! Please!" Then at the end she'd shout "Oh, thank you!" I don't think it was all an act, but then I suppose I'm probably engaging in wishful thinking, one of the few luxuries left for an old man. You can just imagine after a couple of weeks of that she could have led me over the cliffs of hell and I would gladly have followed. Which, come to think of it, is pretty well exactly what I did!

---

* **FACT:** The Chalk River Nuclear Research Laboratories were opened in 1944. The following September (the month of Gouzenko's reported defection) the first nuclear reactor outside the United States went into operation at Chalk River. On the Ottawa River about 125 miles upstream from Canada's Capital, Chalk River was part of the Manhattan Project that developed the nuclear bomb. Among those who visited Chalk River at least once was Klaus Fuchs.

She has it firmly in an encouraging grasp, trying to breathe some life back into a pretty weary little fellow when she launches the pitch that almost kills me. Taking an even firmer grasp, she feeds me the news that we've been invited to dinner with a friend of hers the next night. With something else very much on my mind, I don't actually recall if I agreed, but the following evening, there we are in a lovely semi-mansion on the edge of McKay Lake in Rockcliffe Park. Ferried from my dumpy little second-floor, one-bedroom apartment on Delaware Avenue in downtown Ottawa by a white-gloved, uniformed and apparently mute driver at the wheel of the latest edition of a Hudson Super Six* Impressed? Well I guess so!

If you have ever been inside one of those embassies, high commissions, or millionaires' homes in Rockcliffe Park you'll have a pretty good idea what confronts us. Thick broadloom and much bowing and scraping from servants, dark polished wood, sparkling glass with not a hint of fingerprints, and huge crystal chandeliers screaming money in every room. All the while Patsy is clutching my hand and oohing and ahhing like she's floating off into another one of her noisy orgasms.

If I had been just a little smarter I would have beelined the hell out of there, realizing this was no place for a little Irish girl and a guy who grew up on a threadbare collective farm where a sign of opulence was a lump of pork floating in a pot of boiling cabbage.

Our "host" for this gay little gala is a tall, thin, very friendly and polished man named Harry Sowell. International man of business, he claims. He's all charm. You know the kind—perfect-toothed

---

* **FACT:** That would be a 1942 model, since no Hudsons were built from mid-1942 until late 1945 because of the war.

smile, hangs on to your every word as though it was the most fascinating thing he's ever heard. "Patricia here is my favourite niece," he smiles as he puts his arm gently around her shoulder. This is a little puzzling since blood hasn't been mentioned before, but let's face it, the Irish can be a little strange. I know a fellow who swears he once attended a wake in an Irish pub where the patrons kept plying the poor dead chap with Guinness!

I admit to being pretty impressed with the fact Harry doesn't quiz me about my work at the Soviet Embassy or even about life back home. My brief experience in the West until then has been that once people find out where I work, they start pumping me with questions: " What do I think of Stalin? Are you really a Communist? What is life like in the Soviet Union?" You know, honest-curiosity things like that.

Fully aware that anyone even slightly critical of "the good life" back home is likely to just mysteriously disappear from the face of the earth, or show up bleeding in the dirt, you can be certain all my public reviews are very glowing indeed. Two big thumbs up, as they say. Amazingly, many people seem to actually believe me! But all Harry Sowell seems concerned with this night is making sure his favourite niece and her consort are having a wonderful time. After the second bottle of wine I stop wondering why.

In spite of the 6.5 Richter scale hangover the next morning and a gut ache from all the rich food, it was indeed a wonderful evening. Harry, bless him, helped us into the Hudson sometime past 2:00 a.m. grasping my hand with both of his with a good-old-embassy-row really, really sincere handshake. Patsy gets a little uncle-peck on the cheek. "We must do this again," he says.

All in all I have little choice but to conclude I am truly a marvelous fellow to deserve all this.

"I guess Uncle Harry was doing a little, not so subtle, boasting about the benefits of capitalism last night," I muse the next day, as the pains and rumblings begin to abate. Patsy smiles in what I believe is full agreement.

I now know that good old Harry was just sizing me up. Seeing just what kind of suckerfish his "niece" has hooked onto.

• • •

The official line today is that I was married at the time to someone named Svetlana, or Anna as some accounts claim. All the history books and even a couple of movies made about the so-called "Gouzenko Affair" portray me as a kind and gentle, if somewhat erratic, family man so struck by a sledgehammer of conscience, I decide to save the world from the evils of communism and betray my own country. The fact is, to this day, I have never been involved with anyone named Svetlana and at the time had only one thought on my mind—getting more "pleases" from my little Irish lass! Those who claim young men can only think about one thing at a time aren't all that wrong you know!

If I had been thinking I might have wondered how a beautiful woman like Patsy Regan fell so easily into my lap. Bumping into me like that on the street as I walk home from the Embassy. The twisted ankle. Her phone call that evening to thank me for assisting her to her home, or what she claimed was her home, and the breathless invitation for me to join her for lunch the next day. All of it fairly commonplace in today's world with its terribly loose morals and speed dating, but in 1945, I assure you it was a young man's dream-come-true. Especially for one as shy and inexperienced as I when it came to romance.

As I look back on it today I don't blame myself for what happened. I now realize there was no possible way I could have believed that it was anything other than good looks, good fortune, and the pure, sweet innocence of youth that made Patsy notice me.

I must confess the word "innocence" does not roll easily off the tongue as I tell you about Patsy Regan, but I digress.

To this day I am not sure where she lived. Certainly not in the house I helped her to that first fateful night of the "twisted ankle." Each time I broach the subject with her or suggest we might play a little "please, please" in her house to escape the ever present stink of cooked cabbage which drifts up from the apartment below, she makes some excuse about a landlord who won't allow male company.

She claims she doesn't mind the cabbage fumes and when I explain that I rented the tiny apartment in the first place because the smell reminds me so much of home, she falls on me with such force I am knocked to the floor.

"I'm going to give my big strong Russian something he never got at home," she says. And she does!

· · ·

Anyone who lived in the Soviet Union when "Uncle Joe" Stalin was in one of his purging moods will tell you what they feared most was a knock on the door. Friends never knocked, but Lavrenti Beria's dreaded secret police, the NKVD,* always did and when they came calling it would be a good idea to put a bullet in your brain right then and there—that is if you could afford a bullet.

---

* **FACT:** The NKVD (People's Commissariat of Internal Affairs) eventually became known as the KGB (Committee for State Security).

You'd think that after two years in Canada some of the trepidation would have abated but as they say, old fears die hard. Besides, let's not forget, even in Ottawa, the specter of Soviet "secret police" hovered over all who worked at the Embassy like the little black cloud that used to follow the Al Capp cartoon character around. Joe Btfsplk from Dogpatch in the comics; Joe Stalin from hell in Moscow! Definitely two people you did not want to come calling!

When the knock on my Delaware Avenue door comes, it isn't a delegation from "Uncle Joe" summoning me to a protracted Siberian "vacation," but a missive from "Uncle Harry" requesting my presence at a special dinner party he is throwing the next night at his home. The note pressed into my hand by the white glove of the Hudson Super Six chauffeur concludes, " I hope my niece can join us as well."

"White Gloves" does talk after all! "Shall I tell Mr. Harry you will be able to join him and his other guests?" he asks. With my heart still pounding and having some difficulty catching my breath, I only nod. What I should have done was bounced the chauffeur down the stairs, jumped into the Hudson and roared off in any direction. Where I'm not sure. Anywhere!

Terror was in the driver's seat...death its cargo!

The Black Crows

IT WASN'T HUDSONS OR FORDS that came calling for you in Belarus. It was the "black crows." The NKVD secret police in their black cars, engines fueled with terror, stalked the streets of our little town.

You never knew when it would be you hauled away to God-knows-where, never to be seen or heard from again. If they passed your house and stopped at a neighbour's you cried with relief. The rank odor of fear and suspicion permeated the air we breathed.

Millions of my fellow countrymen in what was then known in the West as White Russia were murdered or disappeared during the years I was growing up. The history books talk about executions. They make it sound civilized. It was slaughter. The madness reached its peak in 1937, the year I turned 18.

That was the year Stalin ordered all individual peasant farms, which in most cases had been in the same families for generations, taken from their owners and formed into collective farms—*kolkhozes* they called them. Those who objected or even questioned the action were usually shot on the spot, their bodies left to rot.

Anyone attempting to bury the dead was considered either a traitor or something called an "inner enemy." They were ordered to lie down beside the corpse and were either shot or, depending upon the depravity of the NKVD agents, buried alive by neighbours forced at gunpoint to man the shovels.

I watched in horror one day in our little town of Rahachow when a "black crow" pulled up in front of a house only a few metres down the street. Two of Stalin's henchmen, armed with machine pistols, strode to the front door, knocked briefly and when there was no response shouldered the door open. In a heartbeat they reappeared dragging an elderly man down the front steps. A woman, her hair flying in all directions, holding a coat or large rag of some kind, suddenly appeared on the stoop behind them and began screaming oaths in German and Russian. As the entire street watched through trembling curtains, one of the "crows" kicked the poor old man into the street, then began methodically shooting him.

I have seen some horrible things in my life, but till the day I die I will never forget how his body jumped and jerked and shuddered as each bullet thudded into him. Calmly, as though they'd just finished a light lunch, both of the "black suits" climbed back into their black car and took a leisurely cruise down the street before disappearing around the corner. The old man's body lay there for hours, the deathly silence on the street broken only by low moaning from somewhere inside the house and the sound of swarming flies and wasps gorging themselves on the blood and the horror.

It should not surprise you then that when Hitler launched Operation Barbarossa and attacked the Soviet Union in June of 1941, many Belarusians, myself included, welcomed the Nazis as liberators. Some villagers, dressed in their finest, threw flowers at the Tiger tanks racing by! *

It didn't take long for us to learn that compared to the Nazis, "Uncle Joe" Stalin was a pussycat!

---

* **FACT:** It is true that, at first, many of those subject to Stalin's oppression welcomed the Nazis. Pictures of flower-laden German tanks invading Belarus are on display at the United States Holocaust Memorial Museum, 100 Raoul Wallenberg Place, SW, Washington, DC 20024-2126, or on their website at « http://www.ushmm.org/ ».

Barbed-wire fence surrounding the Minsk Ghetto, 1941.
The sign warns: Anyone approaching the fence will be shot!

The Ghetto

WE DIDN'T KNOW IT AT THE TIME, of course, but that filthy little monster Heinrich Himmler had already issued orders to the SS that fully three-quarters of the entire Soviet population, some 140 million people, were to be exterminated to make way for German "Lebensraum," which means "living space" in English.

The written instructions handed to all German soldiers read, as follows:

> You are not able either to take things to heart or to worry about what you see, or show any compassion. Kill any Russian or Soviet citizen. Do not stop at anything. When you see a man, woman, a boy or a girl in front of you, kill. It will save you from death. It will ensure your future. It will bring eternal glory to you.

Hitler himself declared, "The war in the east is a war of annihilation."

Most German soldiers had little difficulty following Himmler's orders. Many were enthusiastic about it all. Public executions, usually public hangings, began almost immediately in the Belarus capital of Minsk only a few kilometres away from our little town.

"The only ones to be left alive," said the directive, "are those with light-coloured hair and blue eyes." The "cleaner ones," according to Himmler. They were to become slaves for the Germans.*

What many people don't realize is that when Germany first attacked, about 40 percent of Belarusians were Jews. You can say what you like about Stalin, but at least he didn't select the Jews for special treatment. He was equally cruel to us all. However, by the time the war was over, less than 1 percent of the population of Belarus was Jewish. I don't have to tell you what happened, but let me fill you in on a few details from someone who lived through it. What I'm about to tell you may sound a bit like a history lesson, but you've got to understand what happened to me before I arrived in Canada, in order for you to believe me when I tell you I would sooner die than betray my country.

---

* **FACT:** Lebensraum was a plan, conceived by Hitler, in which those deemed non-Aryan would be exterminated or expelled to make way for German colonists, while the citizens who remained would be subject to forced Germanization. This information is widely available, from such sources as *Bolshevik System of Power in Belarus* by M. Kasciuk, Minsk, Publishing house Ekaperspektyva and Belarus; and *From Soviet Rule to Nuclear Catastrophe* by David R. Marples, New York, 1996 St. Martin's Press. Much of this information is available at the State Memorial Complex in Khatyn. (Khatyn's entire population was murdered and the town burned to the ground by the Nazis early in 1941 as part of the policy of genocide.) In addition, much of the information concerning the Belarus genocide is available from the United States Holocaust Memorial Museum in Washington, DC and its website.

The Germans attacked the Soviet Union on June 22, 1941. Six days later on June 28, they entered Minsk and within hours had rounded up some 40,000 men and boys between the ages of 15 and 45. Almost all were Jews, although there were a few Soviet POWs and some non-Jewish civilians who had run afoul of German authority for one reason or another.

For four days and nights the 40,000 were kept herded like cattle in a field surrounded by machine guns and floodlights. No food, no shelter, no water. On the fifth day, all Jewish members of the intelligentsia were ordered to step forward. About 2,000 men did so, believing they would be freed. Instead, they were taken to a nearby woods and shot. Within days the murder of Jews and others, singly or in groups, became a daily occurrence.

In late July the Germans established a ghetto in the northwestern part of Minsk into which were immediately crowded some 80,000 people. For awhile some of the Jews were forced to work in slave labour camps and factories. Living conditions were unspeakable. Each person was allotted 1.5 square metres of living space. Children none. The ghetto was surrounded by thick rows of barbed wire with watchtowers erected at strategic locations. Anyone approaching the wire was shot on sight.

Tens of thousands of people lived among bombed-out ruins with almost no hygienic facilities and little, if any, food. Disease was rampant, as was torture and mass murder.

Thousands froze or starved to death. On the July 21, 1941, a group of 45 Jews were roped together and 30 Russian prisoners were ordered to bury them alive. The Russians refused, so all were shot.*

---

* **FACT:** This is well documented. Source: US Holocaust Memorial Museum.

Himmler himself came to Minsk on August 15, 1941 to watch as 100 Jews were shot. We now know that he was so sickened by the sight he ordered that more efficient and humane methods of solving the "Jewish problem" be devised. More humane, not for the Jews, but for those who had to do the killing! It was from that little bout of nausea that the idea of the gas chambers was born.

It wasn't just the Jews; I watched with unremitting horror and despair one frighteningly cold night in January, 1942 as 6,000 Russian POWs were marched out of the ghetto without coats or hats, ordered to lie down on the side of the road, and not to move. They lay there until they froze to death.*

Yes, I said, I saw this atrocity because I was a "guest" of the Minsk Ghetto, then the nearby Opera House slave labour camp from early August of 1941 until the following March. But I won't burden you with more details of the brutality of which men are capable. Similar atrocities have been well documented in other ghettos, concentration camps, and extermination camps.

Most historians agree that of the well over 100,000 people forced into the Minsk Ghetto, including many transported from Poland and Germany, only a tiny handful were still alive when Minsk was liberated by the Red Army on July 4, 1944. As is only too typical, your wonderful "highly civilized" and ever "compassionate" citizens of the "morally superior" West have paid little, if any, attention to our agony. We were after all, according to Hitler, and I suspect many of you, a relatively inferior Slavic race not really worthy of headlines.

---

* **FACT:** The accounts concerning Russioan POWs are accurate. According to Nazi statistics, between the occupation of Minsk and February 1, 1943, 86,623 Jews were killed in the ghetto. Source: US Holocaust Memorial Museum.

About 10,000 of us did manage to escape, myself included, forming numerous partisan groups whose members killed far more Germans and destroyed a great deal more military equipment, infrastructure and industrial capacity than anything you saw from that pitiful so-called resistance movement in France. Research it. You'll see what I say is true. In Belarus we were fighting for our very existence. The French, when not jumping into bed with the Nazis or rounding up truckloads of Jews for the ovens, were mostly concerned with settling into some well-aged *fromage* and a robust Bordeaux. I can tell you this. We didn't have to chop any hair from the heads of our women when the "supermen" finally left town!

What you'll find, if you check, is something that to this day makes me very proud of my Belarusian heritage. Once again allow me to give you just a bit more background of what I lived through and the real story of who I am and why I came to Canada.

The history books will tell you that more than 1,000 various partisan groups were formed in Belarus with more than 400,000 of us, including thousands of women, fighting the Nazis. Believe it or not, the records, which by the way are available from the Holocaust Museum in Washington, show that we killed or incapacitated more than half a million German soldiers and blew up 34 armored battle trains, 29 railway stations, 948 military headquarters and destroyed more than 18,000 cars and trucks being used by the Nazis. No other occupied country fought the Germans as hard or as successfully.* Mind you, it was a matter of life or death for us. The Nazis killed many of my fellow partisans and at least a million other Belarusians.

It was pure luck and accidental heroism that saved me!

---

* **FACT:** Source: US Holocaust Memorial Museum.

It's just one of the reasons I have to shake my head with anger and sadness when I read and hear the stories about my "betrayal." Do you think I would betray my country to help the West whose leaders essentially just stood by while all of this was happening? Not on your life!

And let me tell you something else. There is plenty of evidence that Churchill, Roosevelt and, yes, even your prime minister of the day, Mackenzie King, knew very well what was going on. They understood perfectly well that Hitler planned the greatest act of genocide in the history of the world, but not only did they do nothing, they kept silent at a time when news of what was happening might very well have prompted the United States to enter the war much sooner and thus shorten the conflict and save the lives of millions.*

I'm telling you all of this so that you will understand why it would be unthinkable for me to betray the country of my birth. A country I fought for. A country I loved and still love. A sad and tragic country betrayed and abandoned by all, but most of all betrayed by

---

* **FACT:** The idea that the Allies knew Germany's plans for the Jews and the entire Eastern Bloc is very controversial. However, Richard Breitman, Professor, Ph.D., Harvard, author of five books detailing the history of the Holocaust and now director of historical research for the US government agency called Nazi War Criminal Records Interagency Working Group, claims that 282 pages of radio intercepts from SS and police commanders in Belarus and Ukraine, taken with other documents, establish that the British knew that Jews were being targeted for atrocities as early as September 1941. This would be more than a year before Britain or the United States publicly acknowledged the plight of European Jews. "By late 1941," Professor Breitman says, "the British knew a lot about the shootings in the Soviet Union and had concluded that it was perfectly obvious that the Nazis were executing every Jew they could get their hands on." Source: Dr. Breitman's book *Official Secrets: What the Nazis Planned, What the British and Americans Knew*, available from the US Holocaust Museum, Washington. While Dr. Breitman doesn't state this, other historians suspect the British were reluctant to let the Nazis know they had broken their codes.

the great civilizations of the West. Mine is a country of brave and noble people on whom all of you turned your backs.

Shame on all who knew!

[There is a slight gap in the tape here, some background noise, and then the voice returns.]

"Sorry, I dropped my notes, but let me continue."

As I watched and suffered the horror of the Minsk Ghetto and the slave labour camps and even more so as I fought against the Nazis as a member of The Mstitel Partisan Party,* I made a pact with God that if He would allow me to live and let us defeat the Nazis, I would spend the rest of my life helping to rebuild my poor shattered country. I must confess that dreams of endless retribution against the Nazis who carried out the carnage continue to dance through my head even to this day. And unlike some of your more recent prime ministers, I make no apologies for my thoughts or the hate that sustained me during the darkest days.

As you now know, my prayers were answered. God did allow us to defeat Hitler and me to live. He did even more. It was His hand that guided me as I struck at the very heart of the beasts destroying my country. He helped me remove a terrible scourge from Belarus— to wipe a Satan from the face of the earth.

---

* **FACT:** Mstitel means "Avenger." Leonid Smilovitsky, Ph.D., researcher, Diaspora Research Institute, Tel Aviv University, refers to this group of partisans in a 1995 article which first appeared in the publication *Shvut* entitled "Minsk Ghetto: An Issue of Jewish Resistance."

Generalkommissar Wilhelm Kube

"Satan!"

IN MINSK, Satan's name was Wilhelm Kube, Generalkommissar Kube—General Commissar for Belarus with his headquarters in Minsk. A rabid and vile Nazi from the earliest days of the Party and incongruously, superintendent of the Lutheran Church in Brandenburg and head of the Berlin synod of the Lutheran Church. A man of God, indeed! *

---

* **FACT:** This information is accurate. Source: Ernst Klee, *Das Personen-lexikon zum Dritten Reich* (Fischer Verlag 2005).

When not busy saving souls in Berlin and Brandenburg, Herr Kube was busy destroying lives by the thousands in the Minsk Ghetto, a job he appeared to relish. On July 31,1942, the good General boasted in writing to the Nazi High Command that he had personally overseen the killing of 55,000 Jews in Belarus in the preceding 10 weeks, including several thousand German Jews. He expressed hope that all the Jews of Belarus would be completely liquidated as soon as the German Wehrmacht no longer needed their labour.*

His worst atrocity occurred on March 2, 1942, when 5,000 Jews were murdered to mark the Jewish festival of Purim. While it is almost too horrible for me to relate even today, I must tell you the following terrible atrocity since it played a significant role in determining my fate.

[Here there is a long pause on the tape. At first I thought there was a technical problem, but he picked up his narrative again with a trembling voice.]

How could I ever forget the evening of the Purim slaughter? I had seen a large group of slaves forced to dig a deep pit at the Ratomskaya Street ravine in the center of the ghetto, which I presumed was to accommodate the bodies of some of those who had been shot that afternoon. I didn't see what followed, but relate here only what was told to me by dozens of those forced to watch.

---

* **FACT:** Source: US Holocaust Memorial Museum.

The SS had apparently decided the small school that was being used as an orphanage needed to be cleaned out in order to make way for a new batch of children on their way from Poland. So all of the Minsk Ghetto children, some as young as two and still in diapers, were herded by men with submachine guns out of the orphanage, down the street, and thrown into the pit.

As those poor little children screamed in terror, some crying for their dead mothers, that great man of God, Generalkommissar Wilhelm Kube, dressed, as usual, in an immaculate uniform, arrived on the scene with a group of laughing SS officers. Kube reached into his pocket, pulled out a handful of candies, and tossed them to the terrified children below. Then waving cheerily at them, he ordered the pit to be filled and the children buried alive.*

I could hear their screams several blocks away as I sorted through a room full of looted Jewish property in what was once one of the most beautiful opera houses in Europe.

You can hear the sadness in my voice as I tell you this. It still provides nightmares. When you are faced with daily horror and un-speakable conditions such as existed in the Minsk Ghetto, you either develop an ability to block everything out or you die. You shut down a part of your brain. The more you endure, the more layers of a co-coon of denial you wrap around your soul. A dozen women ma-chine-gunned on the street—the shock, the revulsion, and the rage get buried deeper and deeper. A body still twitching from the hang-man's noose—thank God it's not me! Move on!

---

* **FACT:** This atrocity is confirmed by Ernst Klee in *Das Personen-lexikon zum Dritten Reich* (Fischer Verlag 2005), page 346, as well as by M. Gilbert in *The Holocaust*, page 297, Fontana/Collins, 1987, and Reidlinger 1960 as quoted in *Turonek 1989*, page 118.

Nothing matters but your own survival. But children? How do you ever get used to the sight, or as with me, the sounds of terrified, helpless children being buried alive? There is no blanket of denial thick or heavy enough to repress those memories for long. Believe me, I know. Oh, how I know.

Many concentration camp survivors say they still feel vestiges of guilt. Why did they live when millions around them died? I have no such feeling. I have many painful memories that still haunt me, but no guilt. My guilt was cleansed by Satan's blood!

Until the night of the Purim slaughter I now realize that I was in a state of shock. A zombie, I think, is how some would describe it. It's a wonder I could function at all when you consider what happened.

The Rahachow Slaughter

THE GERMANS CAME TO RAHACHOW the morning of August 4, 1941, rounded up almost everyone over the age of 50, more than a thousand people, including my mother, father and two uncles, took them into the nearby woods and shot them. Those of us like myself, young and strong enough to work in their slave camps and factories, were forced to lie in the streets where we could hear the machine guns, then as the last bullet found its mark we were handed shovels and ordered to bury the dead.

I found my mother's poor shattered body amidst the carnage and as l laid her gently in the shallow grave I had dug, an SS officer shouting "*schnell, schnell*" jabbed me viciously in the ribs with his rifle barrel as he urged by to hurry, hurry. I could not find my father or uncles. Perhaps because of the tears that obscured my eyesight.

The Nazis quickly discovered that thanks to a schoolteacher uncle, I possessed excellent handwriting in both German and Belarusian and had considerable clerical skills, so they made me an offer I couldn't refuse: Help unpack, sort, and carefully record all items looted from Jewish and other wealthy homes, churches, and institutions, which were brought to the Minsk Opera House prior to distribution to the Nazi hierarchy, or be shot. I chose not to be shot.

One of the few things I do remember of that terrible time is that I was ordered to write that fat turd Goebbels' name on many of the more valuable items. Albert Speer once showed up with a military escort of about twenty SS officers and with much motorcycle revving, heel clicking and "Heil Hitlering," Herr Speer picked out a Rubens, thus beating poor old Herr Goebbels to a choice prize!

I suppose it is amazing I can recall anything from those bleak and desperate days. I am unclear whether it is my advancing age or the deep fog into which I had descended at the time that clouds my memory of those few months in Minsk.

It was the screaming of the terrified children in the pit that awakened me from my slumbering fugue. I recall, as though it were only yesterday, looking up as the sounds of the terrified children pierced the windows of the opera house and seeing, as though for the first time, the poor emaciated slaves, clothes hanging from sharp shoulders, toiling around me. Some were surely only days from death.

As a non-Jew with light hair and blue eyes, one of the "cleaner" ones according to Himmler, I was given better rations and accommodation than those slated for eradication. No doubt the intent was that I should be kept alive in reasonable condition so that after the Nazis had won the war I would be shipped off to Germany or one of the conquered countries as a slave, although I didn't realize it at the time.

The sound of the doomed children shook me free of the paralysis that had engulfed me and it was at that moment that I resolved to escape, despite the terrible fate that awaited those who were caught making a break for freedom. In the belief it would discourage further escape attempts, the Germans made sure we could hear the nightlong screams from those caught trying to flee. Hundreds of us were forced to view the public hangings that followed the torture. It was a very effective deterrent.

Many of those who escaped from the ghetto did so by slipping away from work parties sent outside the city to repair railway lines, roadways and bridges destroyed or damaged by the partisan attacks that had already begun to bedevil the Germans. Later, a highly organized underground was established in the ghetto that helped hundreds to escape through sewers, holes in the fence, and tunnels.* Since I worked well into the night at the Opera House labour camp just outside the ghetto, surrounded by barbed wire and armed guards, no such opportunity presented itself to me. My escape would have to be more creative.

---

* **FACT:** Many details concerning life in the Minsk Ghetto, the Opera House labour camp and the atrocities, including the above event, are all available from the US Holocaust Memorial Museum.

Minsk after WWII, with the Opera House in the background

The Unasked Question

I WANT TO PAUSE HERE in my story for a moment to ask a question of you. How in the world could a young, fit, trained soldier of the Soviet Union end up in Ottawa in 1943? Because in that aspect, the history books are accurate. I did arrive to begin working at the Soviet Embassy in the fall of 1943. Why have the media never asked how that could possibly be? That is if in fact I really was a trained Soviet soldier who was moved to Canada as a cipher clerk!

Think of it. Refresh your memory. Even though Hitler had failed in his attempt to capture Moscow during the winter of 1941, when I arrived in Canada in October of 1943, the 900-day-long siege of Leningrad was still underway, and more than a million were dead.

Only two months previously, at Kursk, the Soviets and Germans fought in the largest single land battle in history. More than a million men and five thousand tanks took part in that epic seven-day struggle. The Germans were finally thrown back, but in the fall of 1943 they still held large tracts of the Soviet Union, including my own country of Belarus. Millions of Soviet soldiers lay dead. More than three million had been captured and faced God knows what fate. Don't forget, in 1943 the Soviets were all alone in fighting Hitler in Europe. D-Day and the launch of the Western Front didn't occur until June of 1944.*

So I ask the question again. How could it be that a perfectly fit, well-trained Soviet soldier was not fighting shoulder to shoulder for the Motherland with his Red Army compatriots?

In all the attempts to convince everyone that I betrayed my country to help the West, this question was never asked: How I (if I really was a soldier as they still claim) got to sit out a life-and-death struggle in the Soviet Union in the safety and comfort of Ottawa while my countrymen were dying by the millions? Why would the Soviets not have sent someone too old to fight, or a disabled soldier, perhaps even a woman unfit for battle?

Don't you find that a little strange? Could it be that not everything you were told about Igor Gouzenko is true? Is it possible that everything the history books and even the movies claim about me was a giant lie? By the time you hear me out, that is the conclusion you must come to.

So let me tell you what really happened and how it was that I escaped the carnage of the Eastern Front to assume a minor role in the Soviet Embassy in Ottawa, Canada.

---

* **FACT:** This is not exactly true. The allies landed in Sicily on July 10, 1943, and by the fall of that year were fighting their way up the "boot" of Italy.

Miracles

I SUSPECT I AM AS BRAVE as the next man, but the thought of the knives, testicle crushers, and other fiendish devices awaiting those caught trying to escape from Minsk is too frightening for me to even contemplate. If I am really going to proceed with an escape attempt, I must first devise some method of cheating the torturers. I do not fear a quick death. "What I must find," I tell myself, "is a means to achieve it if caught."

I am allowed a small knife, hammer, and crowbar with which to open some of the packing cases containing the pillaged treasures, but all such tools must be returned to the guards at the end of my working day, usually close to midnight. Even if somehow I am able to conceal the knife, it is too small to do the job properly. Death will have to be swift and certain!

They say there are no atheists in foxholes; I doubt there are many in ghettos either, but until that time I had been one. What overcame me that terrible night of the Purim massacres, I cannot tell you, but for the first time in my life I find myself on my knees praying for strength and deliverance.

God arrives the very next morning. Well, to be completely accurate, it is a huge, beautifully carved marble statue of Jesus on the Cross, pillaged from a Warsaw cathedral, probably St. John's.* Why it has been shipped from Warsaw to Minsk only God knows. About ten feet tall and weighing, I suspect, close to a ton, it appears to be in perfect shape, but as I struggle to remove the Polish newspapers which crudely encase it, something falls to the floor and rolls to my feet. It is a thorn made of stone; about eight inches long and tapered at one end to a sharp point. A thorn, cleanly broken from the crown of thorns, encircling Christ's bowed head! A miracle! I have my weapon.

Gunfire suddenly rattles from the street just outside the Opera House—all eyes dart in its direction. Stooping swiftly I grasp the stone thorn and stuff it into my shirt.

God is not finished with his miracles. The next day a truckload of lumber and a large tarpaulin arrive along with orders to build a crate large enough to accommodate the statue and its enormous base, which we learn is to be shipped to the cathedral in Berlin known as the Berliner Dom.

My heart leaps when I see what had been sent!

---

* **FACT:** I have been unable to determine if such a statue existed at St. John's or any other cathedral in Poland prior to the war. Six-hundred-year-old St. John's Cathedral was partially destroyed by the Germans in 1944 during the Warsaw Ghetto uprising. Following the collapse of the uprising in November 1944, the remains of the magnificent cathedral were blown up by the Germans as part of their planned destruction of the entire city. The cathedral has since been rebuilt and is one of Poland's national pantheons.

Ghosts

TODAY THE RENOVATED AND VERY MODERN Minsk Opera House on Parizhskaya Kommuna Square is one of the most beautiful in all of Europe, home to the National Academic Great Opera Theatre of the Republic of Belarus.

Three years ago, I decided the ghosts had been sufficiently banished to allow me to return to the country of my birth for the first time since the war and, at my wife's encouraging, to once again walk through the doors of the Opera House, this time as a free man. My own safety surely was no longer an issue. The "hunters," convinced I could no longer do them any harm, had long ago given up their search, or at least that is what I believed. Everyone involved was dead now anyway. Except me!

With what I guess you would describe as a morbid kind of

fascination, I had for years, here in my little cliffside hiding place, devoured all the news about the Opera House I could get my hands on. I took some pride in knowing it was here that world-famous singers such as Ludmila Shemtchuk and Maria Gulegina launched their brilliant careers and that the children's matinees featuring performances such as *Peter Pan*, *Puss in Boots* or *Magic Music* were also renowned the world over.

"Today," I tell myself, as my wife and I join the crowds entering the building, "this place has become a stage for the magnificence that man is capable of. A cathedral of beauty and art and joy and children. A home for angels!"

How very different I think, from the winter of 1941-42 when this was a house of horrors, a place of death and cruelty, hopelessness and despair. Mankind at its very worst. A place fit for no one but devils and their disciples.

When I was last here as a slave of the Nazis, all the wooden seats had been stripped from their moorings and thrown into the street, where residents had spirited them away for firewood. Sadly, we inmates could have used them ourselves to feed the basement furnace whose spasmodically flickering flame was seldom able to bring the winter temperature above freezing.

Today as we enter this splendid new Opera House, my wife takes one of my hands in hers and softly caresses it. "You're trembling," she says. I haven't noticed. "Would you like to go back to the hotel?" I shake my head, but my heart pounds.

I think I am doing fine, walking briskly down the aisle to our seats, when suddenly, there it is: a pile of filthy rags, through morning-clouded eyes; a dark smudge amidst the clutter; beak-like fingers curled in final terror around the grillwork of the floor vent. Just in front of me. A frozen corpse!

My wife gives a soft cry, "What's the matter? Are you all right?"

I am clutching her arm hard enough to cause her pain.

"Ghosts," I say, "just ghosts."

I recall how the poor fellow must have climbed down from his frigid bunk during the night while the guards slept and how, not realizing, or perhaps not caring that the furnace was out, he lay down on the floor vent trying to suck some heat out of it and froze to death.

She strokes my hand, "Shhh, the music; it's beautiful."

The thing that strikes me is that there is very little inside that appears familiar. The seats are all new and very modern, much of the architecture has been altered, and the stage is completely new. I know that only too well, because during that terrible winter we ripped and hacked it to pieces in a largely vain attempt to keep the furnace fueled and thus ourselves alive.

The German guards in their greatcoats, heavy boots and thick gloves laugh as the once proud stage slowly disappears into the voracious maw of the furnace. From somewhere they have acquired a large gas heater, which, as they often tease us, keeps them "nice and toasty" in the balcony office they have converted to a small barracks.

I remember too, how the basement and back rooms are jammed with looted treasures from Belarusian homes, churches, cathedrals, and theatres. All being stored for that "glorious" day when Herr Hitler rules the world and the Swastika flies from every flagpole. Tapestries, antique furniture, silverware, paintings, sculptures, and other priceless works of art await that "new dawn" when they will adorn the homes, churches, cathedrals, and theatres of the new "supermen" who are creating for us all Hitler's Thousand-Year Reich.

As with cream, the very best is being skimmed off the top almost daily by those destined to be the leaders of this grand "new world order."

It is my job to record all items as they are dumped onto the main floor of the Opera House and present my list to SS General

Kurt von Gottberg who arrives each evening in a chauffeured black limousine accompanied by six armed guards.

The routine is the always the same. Each evening I stand, "loot list" in hand, just outside the main entrance to the Opera House. At precisely 6:30, the limousine pulls up, a rear window rolls down, a gloved hand extends, fingers snap and the list is slapped into the glove which quickly disappears into the darkness of the rear seat as the heavy vehicle and its guards speed away. I never really get a good look at the General who, although neither of us knows it, will soon replace Satan himself.*

If the looting and pillaging has gone particularly well and things get a bit bogged down in the Opera House with an over-abundance of "loot," I will sometimes be ordered to pick up a hammer or crowbar and either help unpack some of the arriving boxes or, if a treasure is heading out the door to a "superman's" home or office, I might cobble together a crate sufficiently strong enough for shipment through what is becoming increasingly dangerous territory for the Germans.

Sitting now in the warmth and comfort of this splendidly refurbished Opera House, I am startled as Aida appears to turn directly to me and begins to sing "Oh, my country, what you cost me!" Raising her arms she points and there it is! Yes, over there, just to her left. The memories flood in! I see it again as though it was only yesterday: a magnificent marble statue of the crucifixion! Look closely, Aida. One of the thorns from the crown that adorns Christ's head is missing!

---

* **FACT:** Kurt (sometimes spelled Curt) von Gottberg did replace Wilhelm Kube as Generalkommissar for Belarus.

Escape

THE GHOSTS TAKE ME BACK now to the time of deliverance from this place—March 5, 1942.

During the night, I tape the marble thorn to the inside of my left thigh, using a stolen strip of masking tape.

At dawn the next day we set to work building a solid wooden crate large enough to accommodate the ten-foot high statue with its nearly six-foot-wide cross. We are told the statue will be loaded aboard a transport truck that evening, but we know it won't actually leave Minsk until well after dark, in order to lessen the risk of partisan attacks.

Fully believing I am under God's protection and having observed previously that none of the guards know anything about carpentry, I begin to construct a base for the crate that is more than six feet square, with full expectation that no one will recognize it doesn't need to be nearly that large. I am right. By the time our breakfast of black bread and thin potato soup arrives, I have completed the large platform my plan requires.

It's early March and all the Jews have "disappeared" from the Opera House work camp that now accommodates some 20 of the "cleaner ones" like myself, all in reasonably good condition. It takes all of us to hoist the statue onto the base. The rest is relatively easy. With the assistance of two other "slaves," we complete the crate well before the truck arrives.

As the time for my salvation draws closer, my heart begins to beat faster. Adrenaline pounds in my ears. "Stay calm," I warn myself, "slow your breathing. Don't give them a reason to suspect anything. Slow down, slow down!"

I touch my thigh. The thorn is still there! The panic abates.

As it is obvious I am the only one with the faintest idea of what is required to build a crate large and strong enough to protect a prize this valuable, the guards are only too happy to "let Igor do it." If anything goes wrong you can guess where the fingers will point, which is exactly what I am counting on. That and the fact the Opera House guards are lacking in a good deal more than just crate-building skills. Describing these wormy slugs as not exactly Rhodes Scholars is an understatement!

Thus I had no qualms yesterday suggesting that while the top of the crate could be left open, a large tarpaulin was needed to cushion the statue against the bumps, jolts and flying stones bound to be encountered on the long trip to Berlin. When I saw the tarp unloaded along with the lumber last night, I knew for sure God hadn't finished with his miracles!

My main worry is that my plans may be thwarted by the Berlin-bound truck arriving before I am able to hand my "loot list" to the good general. When a guard finally points at me and then to his watch, I breathe a sigh of relief. Almost 6:30; no sign of a truck yet. Out the front door the limousine pulls up, right on time, the list is slapped into the gloved hand, and I am quickly back inside. Now deadly calm.

As usual at this time of evening, my fellow "slaves" are gathered over the feeble heat of the furnace grate, devouring their meagre meal. The guards, also as usual, having finished their meal, are off in a far corner playing their nightly game of cards. No one pays the least attention to me. They aren't really worried about anyone escaping anyway. All the doors are barred; besides, in our tattered and filthy clothes, and with no identity cards and Minsk crawling with German troops and police, where would we go? Unless you have outside help and a good plan, your chances of escape are virtually nil. I have both. God is my outside help. The time has come to implement my plan.

Quickly, in the darkness settling over the Opera House, I climb up the side of the crate, silently drop down inside, crawl beneath the tarpaulin draping the figure of Christ, wrench the thorn from the tape on my thigh and with an astonishingly steady hand ready to plunge the cold stone into my breast, I huddle against the base of the Cross.

With Christ's feet caressing my head, I wait. And pray the truck will arrive soon. I know full well that the longer the delay the greater the chances of a guard noticing my absence. I have nothing to fear from my fellow inmates whose senses are so blunted by cold, hunger, fatigue, fear, and hopelessness they would scarcely notice if I, or anyone, dropped dead in front of them.

I need not have worried. The shouts and laughter of the card-playing guards are abruptly stilled by the whack of the massive front door of the Opera House being thrown open and a truck, a large one by the sound of its engine, backs up to the entrance.

Cards abandoned, the guards become the models of efficiency. I hear them shouting orders now, much running about, confusion, more shouts, more orders, and then the crate with its precious cargo—the statue and me—is jerked into the air.

For once I am glad of the starvation diet that has reduced my weight to the point where it will be masked by that of the statue.

For a moment my heart pounds as the crate tilts and we come perilously close to being spilled onto the floor. I clutch my weapon even more tightly. There's more shouting and the dangerous tilt becomes slightly less precarious. Slowly, with much grunting, groaning and cursing in several languages, I sense us moving forward, until with a great thump and more shouting we land inside the truck, thank heavens upright.

This is something I had not considered. I don't panic, but I am very worried. Instead of being loaded onto the back of an open truck, as I had expected, it is obvious from the sound that this time they have sent an enclosed van. I hear the door thud shut and a scraping noise that I fear sounds very much like a lock.

My plan has been to simply crawl out of the crate as we drive in the darkness through the Kurapaty forest that crowds the outskirts of Minsk, jump off the truck as it slows around some of the dangerous curves, then somehow hook up with a partisan group, several of which I know are operating there.

A simple plan made far less so by being enclosed and probably locked inside a van. As the truck lurches forward, I scramble out from under the tarpaulin but am confronted with a crisis. The top of the crate is within an inch of two of the truck's roof. It takes me nearly half an hour to finally pry off sufficient boards from the side of the crate to allow me to squeeze free and roll onto the floor.

Now I am beginning to panic. With time running out, I've got to find a way to get out of here. I know we will soon be through the forest into open countryside and my chances of escape grow dimmer by the moment. I frantically attack the wooden rear door of the van with my stone thorn, hoping to somehow hack a hole large enough to get my arm out and reach the latch. I am only too aware that even if I can reach the latch but find it locked, my goose is cooked, as you Canadians would say.

Soviet partisans in Belarus 1943. The partisan on the left is carrying what appears to be a Soviet PPD-34/38. His companion is equipped with a Mosin-Nagant rifle (with factory bayonet), plus German bayonet/dagger (on waistband) and two RGD-33 hand grenades.

— Russian state archive

Freedom

I DON'T NEED TO FIND THE PARTISANS. They find me! I am digging frantically at the door with my stone weapon when the world explodes beneath me.

When I awake I am lying in what appears to be some kind of underground hut with my broken right leg encased in primitive splints fashioned from boards that look suspiciously like those which, when last I was conscious, enclosed a statue of Christ on the Cross and a stowaway. Strangely, I feel almost no pain from my leg, but my buttocks are screaming at me, as though someone has been digging around with a shovel. Which, as it turns out, is pretty much what has been going on.

My groans rouse an old woman who is nodding off in a corner. Stiffly, she rises to her feet and hobbles to the pile of rags that serves as my bed. Bending over in the dim light is a face the weather has beaten into something resembling a burlap bag. Picture Willie Nelson without the beard, bandana or guitar! Her laugh, as she holds up a jagged piece of metal nearly the size of my fist, reveals a fine set of gums but not a single tooth. Saying something in Polish that I cannot understand, she whacks her rump with the chunk of metal then yanks it away quickly with one hand while pointing to my rear with the other. Another laugh. I hate to say cackle, but in truth that's more descriptive. An unlikely angel!

Someone, I hope to high heaven not her, has removed what is obviously a chunk of shrapnel from my buttocks. What I am able to piece together in the coming days is that, in fact, it is this old lady who set my broken leg, hacked out the shrapnel and patched up several less serious wounds to my legs and back, thus undoubtedly saving my life.

Even with the primitive equipment available, her skill is such that all I have to remind me today of a partisan's roadside bomb that shattered the truck and killed the driver and the armed guard, is a small star-shaped scar on my right buttock and as I grow older, a slight limp.

I have no idea what her real name is. She never tells us. To all of us who spent time in that tiny hole in the ground, she is simply Babunia, or sometimes Baba, which I eventually figured out, is Polish for old woman or grandma. I am told she escaped from Warsaw as the Nazis were jamming Jews into that infamous ghetto and that while she spent most of her life milking cows on a dairy farm, she had some training as a veterinarian.

Her experience may have been with animals, but she tends me with great care for much of that spring, changing my dressings, feeding me and brewing up a painkiller from the bark of surrounding birch trees. Morphine is far too valuable to waste on broken legs or injured flanks!

During the summer, several wounded partisans are brought into our zimlanka, which is what these concealed hiding places deep in the Belarusian forests are called. As quickly as the partisans are patched up and able to walk, they disappear back to whatever fighting units they are attached to. I never talk to any of them, the theory being that the less we know about each other, the less information the Nazis' torture can extract.

One of the wounded is a young, quite attractive Polish woman whose right hand has been partially blown off by the premature exploding of a mine she was setting near a German checkpoint. One day as she and Babunia are chatting quietly in a corner, I notice them throwing amused glances in my direction. With a slight nod, Babunia stiffly clambers up the short ladder leading to the surface, leaving the two of us alone.

Babunia's legs have barely disappeared from view when my little Polish partisan, without a word or warning, tears off her clothes, yanks down my blanket and with a fierce cry, mounts me with marvelous vigour!

Startled and fearful for the safety of my damaged limb, I try to push her off; then, realizing that my leg is as much up to the task as everything else, I quickly get into the spirit of things, and there on a sorry bed of rags in a Kurapaty forest zimlanka, surrounded by a world gone mad with death and destruction, we take of life what life can give. Finally exhausted, we clutch each other like desperate lovers. It's not love, but it's all we have.

Sadly, the opportunity never presents itself again and several days later she too disappears. I have often thought about her and on one occasion tried to track her down, but I suspect that she, as with many partisans, was eventually caught and killed by the Germans.

Belarusian partisan in a forest dugout (zimlanka) with his family, 1944

The Avengers

BY LATE MAY I am almost fully recovered. "Tell somebody I'm ready to fight the bastards," I tell Babunia. The next day they come for me. Two armed and very dangerous looking women, who lead me, blindfolded, for several kilometres through the forest. "When we see what kind of stuff you are made of," explains one of them, "then we may let you know how to find us." I understand only too well how persuasive the Gestapo can be and I no longer have my thorn. It disappeared in the explosion that destroyed the truck and as yet I have nothing to replace the comfort that precious bit of stone provided.

Thus it is that in May of 1942, I join the Mstitel partisans. A loosely knit but surprisingly well trained group of about 100 men and women hiding in a small and scattered collection of zimlankas deep in the forest that pushes almost up to the Minsk City limits.

Some of the partisans are Jews who escaped from the ghettos of Minsk or Warsaw, but most are men and women like myself, who have refused to become slaves to the Nazis.

Food and other supplies come from nearby villages or Minsk itself—usually donated, but sometimes taken by force. Most of the guns, ammunition, knives and other military equipment, as well as whatever medical supplies we are able to round up, come from the Germans. Always by force!

I discover the reason for the high degree of training when we are joined by a member of the Red Army who has been ordered by Moscow to teach combat skills to several partisan groups operating in the Kurapaty forest. He is only one of dozens, perhaps hundreds, of professional soldiers carrying out similar training operations throughout Belarus, in particular in the Naarutz, Chinchivi and Belovezhskaya forests, as well as here in the Kurapaty where thousands of partisans are gradually taking control of large sections of territory as more and more German soldiers march eastward to confront the encroaching Red Army.

We learn how to use a gun and a knife, how to make and set mines and bombs, and how to throw a grenade, but most of our time is spent learning how to defend ourselves and attack without weapons. Our instructor is an expert in a highly refined and deadly Russian method of hand-to-hand combat called "spetsnaz."

I learn the points on a man's body that when pressed will render him unconscious. I learn how to destroy a man's knee, break his arm or leg, and yes, it is here that I learn the skill that later saves my life in Ottawa: I learn how to kill a man with my bare hands!

My first combat operation is a relatively easy one, but a good test for my newly repaired leg and my fitness. Accompanied by our Russian trainer and following a woman who obviously knows these bush paths very well, we run and jog for the better part of six hours until we're halted at the edge of an open field. We don't see any Germans, but wait, concealed in underbrush until well after dark before darting across the field and throwing ourselves against the base of a railway embankment.

Fearful that the sound of our running has alerted the patrols that routinely check this part of the tracks leading from Minsk to the Eastern Front, we still our heavy breathing and listen. Nothing! At the all-clear signal, we clamber up the embankment, and keeping as close to the ground as possible to avoid silhouetting ourselves against the faint glow of a fire burning in distant Minsk, we lay more than twenty sticks of dynamite and fuse along the track, light the fuse, and then run for the welcoming forest with all the speed and strength we can muster.

I don't quite make it and am knocked flat from the force of the blast that sends at least 100 metres of railway track and ties skyward. Thankfully unhurt, I bounce to my feet, join the rest of our "merry band," and as dawn breaks we are back in our forest retreat where there is much joking about maybe overdoing it just a bit with the dynamite! "We could have blown up the Great Wall of China," suggests one of my comrades. "Hell, we could have blown up Berlin," I say, to much laughter. I am elated. At last, some payback!

For the rest of that year and well into the next, we carry out more than two dozen similar raids, blowing up railway tracks, a bridge and several truck convoys. On one occasion we stage a raid on a German roadblock as a distraction while another group of partisans rescues several Russian POWs about to be put to death. Only once do we get into a firefight with a German patrol. We escape with only one slightly wounded comrade, but it's a close call. Most other partisan raids aren't as fortunate. God must still be on my side!

Once in the fall and again in the winter when they think they can follow our tracks in the snow, the Germans make an attempt to locate our encampment and wipe us out. Unable to use tanks or any heavy armament in the deep woods, the *Boche* foot soldiers are less than enthusiastic in their pursuit. They don't know the forest, but we do. Our tactic is to send a few snipers out to pick a few of them off and then melt back into the woods. Classic guerilla warfare.

On several occasions the Germans are able to locate partisan zimlankas in our forest and others, but by the time they arrive, the partisans are usually long gone, and more often than not the enemy pays a heavy price on their way out of the forests. Fortunately, we are now confronting the dregs of the German Army. Soldiers who can shoot straight are being pressed into the bloodbath of the Eastern Front.

I am told that in the early days of the partisan operations they did come under attack from the Luftwaffe, whose planes were roaming freely in the skies, but when the quick victory they had expected is denied in Russia, it becomes obvious the German High Command has more pressing problems than Belarusian partisans.

On one memorable occasion, the Germans haul several 105 mm howitzers to the eastern end of the Kurapaty forest and begin lobbing shells at what they think is our location. They miss us by several kilometres, shattering a broad swatch of trees that after another attack, this time from our axes, makes good firewood.

The guns are obviously in much greater demand elsewhere and despite our attempts to sabotage them, after two days of killing only trees, they are successfully loaded aboard a train and shipped east to kill Russians.

By the spring of 1943, the Germans have pretty well given up trying to root us out of our forest lairs and settle instead on increasing patrols in usually vain attempts to protect vital rail lines, bridges, roads and buildings. As I have already told you, what we did in Belarus is by far the most successful of all the resistance movements in Europe.

I have no doubt that even if the Red Army had not arrived in June of 1944 to liberate us, we partisans would have done it on our own. I often wish that is what had happened. We would certainly have been better off.

As the winter snows fade away, it becomes apparent that I am being kept away from the riskier ventures. It troubles me deeply since I have every reason to believe I have been as effective at sabotage as any others in our group. I take part in a couple of minor raids on truck convoys, but even then, my role is kept to a minimum, far from flying bullets.

When I ask what is going on, I am met with nothing but shrugs. None of my comrades knows what's up either, only that they have orders that my life is not to be placed at risk.

It is mid-summer when I find out why.

There's a stir in our camp. Word quickly flies around that none other than Urie Labonak,* one of the most famous partisan leaders, has arrived from Moscow.

My life is about to take a dramatic turn!

---

* **FACT:** Russian state archives lists a U. Labonak as a key partisan commander.

Soviet caricature. Inscriptions—Ideal Aryan must be: tall (above Göbbels),
slim (above Göring), blond (above Hitler). The author of this caricature is famous
political cartoonist Boris Yefimov, who died on the 1st of November, 2008, at age 108.

Chosen

"**Y**OU WILL HELP US KILL the Generalkommissar!" Realizing I don't understand, Labonak impatiently adds, "Kube, Wilhelm Kube, you're going to help us kill him!"

I am stunned! Labonak gets up from behind a small table covered with maps. He's a short but powerfully built middle-aged man; thick thighs bulging through the ill-fitting Red Army uniform he's wearing. Still unable to fully understand what's happening here, my mind is thinking, "Pear! The man is built like a pear!"

He circles the table and stands in front of me. "Stand up," he orders. "Look me in the eyes."

I don't hesitate.

"Yes," he gleefully shouts to several nearby aides, "they are a beautiful blue; perfect. Take off your hat." This time he almost does a little dance. "Yes, look at that, almost blond!" He walks slowly around me, peering intently at my head as though to check that my hair is the same light colour on all sides. "Yes, yes, yes, wonderful, wonderful. Say something to me in German."

"What?" I ask.

"Come, come—say something in German, let me hear your German; they tell me it is very good."

I rattle off a couple of words.

"No, no. Give me some sentences, tell me what a wonderful fellow I am or something like that," and he chuckles.

So, standing there in the stifling heat of a sod hut, bathed in sweat and confusion, I break into German and tell one of the most powerful men in all of the Soviet Union that I really do think he is a wonderful fellow and so is everyone else in the entire partisan movement. This mighty little pear of a man breaks into a toothy smile, claps his hands in approval and dismissal and my fate is forever sealed! It seems my German is good enough to qualify me for what I fear will be a suicide mission.

The Hot Water Bottle!

It HAS NEVER BEEN CLEAR to me whether Yelena Mazanik was Wilhelm Kube's lover or his maid. Some history books say the former, others the latter. One thing I have no doubt about is that if she is having sex with the Generalkommissar, the mass murderer of Minsk children, it's not for love of anything but her country.

She certainly doesn't hesitate when the partisans make contact with her and ask if she will help kill him. "With pleasure," is what she is reported to have replied.

And so it is agreed that some kind of bomb with a delayed timer will be the method that gives Yelena the best chance of carrying out her dangerous mission and escaping. It is Yelena herself who comes up with the brilliant solution. "The hot water bottle," she says. "He's got circulation problems, so I put a hot water bottle in his bed every night to warm his feet. Can you put a bomb inside a hot water bottle?"

It takes our explosives experts only a few hours to figure it out. Moscow is providing us with small amounts of plastique and detonators to be used only for blowing up important bridges. We don't think Stalin or anyone else around Red Square will object too strenuously if we nick off a little bit of it to blow up a German general, especially one as nasty as Wilhelm Kube!

The problem is how to get the plastique, detonator, and timing device into a rubber bottle and then fill it with hot water.

It's a somewhat embarrassed young woman who almost immediately hits upon the answer. "A condom," she says. Eureka! And thanks to our Nazi friends, who usually have their pockets full of them, condoms are one of the few things we've got plenty of around here. Put the explosive, the detonator, and the timer into a condom, tie off the top, drop it into the bottle, and then you can add the hot water whenever you want! Brilliant! Except for one problem…since we don't know when we'll be able to plant the bomb under Herr Kube, how do we rig up a timer that won't go off until well after Yelena has fled?

In the end what they design is fairly simple. I have no idea exactly how it works, but they rig it up in such a way that screwing the top of the hot water bottle on tightly will activate the timer, which is made from a pocket watch. It gives whoever plants the bomb exactly one half hour to make a getaway.

All that needs to be done now is get the bomb into Yelena's hands.

"Easy," says Moscow, "No problem. No problem at all. Just find a partisan who can pose as a German officer. Put him in a captured car or a motorcycle with a sidecar, have him drive into the heart of Minsk, past all the checkpoints, present the bomb to Yelena Mazanik, hang around until she plants it beneath Herr Kube, then flee the city with her when the deed is done. No problem!" Or words to that effect…

The Germans used motorcycles extensively in Belarus.

The Perfect Partisan

NATURALLY, I AM THE PERFECT PARTISAN for the job. I speak German very well, I'm tall, fair-haired and blue-eyed—Hitler's perfect Aryan!

Not being the perfect person for the job if dead or wounded, I have been quarantined away from battle in recent weeks, during which they've "requisitioned" an almost perfect German officer's uniform. Only lacking in complete perfection by a fair-sized bullet hole and a neat little patch of blood where someone's chest used to be. One of the older women fixes that little problem so well with a needle and thread you'd be hard pressed to spot the defect with a microscope.

I'm not sure if they measured Fritz before they shot him, but the uniform fits me very well, although the officer's cap is a couple of sizes too large, remedied with a bit of wool stuffing under the lining.

A motorcycle arrives on the instalment plan, one piece at a time. Wrecked vehicles of every kind litter the roadsides, so gradually, a steering wheel here, a tire there, a few sparkplugs; my comrades acquire sufficient operational parts to cobble together a motorcycle with a sidecar that runs amazingly well. Rather reluctantly, it seems to me, they remove the sidecar so that I can take a few practice runs along forest trails and into vacant clearings until, as you would say in the West, I get the hang of it.

As I tell you all of this, you may think I am being rather flippant, but to tell you the truth, I was very frightened. Scared out of my wits! My Waffen SS officer's uniform includes a loaded Luger pistol that I try to convince myself is an appropriate substitute for a thorn of stone, but the thought of going back into the heart of the horror from which I have so recently escaped is terrifying.

Nightmares of buried children and mangled corpses fill my nights. I find that resorting to prayer again helps to calm me. God, I desperately want to believe, is still watching over me. What I seek most is courage.

Yelena

[At this point there is a series of clicking noises on the tape.]

AS YOU CAN IMAGINE I very often listen back to what I have dictated on these tapes and I've got to admit to being embarrassed at this last little bit about me being terrified of what lies ahead in Minsk. I'll leave it up to you if you wish to include this admission in whatever account you are keeping of all this, but for the record I would like to say the following.

• • •

If I am frightened of what lies ahead for me in the Minsk hellhole in the late summer of 1943, can you imagine the terror that Yelena

Mazanik* must be experiencing as she goes about her daily routine? Sharing a dwelling with the man she intends to kill, perhaps sharing his bed, as well.

All I must do is masquerade as a German officer, bluff my way through checkpoints, deliver a bomb to Yelena, and then help her escape. Yelena, on the other hand, must risk meeting me during daylight, acquire the bomb from me, and somehow hide the deadly device from the guards who will search her as she re-enters Kube's compound in the center of Minsk.

Once back on duty, whatever that may entail, she must show no unusual emotion, perhaps even while having sex with him, wait until Herr Kube retires for the night, fill the bottle with hot water, tighten the cap, place it under the Generalkommissar's chilly feet without giving him even a hint of her real intent, then somehow flee the building. All in less than half an hour.

To even contemplate what she is about to do requires nerves of steel. Always knowing the horrible fate that will befall her if she fails. Death will be certain but slow and very painful. Female partisans often have a breast cut off before they are hanged.

The plan is that we ride to freedom together aboard my trusty motorcycle, even as the bomb is hopefully blowing Kube into tiny pieces. Looking back on it today, I suspect no one really believes we will make it out of the city alive.

But just think of it. Here is this young woman—she was only 22 at the time—with no training or experience in anything other than household duties, the daughter of a minor clerk, called upon to carry

---

* **FACT:** Yelena Mazanik's memory is still revered throughout the former Soviet Union.

out one of the most dangerous assassinations of the entire war! Her only condition is that her 18-year-old sister Valentina be smuggled out of Minsk before any attempt is made on Kube's life.

At Labonak's insistence, I meet with Valentina shortly after she arrives in our camp. A truly beautiful girl; tall and slim, and proud, with long black hair tied back with a partisan's bandana. Without saying a word, she takes my hands in hers and stares at me for a moment with the most startlingly beautiful brown eyes I have ever seen.

"My sister is ready to die for her people," she says. "She expects to die, but please don't let her die in vain. Help her destroy that monster." Tears glistened in those incredible eyes. "He was laughing when they hanged our brother!"

Without thinking I throw my arms around her. "She won't die. I won't let her. I swear to Almighty God she will wipe that Satan from the face of this earth and she will live. I promise you!"

She hugs me tightly and kisses me lightly on the cheek. I am trembling.

Can Yelena do it? Could I do it? Could you? But the fact that she places herself at risk of a horrible death in hopes of one small victory in this terrible war, is as fine a testament you will ever see of the ability of ordinary people to perform extraordinary feats in desperate times.

Yelena Mazanik was by no means alone in her heroism.

Just the other day I was watching a television show entitled "The Colour of War"* that showed old-fashioned home movies taken in colour during the later stages of the war. Featured in one memorable scene was the triumphant march of the Red Army into

---

* **FACT:** At the time of publication, this film is available at
« www.thehistorychannel.co.uk »

a shattered Berlin. The number of women proudly and joyfully marching side by side as equals with the conquering men was truly astounding.

It didn't surprise me, however, because I could see with my own eyes the fearless and truly magnificent role played by millions of our women in defeating the Nazi scourge.

The torture reserved for female soldiers and partisans is especially horrific, and they all know it, but I doubt very much if the threat of it deters any more than a tiny handful of women from fighting with or even leading the men. There is no doubt, and the facts bear this out, that without the women fighting shoulder to shoulder with us we would never have thrown back the German advance on Moscow.

And our women don't just fight for the Motherland as partisans or in the trenches; they drive and command tanks, and man the huge guns of the artillery. As snipers, they pick off thousands of the enemy and what few people know today is that we had many women flying combat missions both as fighter pilots and with bomber regiments.

One of our most famous female fighter pilots was Eugenia Ustimchouk who flew as a "wingman" with her husband, but the most famous of all were the group of women that comprised the 588 Night Bomber Regiment that incredibly flew a total of 24,000 sorties.* The Germans came to fear them so much they dubbed them "*Nachthexen*," which translates to "Night Witches."

---

* **FACT:** When I looked into this, I was fascinated to learn that there were eventually three regiments comprised entirely of women—the 586th, 587th and 588th. The women were mechanics, navigators, bomb loaders, pilots and officers.

In recognition of their feats the Soviet High Command ordered that they be allowed to take part in the final onslaught of Berlin.*

All that I am telling you now I hope gives you a better understanding of why I am so proud of my country and its people. Even to this day I sometimes weep to think of how heroically we resisted the worst tyranny of modern times and how terrible was the price we paid.

---

* **FACT:** All of this is true. The heroism of women at the Eastern Front is well documented. Much additional information concerning the role women played in the Eastern Front air war is available by Googling "Soviet female combat pilots WWII."

Yelena Mazanik, 1965

Red Army woman sniper,
July 1944

Four women partisans in liberated Minsk, 1944

The Murderer of Minsk

MY MOTHER, GOD REST HER SOUL, tried to instill in her children the belief that there is an angel in all of us. "No matter how terrible you think someone is," she would admonish us, "just remember, no one is totally bad; every one of us has some goodness inside that needs to be given a chance to blossom. You just need to look for it." "Does that include Stalin?" my father once asked as the "black crows" made their daily rounds of terror. Her response was a glare in his direction.

And I remember too, during the Detroit race riots of July 1967, the TV screen showing us a tearful black woman cradling a young rioter gunned down in the streets. "He was somebody's baby," she said softly, "somebody's dear sweet baby!"

No doubt Wilhelm Kube was somebody's dear sweet baby once.

Why his journey from cooing and suckling baby to the man in charge of murdering tens of thousands of my people took him down such a twisted path we will never know. How does one suck from a mother's breast the curdled milk of bestiality?

Out of respect for my mother's memory I searched long and hard to find any sign of an angel in Herr Kube. I read every history book, every account of those terrible days in a mostly vain attempt to detect anything in him other than the very heart of darkness; a Satan walking among us posing as human!

The accounts vary somewhat, but there do appear to be two instances where Kube emitted a faint whiff of humanity.

On one occasion he is reported to have suggested that Jews who had won Iron Crosses in the First World War should receive more humane treatment than those being stuffed into the ovens.

The other instance, of which there is much written documentation, occurred when he complained in writing that the special extermination squads, known as the Einsatzgruppen, should make sure their victims were dead before burying them. "The sight of badly wounded people digging themselves out of their graves is just too cruel," he wrote. "The Führer must be notified."

Not too cruel for the victims mind you. Kube's complaint, similar to Himmler's, was that this kind of thing tended to put extra stresses and strains on those witnessing the events.

Whether Hitler ever heard the complaint is highly doubtful. The only response from High Command was that Generalkommissar Kube was too soft!

That Kube was considered too soft was yet another example of how depraved the Nazis had become. The truth is, Kube insisted on personally viewing all of the executions and took special delight in those in which children were killed. On more than 600 occasions, he ordered that the residents of entire villages be rounded up, herded into churches or municipal buildings, and then the entire village set on fire, often with the occupants locked inside and burned alive.

The most egregious example of this is the village of Khatyn where more than 650 souls perished by fire at the hand of this Satan!*

I can assure you, nothing I have learned about the murderer of Minsk makes me regret what happened on September 22, 1943. What happened the following day is another story!

---

* **FACT:** This information is accurate and available from the *Encyclopedia of the Holocaust*, Gutman Israel, editor, Macmillan Publishing Company, 1998 New York and *The Holocaust* by Sir Martin Gilbert, published by Collins, London, 1986.

Generalkommissar Wilhelm Kube (left) receives power as head of
the newly formed Minsk German Administration, August 31, 1941

September 22, 1943, Daytime

"**W**HO ARE YOU? What's your name? What's your rank?" He's almost spitting in my face as he shouts the questions in German. My reply is hesitant. I stumble over the words. "SS Hauptsturmführer Franz Gehlen of the Vorkommando, Einsatzgruppe B."*

"Not good enough. Not nearly good enough; *verdammt!*" he shouts again. "Look, can't you get it through your thick head you're a member of an elite squad? You're Waffen. You're proud, you're arrogant—act it for God's sake!"

---

* **FACT:** Hauptsturmführer means "Captain." Einsatzgruppe B was a mobile squad that specialized in running concentration camps and conquering territory.

My inquisitor, cum lecturer, is a roly-poly little fellow who looks remarkably like a condensed version of your Santa Claus, even with the white beard and belly. His eyes are not buttons though, and he's not laughing. He's frustrated with me because I am an abysmal pupil. An arts professor before the war, his job is to teach me how to act the role of an officer of the Waffen SS; a member of one of Hitler's elite squads charged with killing anyone deemed to be a threat to the security of the occupied countries. This of course includes all Jews.

As I think I mentioned earlier, I am by nature rather shy and retiring, at least I was then, about as distant in character from an SS officer as you can possibly get and I'm having great difficulty pulling a John Wayne or a Gary Cooper or anything close to it.

"You're going into Minsk tomorrow," says my instructor, feigning patience. "The young lady has been alerted, the plans are set, so you'd better smarten up here or the first time a Nazi bastard hears you talking like *ein waschlappen* [a sissy] he'll put a bullet between your eyes!"

That focuses my mind in fine fashion, so by the time I'm ready to climb aboard my motorcycle the next day and head into the heart of Minsk, I've got the arrogance thing down pretty well. I'm clicking my heels together and heil Hitlering with the best of them.

My little Santa has even rounded up a riding crop so I can impatiently whack my highly polished boot tops as I listen to "stupid" questions from "dumb" German soldiers and guards. At least that's the plan!

Getting into Minsk is ridiculously easy. I speed past two concrete-bunkered guard posts manned by heavily armed soldiers who barely glance in my direction. The Wehrmacht, I have been told, regards the SS with a combination of resentment and fear, with fear the predominant sentiment. The SS after all, have been especially commissioned by Hitler himself and essentially have a license to arrest or even kill anyone they happen to take a dislike to, including ordinary soldiers of the Third Reich.

My heart pounds and my buttocks quiver as I skid my motorcycle to a halt in front of the striped metal barricade that blocks the main highway entrance into Minsk, but as I reach inside my breast pocket for my carefully forged identity papers, the barricade opens and a bored guard waves me through! I can't believe it!

Bombing raids have reduced large sections of Minsk to rubble. Hundreds of people, including women and children, are in the streets methodically clearing the rubble. In a true testament to the spirit of my people, I even see one instance where they have already begun reconstruction operations. At one point I have to slow to a crawl in order to weave my way through a long line of women, a kind of bucket brigade, passing shattered bricks and stone down from a small mountain of debris into a truck.

Armed guards, some of them Belarusian collaborators, I am sad to say, darken every intersection. It's a warm, late summer day, and some of the guards appear to have been lulled to sleep on their feet. The deep-throated roar of my motorcycle elicits little more than an occasional flicker of eyelids or brief glance in my direction.

The plan is that Yelena meets me sometime in the late afternoon, hopefully between 4:00 and 6:00 p.m., in a small basement bakery where she frequently shops for Kube's dinner. The time must be flexible in order to accommodate any domestic duties that may crop up. Kube sometimes demands a mid-afternoon snack, or perhaps it is something else he demands, which can throw our schedule off. No matter what the weather, Yelena will be wearing a bright red scarf and carrying a basket covered with a red-and-white-checkered cloth. The bomb will be placed in this basket.

We did consider leaving the device hidden under a pile of bricks someplace where Yelena could pick it up later, but concluded there was too much danger of one of the cleaning squads accidentally stumbling across it. Besides which, we must devise some method for her to smuggle the bomb past the guards who will search her basket and her clothing as she reenters Kube's heavily guarded compound.

She has also demanded that we see each other to avoid any misunderstanding during the rescue attempt. The possibility of another SS officer being near as she flees the scene is remote, but Yelena insists that we meet, no matter how briefly, prior to her planting the bomb in Kube's bed.

I have studied maps and know exactly where the bakery is, so finding it is not a problem, but trying to remain inconspicuous for perhaps as long as two or three hours, waiting for her to appear may be difficult. First, I have to give my acting lessons another test.

It's shortly after noon as I wheel my motorcycle onto what remains of a shattered sidewalk in front of a partially bombed out building that houses a tiny bakery. My unexpected arrival scatters a large group of haggard and anxious looking women already lining up for an all-night vigil to assure themselves a front-of-the-line position for tomorrow's meagre supplies. All of this is under the watchful but somewhat bemused eye of a member of the Minsk *polizei* with his dreaded black armband.

I know the bakery will open at six the next morning and will run out of bread quickly, as it did today, except for two loaves that are set aside for Generalkommissar Wilhelm Kube's maid.

Brushing aside the women on the sidewalk, I pound on the locked door with my riding crop. "Open up immediately," I shout in the most intimidating voice I can muster. There's a moment's delay before the door opens a crack to reveal a florid, floursmeared face whose gender from this perspective is impossible to determine. The voice, however, is unmistakably feminine. "We are closed, Herr General," she says, obviously misreading my insignia, "What do you want?"

"Open the door!" So saying, I give it a shove, knocking her aside. I stride in.

A young man behind a makeshift counter looks up, startled. I slap my gloved hand sharply with the riding crop. "Give me two loaves of your best bread. White bread, do you hear me? Not that black garbage you're stuffing full of sawdust." The woman's face reddens even more beneath its floury dusting. "I am very sorry Herr General, but the only bread we have left today is reserved for a special customer."

I narrow my eyes and give her what I hope is a menacing stare.

Without saying a word, I reach into my pocket and extract a small notepad and pencil. "Your name please and your address!" Fear leaps into her eyes. She darts through a small curtain and returns in an instant with two loaves of white bread wrapped in brown paper. I slam down enough money to pay for about five loaves, give both of them a view of my back, and march towards the door. As I am about to exit, the man starts to say something about giving me some change. Before he can get the words out, I spin around, click my heels together, snap my right arm over my head, and shout "Heil Hitler!" There is a somewhat stunned and half-hearted response, but I am already out the door.

Several women in the growing crowd outside, seeing my success, rush the door in the mistaken belief that a new supply is available. As I roar away, a melee breaks out among them with much pushing and shouting. As I turn the corner, I see the policeman wading in, baton swinging.

A few blocks away is a small sparsely grassed, rutted park where several young boys are playing soccer with a ball of old rags and black tape. Their game stops abruptly as I pull up; wary eyes, already old beyond their years, watch me; legs prepare to bolt. I strip the wrapping off one of the loaves, fold the brown paper carefully into my pocket, and without a word, I toss both loaves in their direction.

Hunger trumps fear every time and as I pull away they are tearing at the food like a pack of hungry dogs.

It is now approaching 2:00 p.m. Two hours until my stakeout of the bakery begins.

As per our plan, I drive past a large anti-aircraft gun installation to a three-storey, mostly intact building only about a block from the ghetto. After a cursory examination of my papers, I am waved through a guard post, past coils of barbed wire into a parking area patrolled by an armed guard. "No one goes near it," I shout to the guard, pointing to my motorbike. "You understand me?" He nods, and despite a pounding heart and shortness of breath, I march as confidently as any SS officer up the front steps and into one of the most feared buildings in the entire city—*polizei* headquarters!

I exchange a few words with what appears to be a clerk. There's another brief examination of my papers, I sign a large record book and am escorted down a steep set of stairs into a large windowless room crammed from ceiling to floor with filing cabinets. Here are the birth and other vital records of almost every resident of Belarus.

For almost two hours I open cabinets, pull out handfuls of files, rifle through various papers and jot down notes…or pretend to.

No one pays the least attention when I finally rise from the table, walk to the front desk, sign out, and climb aboard my motorcycle. I am surprised they don't bother to search me as I leave. Very obviously they have no intention of, as you would say, pissing off the SS!

Now comes the really dangerous part. My play-acting will have to be Academy Award quality! There will be no retakes when next I take the stage. A missed cue will cost lives. Probably mine!

I know the route Yelena will take, so I park between two shattered buildings about four blocks from the bakery and pretend to observe a nearby group of men demolishing a partially destroyed building.

Thus far the decision to "hide" in full view of everyone seems to be working. There is nothing unusual about SS officers looking for partisans or troublemakers on the streets of Minsk. In fact, two SS officers, one a corporal, another a sergeant, stroll by at one point, giving me a smart salute. It scares the hell out of me, but I manage to return what I think is an appropriately laconic response.

I don't have to wait long. Shortly after 4:30 p.m. I spot the red scarf and shopping basket. Yelena is walking briskly, which tells me I have less than two minutes to go into my act. Firing up my motorcycle, I drive slowly around the block, arriving at the bakery just as the *polizei* takes Yelena by an arm and escorts her through the crowd of grumbling, pushing women lined up outside.

As the bakery door opens to his knock, I leap off my bike, reach into a concealed pocket in the sidecar, grab a package wrapped in the brown paper supplied earlier by the bakery, push through the crowd and just as the door is about to slam shut I give it a solid kick and barge in.

Reaching across the counter, I grab the frightened young man by the collar and between clenched teeth hiss, "You shortchanged me when I was here earlier, you little swindler. Give me the money you owe me, or would you sooner take a nice little ride with me on my motorcycle?" I am afraid I may have overdone it, as he appears about ready to faint.

Turning to Yelena, as though noticing her for the first time, I growl, "And who are you? What are you doing here? They told me I got the last two loaves of bread. What's going on here? Why did this policeman escort you in?" I give him a glare. "Are you involved in this swindle, too?"

Her smile is beautiful; tiny freckles dance across the bridge of her nose. Her black eyes sparkle. I see no fear. The thought strikes me that if indeed Kube is sleeping with this one, he has much better taste than I would have guessed.

"If you bought the last two loaves of bread today then I am in big trouble with the Generalkommissar," she says, still smiling. "Those were supposed to be his! This poor man you are assaulting is under orders to keep two loaves for me to pick up every day for Herr Kube."

I release the young man's collar and he falls back. Giving my best interpretation of chagrin, I gasp, "Oh my God! I had no idea. Those loaves were being kept for Herr Kube?" She only nods but looks carefully at me, sizing me up. Her eyes ask, "Have you got the guts and brains to carry this out?"

I bow slightly. "My apologies to you, Fräulein, and to the Generalkommissar. But all is not lost; I confess I have already eaten one of the loaves, but I still have this one that is untouched. I couldn't leave it outside with that howling mob of vultures. Here, take this and send my apologies to Herr Kube." I hold the bread out to her. She hesitates a moment, gives me a radiant smile and what appears to be a little curtsy, then very daintily she takes the loaf, places it in her basket, thanks me, smiles again and walks out.

If I could have, right then and there, I would have leapt for joy. The bomb is in her basket!

Just as importantly, unless they start poking around in Kube's dinner, Yelena will have no trouble getting it past the guards. After all, she has been ferrying fresh bread through the gates of Kube's compound for months.

Never a loaf like this one, though—baked over an open fire, deep in the Kurapaty forest early this morning from a very special recipe with ingredients not intended to be enjoyed!

September 22, 1943, Nighttime

ANYONE WHO HAS DONE ANY LIVING AT ALL knows full well that the longer the fickle finger of fate gives you the thumbs up, the more serious the trouble will be when it arrives, and arrive it surely will. In other words, I should have known things were going too well and prepared for a reversal of fortunes.

The plan is that after delivering the bomb to Yelena, I return to my faux search for records at *polizei* headquarters, planning to hide out there until dark. Kube generally goes to bed around 10:00 p.m., so I've got a lot of time to kill, if I may use that phrase.

There is a fairly well organized underground resistance movement in Minsk, but their feeling is it would be just too risky for me to make contact with them in any way. The information they provide, however, is that if I can hide until after dark and then begin to patrol slowly up and down city streets, it should not create suspicion.

Not only that, they have advised, but if I stop occasionally in front of occupied buildings and jot down addresses, fear will likely keep the street empty.

It all seems to be working so perfectly according to plan that I begin to relax a little. "This just might work," I'm thinking, when my blood runs cold. Terror strikes so deeply I have to fight against every instinct, every nerve in my body that screams at me to cut and run, to race away at full speed.

Pulling in directly behind me as I wait to be checked through the gates guarding the police headquarters is a vehicle I recognize only too well: the long low black limousine for which I once waited each night at the Opera House doors. A limousine from which only a few months ago a gloved hand extended to grasp my list of looted valuables. The hand of SS General Kurt von Gottberg, the man who commands the regiment my papers claim I belong to!

I reach for the Luger at my hip. My first inclination is to shoot him first, then myself. God help Yelena!

The guard, thinking I am reaching for my papers, holds out his hand. Months of training kicks in. The Red Army instructor back in the Kurapaty Forest hammered into all of our brains the idea that panic is what will kill us. "No matter what," he pounds into us, "never panic. Keep cool. In tight and even desperate situations try talking, bluffing before you shoot."

I am so frightened I cannot speak, my stomach cramps and for an instant I fear I will die with soiled pants. Then suddenly something very strange happens. As though from a place somewhere outside my body, I see myself reaching into my breast pocket, and extracting documents. Fear has been replaced by an icy calm. My movements, which I am sure are perfectly normal, seem to me to have slowed down. Surreal, I think is the word you might use to describe the sensation.

I learned something very important about myself in those few moments. Never again, as long as I live, will I ever let fear overtake me.

"You were here earlier today," notes the guard, who without a reply from me, hands the papers back and motions me inside the compound.

With perfect calm, I park my motorcycle and wait for the General to enter the building ahead of me. As he passes within inches, I snap my heels together loudly and give him a brisk salute. He barely looks up. I follow and within minutes am once again deep in the bowels of the headquarters, pouring over records until well after dark.

The resistance information is correct. In darkness, I slowly make my way from police headquarters along several Minsk streets, taking great care to avoid some of the debris that litters the roadways. While there have been no recent air raids, Minsk is still under a complete blackout order. It is a clear night, but the tiny sliver of moon casts very little light. It makes driving difficult, but concealment easy.

My instructions are that at 9:00 p.m. I am to make my way to a narrow alleyway about a block away from the front entrance to Kube's compound that is a building on Engels Street, adjacent to the intersection of Karl Marx and Red Army streets.

The building in which he and several other high-ranking civic and military officials and their families live is the former main public library, surrounded on all sides by a two-metre-high brick wall, topped now by coils of barbed wire. A heavy wrought iron gate spans the main entrance that is further protected by a large concrete guardhouse manned by three SS officers armed with machine pistols. Two additional members of the SS patrol the perimeter of the compound on foot and a giant searchlight has been erected that can, at the flick of a switch in the guardhouse, illuminate the front entrance. The underground resistance supplied all this information to us.

Most civilians in Minsk are subject to a strict 10:00 p.m. curfew, but since Yelena is required to remain with Kube until he retires for the night, she has a special pass allowing her to leave the compound at any hour. Each night, she walks the dozen or so blocks to her home in the basement of a shattered house at 48 Engels Street* where she and her sister Valentina live. The police and soldiers who patrol the area know her well. According to our information, they are aware of her relationship with Kube and treat her with deference.

Thus, leaving the compound after setting the bomb in Herr Kube's bed, walking a couple of blocks until she is out of sight of the guards, then jumping aboard my motorcycle for a ride to safety should pose no difficulties for her. That is if all goes according to plan.

The silence of the night as I wait in the alleyway is disconcerting. There is not a whisper of a human voice, no dogs bark. Not even a cricket's song can be heard. After living for the past year and a half in the middle of a forest, I find it very disturbing. Ominous even.

I grow more nervous. It is now well past ten o'clock and still no sign of Yelena. Has she been caught? If so, what has she told her captors? Are they searching for me? Where there was utter silence only moments ago, now I imagine I am surrounded by sounds. Was that a boot scraping the pavement behind me? Was that a whisper I just heard? I hold my breath. Nothing. Silence.

---

* **FACT:** Soviet records confirm this address as that of Yelena and Valentina Mazanik.

Shattered suddenly by a soft "pock" from the direction of the compound and the sound of breaking glass tumbling to the ground. I jump from my bike and peer around the corner of the building that has been concealing me. I see flames shooting from what appears to be the upper right-hand side of the main building. Followed immediately by shouting, the sound of heavy boots running and then a woman's scream. Something has gone very wrong. I am certain the scream is Yelena's.

I react immediately. Jumping back onto my bike, I tear out of the alleyway, turn the headlights on full, and roar down the street towards the compound. I don't need my light; the huge searchlight reveals what I fear the most. Two guards have Yelena in their grasp. They are yelling, she is screaming. Lights appear like so many sparks in several windows. Flames are now licking up the side of the building from a shattered window. The two patrolling officers come racing up. They begin yelling. It is chaos.

Wheeling my bike into the middle of this, I shout, "Halt!" As soldiers, they react to authority just as I had expected. They stop yelling, and still holding Yelena, they stand stiffly awaiting orders. They need to be told what to do.

"You," I point to the two patrolling officers who have just come pounding up. "Find out what has happened." I gesture towards the flames that are spreading up the wall. "Then secure the building." I wave them through the iron gate that stands open and they run towards the building, shouting at several curious people sticking their heads out windows and doors.

The two SS officers, both fortunately below my rank, who continue to hold Yelena, look at me with some puzzlement. Who the hell is this guy? The third officer, as per orders I suspect, remains locked inside the guardhouse where I am certain he has already alerted the fire department.

"Who is this?" I demand, pointing to Yelena. "What is she doing here? Why are you holding her? What has she done?" The officer, who I sense is becoming suspicious of me, replies, "Her name is Yelena Mazanik, Herr Captain, she is Generalkommissar Kube's maid. There's been an explosion of some kind in what we think is Herr Kube's apartment and we've just caught her running away." As he's explaining this to me, I notice him very subtly moving his hand closer to the pistol strapped on his hip.

I turn to Yelena, "You little bitch," I say, and hit her hard enough in the stomach to knock her to the ground out of her captors' grasp. In one swift motion, I pull my Luger from its holster, point it at her head as though to shoot her as she lies groaning on the ground. Then, without warning, I whip the gun up and fire a bullet into the chest of the suspicious officer, spin around, and before the second soldier can do anything but widen his eyes, I shoot him in the head.

Stooping down, I grab Yelena by the front of her blouse and yank her to her feet. "Get up! Run!"

Gasping for air, she manages to stagger to the idling motorcycle and collapse into the sidecar. I leap into the saddle, aware that the third guard has thrown open the guardhouse door and is about to open up with his submachine gun. I fire three quick shots in his direction and he dives back to safety inside. By the time he scrambles back to his feet, Yelena and I are swallowed up by the darkness.

I am driving blindly, full speed down Red Army Street not sure exactly where I am, when Yelena reaches across, grasps my arm and shouts, "Here, turn right here," then a moment later, "turn right again here. Slow down, slow down, they haven't cleared the street yet." I hit a large slab of concrete, which almost throws us out of control. "Now," she says, "look just ahead, do you see that building? The one that looks like it's cut in half?" I see it, but just barely. "Go slow now, turn left just past it and then keep going. It will take us out of the city."

I'm confused. "What do you mean out of the city? They told me every road leading out of Minsk is blocked with barricades or guardhouses." I can't see her face, but from her voice she appears to be grimly smiling. "Tomorrow," she assures me, "this road will be blocked again, but tonight our friends have taken care of it."

I hope she's right about her friends in the resistance, because if they haven't taken care of the barricade we are surely trapped. I hear the rising and falling wail of sirens drawing closer from at least two different directions.

God bless her friends! They did their job well. In a few minutes we roar past two large concrete barricades that have been pushed aside just enough to allow us to pass. Past a huge bombed-out building now, over a set of railway tracks, then through what is left of some kind of industrial complex we leave the sirens behind, bounce wildly across a rutted farmer's field, and enter the blessed silence of the Kurapaty forest. Against all odds, we are safe!

There is much cheering and backslapping the next morning in our little haven in the woods. "You did it, Yelena, you did it," is the cry. Valentina is openly weeping with joy, alternately clutching her sister and hugging me.

And it's true—the murderer of Minsk, Generalkommissar Wilhelm Kube, is dead despite a malfunction that obviously detonated the bomb before Yelena could make her way out of the building. Our explosive experts agree that baking the bomb parts into the loaf of bread must have damaged the timer. "Yelena," they claim, "is lucky the thing didn't explode in her hands!"

There is plenty of praise as well for my quick reaction and fast thinking in rescuing her. Urie Labonak himself shakes my hand and tells me Moscow is anxious to reward both of us for our efforts. My little Santa Claus acting instructor is almost giddy with joy. "I knew you could do it, I knew it, I knew it. You were a wonderful student," he lies. The best reward of all, however, comes from Yelena herself who kisses me softly on the lips and whispers in my ear, "Thank you."

It starts my heart pounding almost as hard as it had on our wild ride to freedom.

The official records available for all to see today record this fact: On September 22, 1943, Generalkommissar Wilhelm Kube, the chief administrator for Minsk and its infamous ghetto, the man who boasted of murdering more than 50,000 Jews, is killed when a bomb in a hot water bottle placed by his maid (or mistress) Yelena Mazanik explodes in his bed.*

---

* **FACT:** This is absolutely correct and well documented in many history books and other accounts of the war.

Retaliation

SADLY, THE OFFICIAL RECORDS ALSO STATE the following: On September 23, 1943, in retaliation for the killing of Generalkommissar Wilhelm Kube, one thousand male residents of Minsk were ordered out of their homes, given shovels, made to dig a deep pit, and then jump into it. All were slaughtered by SS officers who poured machine gun fire into the pit for more than 15 minutes. Other residents of Minsk were forced to bury the dead.*

---

* **FACT:** This atrocity is well documented, in particular by Ernst Klee, *Das Personenlexikon zum Dritten Reich* (Fischer Verlag 2005) and also by M. Gilbert, *The Holocaust*. Once again the US Holocaust Museum in Washington provides full documentation concerning both the assassination of Wilhelm Kube and the subsequent retaliation by the Nazis.

There is no cheering in the Kurapaty forest at this terrible news, believe me. Our shock and sorrow is profound. We expected some kind of retaliation, but 1,000 innocent people? It is almost unthinkable, but of course, we should have known that the Nazis' depravity knows no bounds. What's another thousand dead to them?

Labonak, trying to console Yelena and me, points out that the intent of the Germans is to eventually kill most of our citizens anyway. "We must continue to fight them in any way we can," he says. "What you did was not only brave but noble! We have to send a message to the highest level of the German Command that none of them is safe from the fury of those they would murder, torture, rape and oppress. We will find them and kill them even in their beds at night. No more sweet dreams for Nazis—we are their nightmares!"

It quickly becomes apparent not everyone shares his sentiments.

The grief, shock, and anger are such that I become afraid that Yelena and I may be in some danger. Several of those in our zimlanka have loved ones murdered in this latest atrocity. One sobbing woman begins to berate and then attack me, pounding on my chest with her fists and screaming in agony. Several other women gather around in black silence, their eyes more dangerous than the fists.

Labonak is no fool. He's aware of the feeling among some that Yelena and I are responsible for yet another terrible tragedy. The growing consensus in camp is that the death of one man, no matter how bestial he was, is not worth the lives of a thousand. We are no longer heroes here.

The Land of Great Ice and Snow

THE NEXT MORNING Labonak summons both Yelena and me to his hut and addresses us in formal fashion.

"The Soviet Union congratulates both of you. Joseph Stalin himself has been made aware of your feat and has summoned you, Yelena Mazanik, to Moscow where you will be presented with the award 'Hero of the Soviet Union.' You are destined, I think, to become one of the Motherland's most famous and beloved heroes." Yelena, obviously expecting something far different, becomes flustered and can't seem to get any words out.

I don't suppose Labonak has many pleasant duties to perform and is obviously enjoying this greatly. "Yelena," he smiles, "while you're eating caviar and filet mignon in Red Square, this young man," here he turns to me, "is heading to the land of great snow and ice."

Here he pauses for dramatic effect. "No, not Siberia!" He breaks into outright laughter. "Igor is going to serve us in Canada."

Canada!? I've hardly heard of the place. This is a reward? Honestly, that's my first reaction when told that in recognition of rescuing our brand new "Hero of the Soviet Union," I am being posted to Canada.

Labonak, sensing my consternation, punches me lightly on the shoulder. "Young man, wake up, we're getting you out of this damn war. No more Nazis, no more guns. Think of it, no more bombs, you can take a bath. They tell me Canada even has hot running water. Think of that! Sleeping in a nice warm, soft bed at night." Here he pauses briefly, and then whispers so Yelena can't hear, "Maybe even with someone who's also had a nice warm bath. Think of that!"

Thinking or wanting has nothing to do with it. Stalin, or someone in the Kremlin, has decided I am being posted to the Soviet Embassy in Ottawa, Canada, and that's the end of it.

Yelena kisses me one more time, this time goodbye. She eventually makes her way to Moscow where, at the end of the war, she is indeed awarded the title of "Hero of the Soviet Union." Even after her death in 1996, she remains to this day a much-revered figure in Russia.

Her sister Valentina? Ah, that's another story!

The next evening I am driven for several miles via my now-famous "escape" motorcycle to a large clearing in the forest where a small airplane is waiting.

That night the moon is bright enough for me to catch the odd glimpse of the English Channel, as we skim the waves. I recall very clearly that as the blackness of England looms just ahead, a terrible weight falls from my shoulders.

If I knew what lay ahead, I would not have been so sanguine!

We land someplace in the north of England, and from there a

battered and noisy vehicle I now know was a Jeep, takes me to a small seaport village in the north of Scotland.

It is a strange and mystical place where the mist drifts in and out so that most of the time we can only half see things. The top half of trees, the top half of the nearby hills, and most of all, only the top half of a huge ship whose mooring ropes appear to dissolve halfway down her side. The ship herself is painted a misty grey; even her smoke stacks, so it is difficult to discern where ship and mist begin and end. Only when I am aboard do I realize I am on one of the most famous ships of the war. So famous we've even heard of her in far-away Belarus.

It's the *Queen Mary*, with all the trappings of luxury passenger accommodation stripped away to make way for bunks and hammocks for as many as 12,000 troops on their way to war from the United States, Australia, and New Zealand. On the return voyages, she is converted to a hospital ship taking back thousands of wounded soldiers, sailors, and airmen—and on this occasion, me!

I cannot believe we haul anchor and leave without a single escort vessel, but they tell me that the "Grey Ghost," as she is affectionately dubbed by the crew, is so fast she's almost impossible for subs to catch. Convoys, I am told, would only slow her down.

She's fast all right. We are sailing past the Statue of Liberty into New York Harbour less than a week later.* It's all happened so quickly I am completely disoriented. As the "Grey Ghost" pulls into port, someone on the docks very foolishly sets off some fireworks and I dive for cover behind a lifeboat. No one who sees me laughs.

---

* **FACT:** The *Queen Mary* left the obscure port of Gourock on the northwest coast of Scotland on September 29, 1943, arriving in New York City on October 5.

A train ride from New York into Ottawa's downtown Union Station and three days later they have me sitting at a small desk in the Soviet Embassy near Strathcona Park, close to the University of Ottawa. Because, in addition to fluent Russian, Belarusian, and German, I have a rudimentary knowledge of English, they decide to appoint me assistant editor of the propaganda magazine the Embassy churns out each month entitled *The Soviet Union Today.**

You have been told that I was a cipher clerk. Whatever a cipher clerk is, I most definitely am not! Actually, I'm not really much of an editor either, at least not at first, but the job does pique my interest in becoming one and ignites in me a lifelong love of the study of Russian and English literature. Of course, it's all just a cover for the "real" work I believe I have been assigned—which is "befriending" the Ottawa University professor. Not that I am making much headway there, either.

• • •

There you are, my friend, the mystery is solved. Now you know how it came to be that what the history books claim was a young, fit, Soviet soldier got to sit out some of the most terrible battles in history in the safety and comfort of Canada's capital city.

It was genes and circumstance that brought me to Canada. Genes that dictated blue eyes and fair hair, and circumstances that led to a wild motorcycle escape through the streets of Minsk with a "Hero of the Soviet Union"! That's a far cry from what the history books say isn't it?

---

* **FACT:** This magazine was published well into the 1960s at the Soviet Embassy in Ottawa.

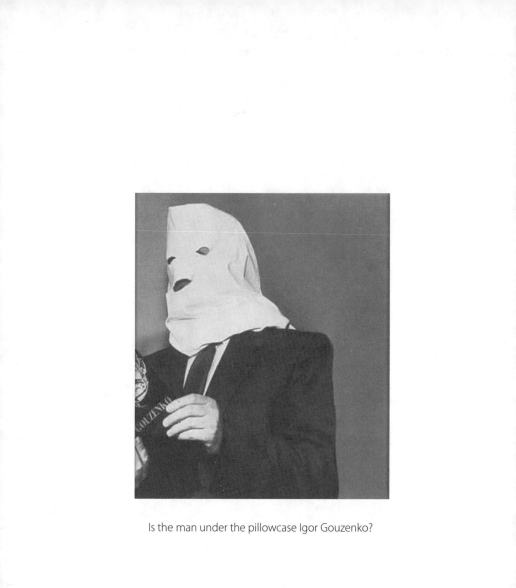

Is the man under the pillowcase Igor Gouzenko?

Why the Pillowcase Over His Head?

BEFORE I GO FURTHER HERE, I want to ask you about something else you must agree is very strange.

I've already raised the matter of the mysteriously missing two months from Mackenzie King's diary, and I've asked you if you don't think there is something very curious about a young, able-bodied, highly trained Soviet soldier kept from the battlefield to push a few papers around in a Canadian office.

Please keep in mind that I'm not in Ottawa to assume a position of any importance, but rather to fill a relatively minor role.

Do you really believe that Stalin sent me all the way from Belarus to fill a job that could easily have been assigned to one of a million or more disabled Soviet soldiers or, for that matter, a grandfather far too old for the trenches?

It's a mystery I hope I have solved for you by explaining how allowing me to escape the carnage of the Eastern Front for the safety of Ottawa was a reward for rescuing Yelena Mazanik.

Now I want to point your curiosity towards something else, which when you stop and think about it, really doesn't make any sense.

The question is this: Why did the man the media, the Canadian Government, the RCMP and the FBI all claim was Igor Gouzenko never show his face in public? Think back. Every time you saw this man who supposedly defected from the Soviet Embassy with his famous list of spies, his head was covered with a crazy-looking pillowcase. Why?

If he was really Igor Gouzenko, the Soviets obviously knew what he looked like, so why try to hide his face from them?

Recently, I found an episode of the Canadian television program "Front Page Challenge"* on the Internet, during which this so-called Gouzenko was the guest they were supposed to identify. Sure enough, there was this faker standing there, hidden from the panelists with that famous pillowcase over his head. Unfortunately none of the panelists ever thought to ask the most important question of all: Why do you have that stupid hood over your head? Dare I suggest that even such famous personages as Pierre Berton, Gordon Sinclair, and Betty Kennedy, some of Canada's most famous journalists at the time, were hoodwinked along with everyone else?

* **FACT:** At the time of publication this show is available at
« http://archives.cbc.ca/polotics/national-security/topics/72/ »

I ask you again. Why? The claim was that the Soviets were looking for him to put that head in a noose rather than in a bag, but they knew perfectly well what he looked like. I mean, the Soviet Embassy must have had all sorts of pictures of him. So why did we never get a look at his face?

From whom was he hiding and why?

I know the answer.

I am the reason why. It was because a newspaper editor saw the real Igor Gouzenko. He saw *me*!

Klaus Fuchs' ID badge photo from
Los Alamos National Laboratory

Defect or Die!

I HAVE NEVER BEEN SO SURPRISED in all my life as I was the night of the second dinner party at Harry Sowell's Rockcliffe Park residence when they threatened to kill me!

One minute my little Irish lass is suggestively stroking my leg beneath a wine-laden dinner table, the next minute I'm being told I either defect with a briefcase full of spy information or I will have an "unfortunate accident."

Actually it's more than a few minutes from table to threat; the shock of it all seems to compress time.

There's an extra guest at our table this night. An older man, almost bald, short with a pronounced pot only partially concealed beneath what is obviously a very expensive grey suit. He is preceded as he strolls over to meet me by a noxious, vile-smelling cloud of smoke he noisily sucks from an enormous cigar then exhales through his nostrils. Altogether a disgusting, but at the same time, fascinating performance. I get the idea he fancies himself Winston Churchill in a fine suit!

"Jonathan Walters," he announces as he holds out his hand for me to shake. "Good friend of Harry's here." Two smoking volcanoes erupt; I instinctively flinch and step back. He doesn't seem to notice. "Yep, old Harry and I go way back, way back. Been friends a long time, long time. Business partners too." Another smoky eruption. The end of his cigar seems to flare for a moment but he pays it no attention. "We're going to have a lovely little dinner here, then Harry and I have a business proposition for you. Yes my boy, a wonderful business proposition."

"But first" says Harry, who battles his way through the fumes that have settled over both of us, "let's all sit down now. Dinner is being served."

The bit about the business proposition floats like a feather in the breeze right over my head. But you know, in thinking it over since, I have come to the conclusion that something during that evening must have fired a warning shot across my brain because I recall cutting back on my wine consumption, thinking it might be best if I kept my wits about me.

How right I was!

"Let's finish up with a brandy in the study," says Harry with a big smile, as the dinner plates disappear. "Patsy, can we steal your man for a few minutes? We've got a little something we'd like to discuss with him." Her hand departs my leg and does a little above-the-table flip of dismissal. "Of course. Now don't you boys be too long. Igor and I have some plans."

She gives me her best dazzler...and I never see her again.

•••

So here we are in this lovely little room lined with dark wood, leather, and books. Carpet deep enough to take a swim in. The "study," according to Harry, who takes a seat in a plush leather chair in a far corner. He leans back, grabs his left ankle with his right hand and pulls the leg up over his thigh. It's a very clear signal that his "good friend" and "business partner" is the man in charge here.

"Have a seat," says Jonathan and points to a straight-backed chair in the centre of the room. He remains standing, still puffing away on what must be his third or fourth cigar of the night. A side door suddenly opens and I am somewhat surprised to see that "White Gloves," the chauffeur, has joined us. He closes the door behind him and stands stiffly in front of it.

The little buzz of concern I am feeling suddenly becomes a definite tingle up and down my spine. Something seems just a little odd here.

I decide I've had enough. "You know, gentlemen," I say, "I'm not feeling so good, so if your driver here can take Patsy and me home now…" I begin to rise from my chair but Jonathan takes me by the shoulder and with surprising force settles me back down. Harry just looks at me and says nothing.

"Would you like one?" asks Jonathan as he proffers a small wooden box containing several cigars. "Man just north of Montreal makes them special for me; grows the tobacco right in his own back yard believe it or not. Nothing else you can buy anywhere with this aroma." I don't have difficulty believing him but shake my head no.

"Too bad," says Jonathan, "they're really very special. Okay then, let's get down to business. How would you like to make ten thousand dollars tonight?" Before I can reply he continues. "We have a job for you tonight and your choice is really very simple. Either do this not-very-difficult job, take the ten thousand or we will arrange a very unfortunate accident for you and we certainly don't want that now do we?"

He steps back to watch my reaction.

They can't be serious! "You're not serious," I say. "You will have me killed? Is that what you mean by this, what did you say, unfortunate accident I'm going to have? You're going to have me killed if I don't do this thing you want?" In anger I spring from my chair, ready to attack. I can handle these two easily.

"Whatever you're thinking," says Jonathan calmly, "look over there."

I turn slightly. "White Gloves'" revolver is pointed at my head!

"Now sit down," says Jonathan forcefully, "and listen to what you're going to do tonight."

Just as occurred more than two years ago when an SS General pulled in behind me at the Minsk police headquarters, anger and fear are replaced by an icy calm. I sit and listen and think.

"Mr. Gouzenko, you are going to become both rich and famous tonight. You are going to defect. You are going to go running to the police, well actually to a reporter, with a long list of Soviet spies operating in Canada and the United States. You are going to expose a major espionage ring."

My anger dissolves into puzzlement. "Why me?" I ask. "If you've got this list of spies, why don't you give it to the police yourself? This is crazy stuff. Why involve me?" Then a thought strikes me. "Where did that list come from? Where did you get those names? Not from me. Who are you?" I turn to Harry. "Who is he? Are you the police?"

"I see you're not without brains," says Jonathan who lights another giant cigar, exhaling clouds of smoke in my direction. "Well, since it sounds like you're being a bit more co-operative this time, I'll lay a few facts out for you."

Pacing back and forth through a thick haze of smoke, the fat man in the grey suit explains.

"Anyone who sees this list we're giving you will know full well it can only have come from the Soviet Embassy in Ottawa. Many of the spies are, in fact, Canadian.

"If the list originates in Canada, then very clearly there must be a leak at the Embassy here. Right? So if we don't give the Ruskies a story about a defector—you—then they'll ship every single person in the embassy back to the good old Soviet Union for some serious questioning. That, by the way, would of course include you, wouldn't it? You know what will happen to you all then. If Stalin has you all shot, it won't bother me one bit, but our source here in Ottawa will dry up and that we cannot allow. Are you following me so far?"

I nod. "So, you've got an informer here in the Soviet Embassy, but you don't want Stalin to find out who he is, so you've decided I'm going to be the fallen one? Why me? Who are you?"

Off in his private corner, Harry suddenly uncrosses his leg and comes to life.

"I think you mean the fall guy, Igor. We don't look at it that way at all. We're giving you a chance to earn ten thousand dollars tonight, more money I am certain than you'll make in the next three years at the embassy and all you have to do is deliver some papers to a newspaper reporter. You'll be a hero. Your picture will be all over the newspapers. You'll be on all the newsreels in movie theatres. Beautiful young ladies will fall all over you!" He pauses for a moment and looks at Jonathan. "And as for who we are, it doesn't really matter, does it? Let's just say we represent the interests of free people, and by the way we know all about your attempts to cozy up to our friend the science professor at the university. Sounds very much to us like spying, wouldn't you say? We could have turned you in long ago."

Anger grips me again but I manage to control it. "You're talking foolish, crazy. You know I will be a dead man if I defect. No newspapers, just a bullet in the head and a grave for me." When I am agitated I sometimes have trouble finding the correct words in English.

Jonathan reaches down and pats me on the shoulder. "No, no, Igor. We will protect you. We will give you a new identity, a new home. You will be safe, Igor. The United States will not allow anything bad to happen to you."

This is the first time anyone has mentioned the United States, but I let it ride for the moment. A voice from the Kurapaty forest jumps into my head. "Keep talking. Keep them talking and keep thinking your way out of this."

"This is nonsense, foolish talk," I say, "no one can hide from Joseph Stalin or Lavrenti Beria and his police if they want to find you. Why do you pick me to do this thing?"

Harry sounds almost as though he's trying to apologize when he replies.

"Several reasons, Igor. First, you are young and eager; easy pickings for Miss Regan, a lovely little piece of prime bait if ever there was one. You're quite an attractive, western-looking fellow; you've begun speaking English very well, so you'll be more likely to receive favourable press. Newspapers, you know, love good-looking heroes. Then, of course, since you don't have any family members back home, in the eyes of our Soviet friends you would be much more likely to defect than someone whose relatives would be prey to retaliation. In short you're just about perfect for the job!"

The perfect partisan in Belarus and now in Canada, the perfect traitor!

I decide my best course is to play along. Keep them talking. If I could fool the SS in Minsk I should be able to figure my way out of this one without too many bruises.

"What happens if I refuse? I don't want to be a traitor to my country. I have no love for Stalin and I am very much afraid of him, but I don't want to betray my people. They have suffered for many, many years while you in the United States did nothing to help. You *are* from America, aren't you?" I ask Jonathan but he doesn't respond.

"If I refuse to do what you want, what will you do? How can you make me do this thing?"

Jonathan's eyes flick past my shoulder to take in the man with the gun. Turning completely around so I am staring at his back, he puffs vigorously on his cigar and beings speaking so quietly I have to strain to hear him.

"You see Mr. Gouzenko, Mr. Hoover and I have an urgent problem. We have a very bad man down there in the United States who's taken to having little boys killed and our government has asked me to put a stop to it. You know who Mr. Hoover is?"

I nod. "Everyone knows he's head of the FBI. I knew that in Belarus."

"Good," says Jonathan, "then you know we are serious people. This bad man's name is Klaus Fuchs. You've never heard of him, I'm sure, but he's one of those hotshot German scientists we've let into our country. Right now he's busy figuring out how to build atomic bombs. You know, the kind we just dropped on the Japs. This little freak thinks he's been feeding all kinds of atomic secrets to your commie comrades in the Soviet Union. Fact is, though, most of the information and documents he's handing over to your good buddies are either garbage or stuff we know you Ruskies already have.

"It's been kind of fun 'till now. A kind of game really. Not helping you Reds very much at all, but Klaus Fuchs is a dirty pervert. Likes little boys and sadly one of those little boys has ended up dead. We think it's because the boy was going to blow the whistle on Fuchs." Here he turns around to look at me. "You know what I mean, blow the whistle?"

I nod.

"Turns out the boy was the son of a very influential congressman. The newspapers are starting to ask questions and if we don't put a lid on it, the mess could blow up pretty nasty, if you understand what I'm saying here. The press might not like to learn we've been playing games with a vicious little pervert and doing nothing to stop him.

"One of the problems we've had all along is how to put Fuchs behind bars without exposing our informer here in Ottawa. That's one of the reasons we need you to show up with the list of spies. All the information we have about him comes from Canada and your comrades would soon be able to figure that out."

He's got me puzzled again. "I understand you want to protect this person, this traitor here in Ottawa, but why do you think going to the police now with a list of Soviet spies will get you out of that problem, that mess, with the murdered little boy?"

Harry chips in again. "Listen, when you show up with that list, which by the way includes Klaus Fuchs' name and dozens more, the newspapers will drop everything else they're working on. It will be spies from cover to cover. Dead boys will be completely forgotten. Besides which, it's time to reel in Mr. Fuchs along with all the other miserable traitors we've got running around here."

"So you want me to be one of those—a miserable traitor? And what happens to your plan if I say no?"

It's Jonathan who spells out for me, what I think you in Canada would say, the facts of life.

"Actually, if you choose to be stupid it doesn't make all that much difference. We have a young man who can pose as Igor Gouzenko if the real Igor Gouzenko disappears!"

The silence that engulfs the room triggers a memory of an alleyway on Engels Street in Minsk. Even the cigar sounds are stilled.

120

My mind is racing. "Keep them talking. Think your way out of this. You've been in more desperate situations than this."

I raise my voice in disbelief. "What? You have an actor? Some kind of actor who can take my place? Makes no sense. They know what I look like at the Embassy. I've been there almost two years. You think they won't be able to tell the difference between the real Igor Gouzenko and some fake man? Some actor?

The cigar is back at work. "It makes a lot of sense. The actor, as you call him, is about your size and height, but he won't be holding any press conferences until our informant is settled on a nice little ranch in Colorado someplace. As for his appearance—well you're right Igor—our substitute is not the handsome fellow you are, but then who will know with his head buried under a bag?"

The apartment on Somerset Street in Ottawa, Canada,
where it is claimed Igor Gouzenko lived in 1945

Photo: D. Dean

One More Mystery

LET ME NOW PRESENT YOU with something else you must admit is very odd about the Gouzenko story as you know it. Something very mysterious, I should say.

If you've read the stories or seen the movies, you know that Igor Gouzenko first tried to defect to a newspaper reporter at the *Ottawa Journal*, a newspaper that no longer exists. This by itself must seem a little strange to you. Why would someone show up at a newspaper office with a list of Soviet spies? Why not go directly to the RCMP who were in charge of national security? Then of course, this question: Why would the reporter dismiss him as some kind of kook?

I know the answer because that was Igor Gouzenko who showed up at the *Ottawa Journal*. That really was me. The reporter didn't understand me, because I didn't want him to.

But there is a much bigger mystery.

The second place they claim that Igor Gouzenko appeared was at the office of Louis St. Laurent who was the Minister of Justice for Canada at the time. Yes, the same Louis St. Laurent who later became your Prime Minister.

Think about that for a moment. First, Gouzenko shows up at the *Ottawa Journal* newspaper so agitated he can't make himself understood, and then he just disappears until the next afternoon, when he very mysteriously appears at the offices of the Justice Minister of Canada on Parliament Hill.

I ask you. How could a young employee of the Soviet Union, in Canada less than two years, know where the Justice Minister's office was? How would he even know who the Justice Minister was, for heaven's sake? How did he get there? Who took him?

We're expected to believe that all this time he's lugging around a long list of high-level spies, 109 documents in all, and the Soviets are looking for him everywhere. Frantic to find him! For the Soviets, he's enemy number one—a very dangerous man.

Let's remember here that the espionage network I am supposed to have uncovered contained the names of spies not only involved with nuclear secrets, but the documents identified Soviet agents at work in the US Treasury Department, in the intelligence services, and in the White House! The list even contained the names of traitors serving in the Parliament of Canada.

You don't think someone from the NKVD would be hanging around Parliament Hill in case Gouzenko showed up there? You don't think Gouzenko would be only too aware of what the Soviets would do to him if they caught him?

And another very strange thing. The history books and movies claim that Gouzenko spent that first night after his failed defection attempt, in an apartment building on Somerset Street in downtown

Ottawa. An apartment building in which several other Russian families were living. That's the story you will still hear today. But think about that for just a minute. Would Gouzenko really go back to a building filled with Russians, at least one of whom might turn him in? Coming from Belarus where you couldn't trust anyone, do you really think he would have trusted all those Russians in the building not to betray him? Come on! Please! As a good friend of mine would say, "Use the old noggin, old chap!"

All reports show Gouzenko to be a highly intelligent man. With that in mind, don't you think he might have just picked up a telephone and called the police? At least called someone who could provide protection from a bunch of guys who would probably shoot him on sight? He asks protection from a newspaper reporter and not the police!?

Do you get my point?

Even if you still don't believe what I am saying, you've got to admit there's something a little weird going on here!

So let me continue to tell you what really happened.

The *Ottawa Journal*

I REMEMBER THE NIGHT like it was yesterday. It's one of those cold, crisp early fall evenings. Not a cloud in the sky and an almost full moon. Just a hint of the vicious winter cold soon to follow.

The dark streets of Ottawa are virtually empty, as they are almost every night during the early post-war dinner hour in Canada's capital. I even remember it's a Wednesday because, had circumstances been different, I would have been hauling a load of laundry around the corner from my apartment to the coin wash on Elgin Street. Instead, here I am behind the wheel of a lumbering Hudson with a gun aimed at a vital part of my body. That is to say, my head.

And from the look of grim determination on "White Gloves'" face, I have no doubt he is only too willing to pull the trigger. Strange, when you stop and think about it, since shooting the driver of a moving car can be rather risky.

I do not intend to give my armed escort cause for concern, at least not until the time is right. No sudden movements. I follow instructions issued a few minutes ago right to the letter.

"So do we have a deal then?" asks Jonathan. "Pierre here," he points to "White Gloves" who still has his gun trained on me, "will drive you to the *Ottawa Journal* offices where you'll give this to the editor on duty along with your story."

He hands me a small brown leather briefcase and then holds up a fat envelope and sticks it under my nose. "Then, my friend, when the newspaper gets this briefcase along with your story, you become a rich man."

"You see this?" He waggles the envelope in front of me. "Ten thousand American dollars that you can spend anywhere in the world and it's all yours for just one night's work. Not bad, wouldn't you say? You can buy yourself a villa in Spain. Hell's bells, with ten thousand Yankee bucks these days, you can *buy* Spain!"

He waves the envelope back and forth in front of me again before handing it Pierre, who puts his gun away and stuffs the envelope into the inside breast pocket of his jacket.

"But," warns Jonathan, "any change of heart, any screw up and it's something other than a king's ransom you'll get. Understand me? Mr. Hoover does not take kindly to failure!"

I don't reply, which Jonathan interprets as a yes.

"Okay then. Just so long as we understand each other. Don't get fancy with the editor at the *Journal*. Hand him the briefcase. Tell him you are a cipher clerk at the Soviet Embassy. Explain you're defecting and have documents revealing a major espionage ring operating in Canada and the United States. Tell him the briefcase contains a list of more than 25 Soviet agents providing nuclear secrets to the Soviet

Union. "Demand political asylum. Do you know what that means?"

"Yes, I think so," I respond. "I want police protection so Stalin doesn't hang me. Right? Is that right?"

"Ya, something like that. Just tell him you're defecting, that you've got a long list of spies and you want political asylum. Understand?"

Slowly, I get up from my chair. I don't want to alarm the driver I now know as Pierre. I don't want to signal anything other than resigned acquiescence.

"Yes, I understand. When do I do this?"

A great dark cloud erupts from Jonathan's nostrils, which I interpret as a sign of relief.

"Now!" he says. "Right now!"

The Ruse

BECAUSE YOU CANNOT SUCCESSFULLY DRIVE while pointing a gun at your seatmate, I am behind the wheel. My driving experience is very limited, especially with a behemoth like a Hudson Super Six, but I manage to navigate the downtown streets of Ottawa and pull into the darkened parking lot of the *Journal* building.

I'm watching closely for my chance to strike, but Pierre is a professional and stays well out of my reach with his gun steadily trained on me. I know, however, the odds are on my side.

He has the pistol all right, but I have spetsnaz training and he doesn't know it. He thinks he's dealing with some half-baked kid here and sooner or later I'm positive he'll drop his guard. When he does, his reward, as we say back home, will not be collected on this side of the grass!

I pluck the briefcase from the back seat and start walking towards the front entrance of the brightly lit *Journal* building. Pierre follows, but as we are about to step inside he growls menacingly in a low voice, "Okay, you stinkin' commie, no funny stuff. Any tricks in there and I shoot you *and* the editor. You understand? Try to pull anything and you're both dead men. You know what you are supposed to do. You know what you're supposed to say. Got it?"

I got it all right! My mind is churning but I remain silent as though cowed.

The newsroom is almost empty. One young lady staring down at her typewriter looks up, startled, as we enter. Pierre, I notice, has stuffed his gun into a coat pocket.

It's time for me to go into my act; to launch the ruse I've been planning since I got into the car.

With no warning, I suddenly become extremely agitated and start yelling in broken English with a very thick Russian accent. "You help. I have list. Russia, Russia. It's war; it's war. Must help!" All the while I'm kind of dancing from one foot to the other and swinging the briefcase wildly about.

I'm still shouting about lists and spies and help when an older man with a pencil stuck behind his ear wanders over and gives me a strange look. I now know his name is Chester Frowde,* the man unlucky enough to be the editor on duty that fateful night.

---

* **FACT:** It was Chester Frowde on duty at the *Journal* that night. According to him, Gouzenko kept shouting: "It's war, it's war. Russia, Russia." Frowde always claimed he simply couldn't understand what Gouzenko was trying to say.

I forget exactly what the poor man says to me. An inquiry as to what I want, I suppose. I become even more agitated, demanding protection. I talk about spies and wave my briefcase around. My accent gets thicker and thicker. My acting matches anything I was able to pull off back in the Minsk bakery.

A totally confused Frowde undoubtedly thinks he has an escapee from a mental institution on his hands and in an act that haunts him all his life, he more or less pushes me out the door, briefcase still in my hand.

Pierre is visibly seething with anger. Good! I'm ready for him!

As we walk out the front door, he shouts, "You fucking commie" and steps in close to drive his fist into my stomach. That is the last thing he utters on this earth.

They taught me well back there in the Kurapaty forest.

I don't necessarily want to kill him, but the smash to his Adam's apple unfortunately snaps his neck. I feel a bit badly about it today.

"White Gloves" was only doing his job, but as I drag his body away from the lighted entrance to the darkened side of the building before removing the envelope, his wallet, and the gun from his jacket, his death is the last thing that concerns me.

The Ambassador

THERE'S ONLY ONE MAN WHO CAN RESCUE ME from this desperate situation. A man who asked that I come to him if ever I had a problem and I certainly have a problem now. His name is Georgi Zarubin, the Soviet Ambassador to Canada.*

Last December, while attending a Christmas party at his home, Ambassador Zarubin rushed over to meet me, took both of my hands in his, looked deeply into my eyes and said with what appeared to be the utmost sincerity, in Russian: "Igor, it's so nice to finally actually meet you. It's an honour. I want you to know it was I who asked that you come to work for us here in Canada. I know what

---

* **FACT:** Georgi Zarubin was the first Ambassador from the USSR appointed to Canada.

you have done for the Motherland and we all thank you. I hope you enjoy your stay in this wonderful country and let me say this: If ever you are in need of any assistance, of any kind, please feel free to come to me."

He shakes my hand vigorously, introduces me to several other guests, and then moves on. While saying goodbye to his guests later in the evening, the Ambassador once again takes me aside to say, "I want to again say thank you for what you have done for our country. If ever you need anything, please do not hesitate to let me know. We will answer your call just as you answered our country's call." Another handshake and he is gone.

Finding Zarubin's house on Acacia Avenue in Rockcliffe Park will not be easy in the dark. My superior officer at the Embassy, Colonel Nicolai Zabotin,* drove several of us there the night of the Christmas party and I have only a vague recollection of the direction he took.

Also disconcerting is the fact that Harry Sowell's residence is in the same area. But I have to risk it because the Ambassador is my only hope. If I can tell him what is happening to me, what they are trying to make me do, surely he of all people, can extract me from this terrible mess and help me to get back home. Back to Belarus.

As I make my way from downtown Ottawa past the Parliament Buildings on Wellington Street, a sudden longing for home almost overwhelms me. I fight to keep tears from blurring my vision along these gloomy streets. How wonderful it would be to escape all of this and return to my little village in Belarus.

And there is something else. On my lips I feel again the wonder of that soft warm kiss from Yelena Mazanik.

---

* **FACT:** Colonel Nicolai Zabotin was indeed Igor Gouzenko's boss at the Embassy. He spent several years in a Soviet jail for his role in the "Gouzenko Affair."

The Letter

SINCE IT HAS A DIRECT BEARING on what happens next, I want now to read into the record a letter I received from Yelena Mazanik several months before all this happened. A letter carefully tucked into my wallet even as I speed away from the *Journal* building towards the Soviet Ambassador's residence in Rockcliffe Park. It is a letter I still treasure!

I will translate it from the original Byelorussian as accurately as I can.

Dear Igor.

I hope this finds you well and happy. I think of you often, especially our wild ride through Minsk that desperate night that now seems so long ago. Those were not happy times for any of us and it often occurs to me that I never really had the chance to thank you properly for your very brave rescue. You know very well what they would have done to me and all members of my family had you not arrived when you did.

The terrible murder of those poor men the next day, continues to haunt me sometimes, as I am sure it does you, but for the most part I have come to terms with it all. Those were desperate times and we did what we had to do. I find myself more and more at peace with myself and hope very much that you have been able to do the same.

I remember you were a religious man; that you truly believed that it was God who saved you in Minsk. Are you still religious? I would love to be able to find solace in a belief in God and His forgiveness but have never been able to reconcile your God with the one who allowed such cruelty. If ever we meet again, we must discuss this. When I think of such a meeting it makes me happy!

When we last saw each other we were headed off in different directions. You to Canada and I to Moscow. I wish I had come with you, because life for both my sister Valentina and me has been very difficult here in Russia.

Until recently, Lavrenti Beria kept both Valentina and me in a state of fear. We think he had the paranoid belief that any of us who fought the Nazis as part of the resistance must be too independent to be good communists. Seldom did a month go by without a member or two of his terrible secret police paying a visit to our little apartment, usually on the pretext of investigating complaints from neighbours or fellow workers that we were making derogatory remarks about Stalin or the Politburo.

It was not until the terrible war was over that Stalin finally did get around to presenting me with the title of "Hero of the Soviet Union," which seems to have put an end to the harassment from Beria's "black crows." It is now almost a year since our last visit from them.

If it is possible, please write and let me know how your life is going. Don't send any correspondence to my Moscow address, but rather to the Soviet Consulate in Nassau, Bahamas. I have just been appointed trade commissioner to the Bahamas, but it has been made very clear that what they really want is for me and Valentina, who is coming with me, to keep our eyes and ears open for anything that might be important to Stalin or Beria. They seem to see plots everywhere, even under palm trees!

They tell me things are quite exciting in the Bahamas since the English King Edward who abdicated and that American woman he married settled there in the Governor's Mansion during the war. They're now called the Duke and Duchess of Windsor and hopefully I will be able to get to know them a little bit.

I have to be honest with you, one of the things they want me to do is somehow ingratiate myself into the social circle that has sprung up around the Duke and the Duchess. As you probably know, both of them were pretty enamored of Hitler prior to the war and Beria thinks some escaped Nazis may have made their way to the Bahamas and are now being entertained, or at least being helped in some way, at the Governor's mansion. They want me to make note of the names of people attending any of the Duke's parties, especially newcomers. I guess this makes me a bit of a spy, but if I can help catch one of those Nazi monsters I am more than happy to do it.

Even though I'm a little worried about trying to befriend the Governor and his wife, I am looking forward to the posting very much. The weather, as I am sure you know, is much better in the Bahamas than here in Moscow, and is certainly a lot warmer than in Siberia, which is where I often worried we would end up!

If you are wondering if it is safe for me to write things like this, maybe not, but since this letter is being mailed from Ireland, I doubt if I'm in much danger, although who knows? They may be opening even your personal mail. Yes, Ireland—let me explain.

Shortly after I last saw you, Urie Labonak and I had a brief love *affair that sadly, was doomed from the start. After all that had happened, I was desperate to just settle down in a quiet little corner someplace, raise a family, and never again get involved in politics of any kind. Urie, however, just could not seem to shake his need for some kind of action, or perhaps it is conflict he craves. I would sometimes wake at three or four in the morning to find him pacing the floor with boredom.*

He had a very good job with the Politburo here in Moscow, but remained a very unhappy man until one day some revolutionaries from Belfast, Ireland, somehow contacted him. A few days later, amidst many tears shed, he left, and while I very much fear he will meet a violent death in Ireland, he will die doing what the blood pouring through his veins seems to cry out for.

Before our final goodbyes, he offered to mail this letter from Ireland, thus avoiding the censors. He asked that I tell you he continues to have great admiration and affection for you.

Please write soon. But be very careful what you say, keeping in mind that it is very likely they will open any mail sent to me.

Still with thank you in my heart and thinking of you often, I remain your

Yelena Mazanik

It is a letter that changed my life!

The Traitor

THE TREE-LINED STREETS OF ROCKCLIFFE PARK, home to multi-millionaires, high commissions, and embassies, are a tangle of frustration for the uninvited. Designed, I am sure, to keep common folk and wanderers at bay. On the Greek Isle of Mykonos, streets were laid out in a maze of confusion to foil pirate attacks. In Rockcliffe, the intent must surely be to separate the very rich and influential from people like you and me.

I feel like I am driving in circles. On one occasion I am certain I pass the house where only a short time ago I was served up wine and threats. Since I am driving what I presume is Harry Sowell's car, I am very nervous about being spotted. But finally, there it is, tucked well back from the street behind a solid wall of maple trees—the home of the USSR Ambassador to Canada, Georgi Zarubin.

I wheel up the driveway, park behind a beautiful shiny, dark-coloured Chrysler with diplomat's licence plates, pound on the door and am met, incredibly, by the Ambassador himself! I am safe!

He recognizes me immediately. "Igor, Igor," he says in surprise. "What are you doing here?" He glances over my shoulder. "Come in. Come in, please. Is there a problem? This is a great surprise. Come in. Come in." He closes the door behind me and for the first time appears not just surprised but anxious, a bit flustered perhaps.

A woman appears briefly on the stairs behind him. His wife presumably, although I don't recognize her. She doesn't say anything before quickly disappearing into another room. I hear a quick burst of English voices from upstairs and for the first time I wonder why the Ambassador himself answered the door when there are obviously servants in the house.

In a rush of words, I begin to explain my predicament, but Zarubin waves his hand and says, "Igor, I can see you are very agitated. Here, come with me away from the servants and we will talk."

He is leading me down a long hallway toward what he says is his office when something makes my blood runs cold! I reach into my coat pocket for the gun.

I cannot be mistaken. Yes, there it is—the faint, but very distinctive smell of cigar. A very special kind of cigar made near Montreal of tobacco grown in a backyard. A cigar whose stink still lingers on my clothes. Hoover's man, Jonathan, is here. Somewhere in this house!

The Ambassador's eyes widen with fright as, throwing caution to the winds, I jam my gun into his face. I cannot contain my anger. "You filthy traitor. So it's you they want to protect. You're the one! You're the one who gave them the list of spies! How much are they paying you?"

I am about to reel off a string of curses when I hear a sound behind me. Without looking around, I jam the gun under the bastard's chin and shout a warning, "No closer or this traitor dies!"

"Let's not be stupid here Igor," says the voice behind me. Grasping Zarubin's arm I whirl him around so we both face Jonathan with my gun now firmly pressed against the back of the Ambassador's head.

"There's already one man dead tonight, don't make me do it again." My voice betrays my fury.

"My God," gasps Jonathan, "Pierre?"

"Yes. And it will also be this bastard's fate if you make one move!"

"Wait a minute, Igor. Let's talk about this," says Zarubin. I ram the gun into the back of his neck until I can feel him flinch. "Shut up you piece of dog shit, you're coming with me."

Here I make a serious mistake. I forget the telephone. I should have demanded that they rip the phone off the wall so they would at least have to dash next door to call police, but instead I warn Jonathan not to move and slowly back the Ambassador down the hallway, out the front door, and onto the tree-lined driveway.

At the last minute I remember the car parked in front of the Hudson. "Where are the keys to the Chrysler?" I demand of Zarubin. "In my pocket," he grunts. Still holding the gun firmly to his neck I reach into his pocket, yank out a set of keys, and hurl them as far as possible into the trees.

My first inclination is to force this greasy weasel into the car with me as a hostage, but as I prod him towards the Hudson, I have second thoughts.

As you can well imagine, I've had plenty of time to think about my actions that fateful night and I now believe that instinctively I was afraid of what I might do if forced to spend any more time with this sorry excuse of a man. A wormy traitor for whom I am supposed to take the fall. I'm not a murderer, but in my anger and shock I must have realized it wouldn't take much to push me over the edge and blow Zarubin's head off.

Instead of pulling the trigger I do something that, other than trying to humiliate him, makes absolutely no sense. Removing the gun from the back of his neck, I step in front of him where he can see me and wave the barrel in the general direction of his crotch. "Take off your pants and throw them into the car. My car, you son of a bitch, not yours."

To this day I have no idea why I did this, but it probably saved my life!

"*Blya*," curses the Ambassador. He reaches into his pocket to pull out his wallet. "No, no, the wallet stays in the pants. Fast—off with the pants or I shoot your balls off!"

The pants drop to his feet lightning fast. I wave my gun and he tosses them onto the front seat of the Hudson.

Ordering Zarubin to sit on the driveway, naked skinny legs sprawled in the light thrown from the open front door, I slide quickly behind the wheel of the Hudson. I spin it around on the beautifully manicured front lawn and then careen down the laneway, out through the stone gates, and onto Acacia Avenue trying to remember if I should turn right or left.

In frustration I take several wrong turns, wasting precious minutes before finally finding Sussex Drive, the street that will lead to downtown Ottawa. I'm almost to the large residence at 24 Sussex Drive, when I spot the flashing lights of a roadblock just ahead.

---

* **FACT:** 24 Sussex didn't become the official residence of the Prime Minister until 1951.

Police have several cars stopped and are checking them carefully. I can see that one of the cars, which in the dark looks very similar to my Hudson, has been pulled over to the curb and police are talking with the driver whose face is ghostly white beneath the glare of a powerful flashlight.

It dawns on me. "Of course, how could I be so stupid? The telephone. Damn! The police have been alerted and are looking for me already."

I realize that if I make a run for it I don't stand a chance with this lumbering beast of a car and I am very reluctant to get into a gunfight. The Ottawa police are not the Nazis!

What was it they instructed me back in the Kurapaty forest in situations like this? "Remain calm, don't panic—think, think—be ready to talk your way out."

Something is pinging away at the edge of my consciousness. What is it? I glance down at the pants strewn across the seat beside me. Another ping. What is it? What is it?

Of course! I reach down as I slowly advance towards the roadblock and feel its heft through the fabric. The wallet! Zarubin's wallet. It's bound to, at the very least, contain his driver's licence and with any luck perhaps even his Ambassador's credentials.

Keep in mind in those days, documentation of this nature was pretty primitive compared to today. Thank heavens a driving permit in 1945 contained no picture, but it did show date of birth. Zarubin was at least ten years older than I, but in the stark glare of a flashlight I should be able to bluff my way through. Or at least so I hope. It's a long shot, but essentially the only one I have. I resolve to give myself up rather than try shooting my way out. I've done enough killing for one lifetime.

As I pull to a stop beneath the signalling flashlight of a uniformed policeman, I notice something strange. The police don't appear very concerned. They aren't the least bit cautious. The officer who approaches my window as I crank it down doesn't have his gun drawn; the other two policemen don't appear to be paying much attention to me. I hear one of them chuckle at something one of the other drivers is saying.

It strikes me as very obvious that these police aren't looking for someone who's armed and has already killed a man.

Then the light goes on! The murderous bastards! When they made that phone call to police from the Ambassador's residence they failed to mention I am armed and dangerous because they want me to try shooting my way out of this, hopefully getting myself killed in the process. Jonathan's assumption obviously is that I am not likely to draw my gun if several police weapons are pointed at my head. The temptation to start blasting away will be much greater if it looks like I will get away. He is probably betting that if I do shoot my way through the roadblocks, my freedom will be short-lived. Cop killers seldom ever make it to jail or court. Certainly not in 1945! You must understand that in those days anyone who killed a police officer usually ended up lying in a ditch someplace with a few broken bones and at least a dozen bullet holes. Rough justice that no one seemed to mind.

And something else is clear to me. If I just give up and allow myself to be caught, Jonathan will make sure the charges against me are so minor that by the time I'm hauled down to the police station someone will be there waiting to bail me out before I can, to use Jonathan's words, blow the whistle on their plot. Almost certainly, my next "escort" will be a bit more careful than the late Pierre!

I don't know what these diabolically clever sons of dogs have claimed I've done, but it can't be serious.

The last thing Jonathan and in particular Zarubin, want now is for me to start singing to the police. The only thing worse for them would be for me to blow the cover off their tidy little operation in Ottawa by letting Stalin or Beria in on the treacherous game their Canadian Ambassador is playing. Almost as dangerous for the ambassador would be my telling the whole story to anyone at the Soviet Embassy. That is anyone who isn't in the pay of the FBI, the RCMP or heaven-only-knows who else! The espionage game is far too complicated for me I am afraid.

All of this is jammed into my mind as I ask, "What's the problem, Officer?"

"Can I see some identification please," he says, throwing the beam of light into my face. I hand him Zarubin's driver's licence, which clearly indicates his diplomatic status.

The officer glances at the document, mumbles something unintelligible, holds it close to his face for a better look, and then peers down at me. I shield my eyes from his flashlight which helps camouflage my youthful years.

"Mr. Ambassador." he says, giving me another hard look, "You are Ambassador Zarubin, are you?"

"As you can see, yes. Can I have my document back please?"

"Excuse me sir, I don't understand. We got a call from your home saying that someone had assaulted a guest and left the scene in a stolen Hudson car. This is a Hudson, isn't it?"

Think! Think! Think!

I stall for time. "Was it a man or woman who called?"

"I have no idea, sir. We just got a call a few minutes ago from headquarters; they didn't give us many details. Only to be on the lookout for a man driving a Hudson Super Six."

I give him my best imitation of a really exasperated sigh.

"Damn! It must have been my wife again. Look, officer, let me be very blunt here. My wife and I are having, let's say, some real trouble in our marriage. We had a few hot words tonight and I decided to leave the house and go for a drive to cool down. When she's mad, she does some very strange things sometimes, especially if she's..." Here I make a tippling motion with my hand. "She's trying to get even, I guess; embarrass me because of some of the things I said that I probably shouldn't have."

I look up at the officer who's listening intently.

"Ever have wife problems yourself?" I ask plaintively.

I get a big smile in reply.

"Oooh boy, do I! Sorry to disturb you, sir. Hope you understand. We're just doing our job."

"Officer, I understand perfectly."

Amazingly, he steps back, gives me a kind of half salute and waves me on my way.

My relief is such that I find myself breaking into laughter as I turn the corner onto Wellington Street in front of the Château Laurier Hotel. My little Santa Claus acting instructor back in the Kurapaty forest would be proud of his pupil tonight.

"Maybe when this is all over, I'll head for Hollywood." I think to myself.

The exhilaration is fleeting, however, as the realization settles in that I've got to get out of Ottawa as fast as I can if I have any hope of staying alive. I'm unclear exactly who it is I am up against, but there can be no mistaking their resourcefulness and their determination that I not have the opportunity of blowing Ambassador Zarubin's cover. Let's face it, Zarubin's life is at stake and in all probability so is Jonathan's career, and perhaps his life also.

My first inclination is to continue driving into what I know is the dense bush of northern Ontario and in particular Algonquin Park. I've never been there, but have read a great deal about how rugged and isolated it is just a few hundred miles northwest of Ottawa.

One of the students at the University of Ottawa, where I was attending night classes, tried to give me a crash course in Canadian history and suggested I read a famous book entitled, *Roughing It in the Bush* by Canadian pioneer author Susanna Moodie. Her book paints a very graphic picture of early life in the Canadian woods that I found fascinating and very romantic. Made even more so probably because it was the forest that provided such precious sanctuary for me back in Belarus.

The delightful little fantasy that has been brewing away in my head of building a little "zimlanka" out in the woods someplace and living off the land is shattered as I pass the Parliament Buildings of Canada and spot a police cruiser parked just outside the front gates. My heart pounds as I drive slowly past and watch him carefully in my rear view mirror. He doesn't follow, but I realize it can't be long until a body is found in the parking lot of the *Ottawa Journal* building and some alarm bells begin to go off in the capital.

And then it comes to me: it's not just the Ottawa police I have to fear. Will the RCMP be drawn into this? Are they already involved? How about Jonathan's people that I now am certain are FBI? But most of all, I fear Zarubin and the NKVD—the ruthless Soviet secret police who will surely shoot me on sight.

With these thoughts, my dreams of pioneer life deep in the Ontario woods die. I have no choice. I've got to get out of Canada as fast as I can. Much as I have come to like, even love it, Canada has become far too dangerous a place for Igor Gouzenko!

Escape From Canada

ONE OF THE MOST IDYLLIC DAYS Patsy Regan and I spent was aboard a small motor boat putt-putting around the beautiful Thousand Islands in the St. Lawrence River. We rented the boat for a couple of dollars from a small marina we stumbled across by pure accident in the tiny village of Ivy Lea, near Brockville. The motor proved a bit cranky to start, but after a few minutes it seemed to be running smoothly and we set out for an aimless jaunt of exploration. At the time I didn't think I had a care in the world, if you can imagine that!

It was one of those soft warm days of late summer that, as I now nervously drive along Wellington Street, seems like a lifetime ago, but was in fact only last month. The water was calm; boat traffic was very light, just a few fishermen out lazily casting for salmon or pike. Patsy had suggested we rent some fishing poles, because she claimed the Thousand Islands were where record-sized muskies were frequently caught. I didn't know what a muskie was. "Silly boy," she says, "Fish this big!" And extends her arms as wide apart as possible. We both laugh at her remark about really liking the big ones, but I decline the fishing idea in favour of just soaking up the sun and the scenery. Boating in strange waters is adventure enough for me. In fact, I recall telling Patsy that I'd had enough adventure already to last me a lifetime, thank you very much!

It was a wonderful day made even more so by our getting lost amidst the jumble of islands. When we finally emerged and spotted a little village, we pulled up to a bedraggled old dock and asked a couple of boys fishing from the nearby river bank, "Where are we?" They both began giggling, and then one of the boys, the smaller of the two, pulled his line out of the water, drew himself up to full height, snapped his hand to his forehead in a perfect salute and replied. "Welcome one and all to the great United States of America!"

As it turned out, we were in Alexandria Bay, New York. Illegal visitors in the strictest sense of the word, although we were assured by the boys that boaters from Canada show up here all the time without undergoing any sort of formalities.

Those were truly innocent times!

An older man, puffing away on a pipe, wandered over and when apprised of our difficulties, drew a rough map of the islands on the back of a cigarette pack and marked the route we should take to get back to Ivy Lea.

After that glorious day, whenever we'd enjoy an especially vigorous round of sex, Patsy would sometimes, without warning, leap to her feet, and stark naked, cup both breasts in her hands, thrust her pelvis forward and shout, "Welcome one and all to the great

United States of America." We would laugh till the tears poured down our cheeks.

It was the only time I had ever set foot in the United States and as my mind races now, I begin to wonder if that little motorboat is still there.

There's no question that all the bridges from Canada to the United States will have border guards alerted, but what about that little wooden boat? If it is there, can I find my way through the islands to the American side? Will I be able to start the motor?

The main question right now, however, is this: Can I find my way back to Ivy Lea and that marina before somebody who's after me spots this behemoth of a car and starts shooting? And right now I am guessing that there are a few people out there who want me dead.

I have only a vague idea of how to get back to Ivy Lea. The only thing I do know is that I have to first find the highway to Toronto. I remember this because when Patsy showed up that memorable day with what she claimed was a friend's car, she announced gaily that we were going to Toronto. Whether she didn't know that the trip to Toronto would take us almost all day I have no idea, but by the time we were a few miles out of Ottawa she decided to turn off and head for the town of Smiths Falls where she said her cousin lived. We couldn't find the cousin, and after meandering around dusty back roads for awhile, we finally ended up at the St. Lawrence River and the marina at Ivy Lea.

I'm nearly frantic when finally I spot a little sign, topped with a crown, reading "King's Highway 7" on it, and below, a board that reads "Toronto 221 miles." With my heart pounding each time a set of headlights approaches or follows me, I'm soon out into open countryside and starting to breathe a little easier.

Although I don't know it at the time, they certainly aren't

breathing easy back at Harry Sowell's house, where a command post is being established to accommodate an ever-growing number of worried people. The bird was flying the coop and heads would surely roll!

It's probably a good thing that it wasn't until many years later I learned of the bushel or two of very hot potatoes I'd dumped into their laps back there in the Soviet Embassy. If, while fleeing Ottawa, I had known of the scheme they were cooking up, the forces being aligned against me, and what lay ahead for me, I'd probably have wrapped that Hudson around a tree!

Jonathan

Two days before my 75th birthday, I learn that Jonathan is dying in a London hospital. Lung cancer. The high cost of special cigars!

My wife tries to dissuade me, but after two days of soul-searching, I decide to pay him a visit. There are a few things I want him to hear from me and I have a few questions I want answered now that he can no longer harm me. And I may as well be honest with you; the idea that despite all his efforts to the contrary, I will outlive him is not altogether unpleasant. I am not above gloating.

It's a leisurely two-day trip by automobile, so I offer a few British pounds to the next-door neighbour's son to do the driving. As I position myself comfortably in my nice new Ford I think about the fact that there are no Hudsons available anymore and off we go to London and the Royal Marsden hospital in Chelsea.

But now, as I stare down at this shrunken, grey-skinned, remnant of the man who once ordered me killed and pursued me halfway around the world, I feel nothing but pity. My wife was right. There is no victory here. No gloating to be found. Only death cheated temporarily by tubes and machines.

I am about to turn on my heel and leave when Jonathan opens drug-dulled eyes and says "Igor!" There is no shock, no surprise in his voice. "Igor," that's all he says, to which I reply simply, "Jonathan."

His attempt at a smile is really a grimace, his voice not much more than a hoarse, coughing whisper. But there's still some strength there. No surrender to death or to me. Not quite yet.

"So it ends like this," he whispers, "you gloating, me dying."

I shake my head slightly but can't resist replying, "But Jonathan, until now it's been you chasing and me running!"

What starts as a chuckle from him ends in a prolonged bout of coughing. It abates long enough for him to say, "Igor, you gave us a hell of a scare, we had no idea what a clever son of a bitch you were."

It's my turn to smile. But I want some answers from this man, dying or not.

"Jonathan, I know why you chose me for your great deception, you explained that back in Harry Sowell's house, but after I escaped, left the country even, why did you hunt me down like a dog? Why did you try to kill me? And why, Jonathan, did you murder that poor woman I cared so much for?"

Before he can assemble his thoughts, I add, "There are people who believe I should write the story of my life. You're a big part of it Jonathan. Help me fill in some missing blanks."

Talking is very difficult for him; every precious, gasping breath is painfully squeezed from cancer-riddled lungs, but during the next two days he manages to fill in not just a few blanks but an entire missing chapter.

At times it's hard for me to follow his rambling discourse; occasionally, his clarity of thought is astonishing. He often requires breaks to regain some of his strength. On more than one occasion, he dozes off, so the following is the best I can do at summarizing what he tells me over a period of slightly more than two days as life slowly drains out of him.

"Igor," he says, trying to focus his eyes on my face, "I know how much you must hate me, but I want you to know we never set out in the first place to do you any harm. That wasn't the idea at all. We truly believed you would jump at the chance to earn ten thousand dollars. We never, in our wildest dreams, thought you wouldn't agree to carry out our plan. We knew what Stalin had done to you and your people. All of us were convinced you'd be only too happy to get even with him."

He's gasping for breath when he finishes his little spiel, but it all sounds so phony, so false, that I only grunt in response. He's conscious enough to recognize my grunt as one of disbelief and he is absolutely right. I don't believe a word of it. A cough wracks his body. "You don't believe me. I can see you don't believe me."

"Jonathan," I reply, "neither you nor I have much time left on this earth. No need for lies. I admit that the idea I'm going to outlive you doesn't exactly make me unhappy, but if you want to come clean now and give me some kind of deathbed confession—if you want to tell me why you tried so hard to destroy me—maybe at the very least, you can enter the next world with a clearer conscience.

"Perhaps if you tell me all that happened and why, I can give you some kind of absolution or maybe God can, but then again I suppose, why would you want to bare your soul to me? I would think that doing what you did for a living all those years, trying to kill me was just another day at the office—a venial sin at worst. You've probably got a whole kit bag full of mortal sins to confess."

Jonathan goes so quiet I suspect he's either died or fallen asleep. I'm about to heave myself out of my chair when he groans and coughs again.

"Igor," he says, "you seemed to be such a sweet innocent boy!" And so, slowly, painfully and sometimes tearfully over the next two days he completes the missing chapter.

As it turns out, Jonathan really was telling the truth when he claimed they all believed I would go along with their plan to have me tell the world about the spy ring operating in Canada and the United States, thus protecting the identity of their informer, Ambassador Zarubin.

Patsy had convinced them I had little, if any, loyalty to Stalin or the Soviet Union and had become totally enamored of both capitalism and the western lifestyle. She apparently took some credit for this, assuring them among other things, that after spending a few nights in bed with her, I'd never settle for what she described as "some Russian babushka with flannel drawers down to her knees!"

"Give him ten thousand dollars and tell him women will be falling all over themselves for him and he'll dance barefoot on broken glass for you," were her exact words according to Jonathan and I have no reason to disbelieve him.

When I ask him why the strong-arm stuff—"White Gloves" and the gun—I am told it was at the advice of J. Edgar Hoover himself. The old carrot-and-stick approach, apparently. They wanted to let me know they were serious people and this was a serious undertaking. "I was opposed to the threats," claims Jonathan, "but I was overruled. You just didn't argue with Hoover."

The reason they wanted me to present my briefcase of evidence to a reporter rather than go to the RCMP or even the government was because they knew Prime Minister Mackenzie King was convinced that Stalin was a great friend of Canada. They were worried that Mackenzie King might try to cover up the whole thing in an effort not to offend "Uncle Joe."

As has been well documented, they were absolutely correct in that aspect. When the imposter, claiming to be Igor Gouzenko, showed up the next day in Justice Minister Louis St. Laurent's office with copies of the same list of spies they gave to me, Mackenzie King wanted nothing to do with the whole affair. He was so concerned about offending the Soviets that even after the spy ring was finally exposed, he phoned Stalin in Moscow to tell him that he hoped they could still be friends! It drove the RCMP and the FBI absolutely nuts! *

The consensus was that no newspaper reporter could resist the story I would give him and it would end up splashed across the front pages of every newspaper in North America within hours. Thus, Mackenzie King would have no choice but to act immediately and start ordering arrests. Jonathan and company obviously didn't anticipate my little "crazy man" act at the *Ottawa Journal*.

When I showed up that night at Ambassador Zarubin's residence and then managed to elude the police blockades, it threw them all into panic mode. While I was trying to find my way out of Ottawa, Hoover was screaming at them on his bedside phone in Washington, demanding that they find and shoot me immediately.

"Hoover was beside himself with rage," claims Jonathan. "He threatened to fire the whole bunch of us and at one point even threatened to expose Zarubin to the Soviets. You can imagine the scare this threw into the Ambassador."

---

* **FACT:** This is well documented in Amy Knight's book, *How the Cold War Began: The Gouzenko Affair and the Hunt for Soviet Spies* (McClelland & Stewart).

According to Jonathan, it was RCMP Commissioner Stuart Wood* who finally calmed Hoover down enough to get him to agree to "Plan B" which was to hunt me down with every resource they could muster while prepping their stand-in for me—a local small-time actor named Pedro Thompson.

Thompson, according to Jonathan, was actually a sort of last-minute idea. They were so certain that I would play along with them that only at the insistence of the very cautious Commissioner Wood did they agree to have a backup in the unlikely event I refused to cooperate.

Thompson was chosen for the role for no other reason, from what I can gather, than he spoke perfect Russian, was bright enough to carry out a massive deception, and would sell his soul to the highest bidder with no qualms. His mother had arrived in Montreal prior to the war as a member of a minor Russian ballet troop, met a wealthy Westmount merchant whom she inveigled into marriage, and then divorced him as soon as she received her Canadian citizenship. Why the boy she gave birth to some nine months later was named Pedro no one seems to know, but as we all know now, he did one hell of a great job convincing almost everyone that his name was really Igor!

I stop Jonathan cold at this point because there is something deeply puzzling about what he is telling me.

"Jonathan, I'm having a really difficult time here understanding how you were able to fool the Soviets with this guy Pedro Thompson. I mean, come on now, I was a single man when all this happened, but your stand-in—your understudy for me—was a man with a son still in diapers and a pregnant wife. As soon as that fact became known, the Soviets would realize immediately it wasn't me and this charade was to conceal the true identity of your mole in the

---

* **FACT:** Stuart Wood was the RCMP Commissioner at the time.

Soviet Embassy! The average Canadian or American wouldn't know if Igor Gouzenko was old, young, married or single, but the Soviets obviously knew very well. How did you fool them with some actor with a hood over his head?"

Jonathan falls silent for a long time. "Jonathan," I prompt.

"You really don't get it do you?" He stares intently at me.

And then all of a sudden I do get it.

"Oh my God," I say. "That's why you tried so desperately to kill me. Of course! Of course!"

Jonathan continues to stare. For a moment even his coughing abates.

I burst out laughing. "I do get it. The Soviets knew all along that Pedro Thompson was a fake. You told them. That's why you were so desperate to get me out of the picture. Let me see if I've got this right, okay? When you and your attack dogs didn't get me that first night, you got Zarubin to call Moscow and inform them that Igor Gouzenko had defected with a pile of documents, spilling the beans on a whole raft of their spies. Am I right so far? Am I on the right track?"

Jonathan begins coughing again. "The right track, yes."

"Okay, you tell me what comes next. Zarubin tells Moscow that some faker is going to pretend to be Gouzenko with the incriminating documents? Why would Zarubin do that?"

This time Jonathan sounds angry. "Because, damn it, in order to take some of the heat off himself, Zarubin lied and told Beria one of his men shot and killed Gouzenko, but it was too late, he said. Gouzenko had already turned the lists over to the Canadian Justice Minister, Louis St. Laurent. Zarubin warned that if the Canadians got wind of what happened, all hell might break loose! You've got to remember we were all sort of ad libbing at the time. You really threw a monkey wrench into the works, you know!"

"So let me guess. You struck a deal with Beria. Or was it Stalin?"

Another long pause. "Yes, we struck a deal."

"What kind of a deal?"

"We got two more names."

"Two spies not on the documents I had? Is that what you mean?"

"Yes."

"My God, there were dozens of names on my lists. Who were the missing two?"

This time there is a long sigh.

"The Rosenbergs!"

I am stunned, "Julius and Ethel Rosenberg? The ones executed for spying?"

"That's right," says Jonathan, "those Rosenbergs. I suppose, why not? I mean after all, by that time Stalin knew how to make an atom bomb and had acquired briefcases full of other military information including the work we were doing with nuclear submarines."

What's left of his voice turns bitter. "All those loyal American and Canadian commies did their job, gave Moscow everything they needed to know about the Manhattan Project and how to build atom bombs, so no big deal for Stalin to throw their spies overboard now. Once in jail or the electric chair, they wouldn't have to be paid anymore. Save the Ruskies some money, right?"

I confess, this takes a few minutes to sink in. As you can imagine, I had followed the sensational trials of Julius and Ethel Rosenberg back in the mid-50s with great interest, but I had no idea they were somehow involved in what happened to me.

I finally ask the next question.

"So then what did you give the Soviets in return?"

"Well, remember that their ambassador has informed Moscow that it's one of their men who shot and killed Gouzenko. If this becomes known it'll greatly strain relations between not only Canada and the USSR, but the United States as well. The idea that Soviet agents were killing people in downtown Ottawa is not something likely to create warm feelings or goodwill amongst the Canadian public. It might even result in the closure of the newly opened Soviet Embassy in Ottawa, which, don't forget, was a major source of espionage for Beria and Molotov."

He goes on at some length, and with great difficulty, to describe various details of the negotiations—in some cases the yelling and threatening back and forth between Moscow and Ottawa, but what it all boils down to is that the deal finally agreed to was, we keep Gouzenko's murder quiet in return for the Rosenbergs' names. And since Moscow believes that Gouzenko has already turned over his list of spies to the Canadian Government before being killed, the Soviets are only too happy to pretend Gouzenko is still alive and keep quiet about the fact that a man named Pedro Thompson is hiding behind that hood. That way they get the embarrassment of being caught stealing state secrets, but the reality that they shot and killed someone on Canadian soil is covered up. They didn't like the deal, but it was the best they could negotiate under the circumstances.

"Since the Soviets have a couple of operatives they didn't want caught," explains Jonathan, "the RCMP and Hoover agree to postpone releasing the story to the public until a few sleeper spies Stalin wants saved are safely back in Moscow. As you know, the whole Gouzenko affair didn't blow up until the following February, at which time 11 Canadians and dozens of Americans were arrested and charged with espionage, including that Canadian commie member of Parliament guy, what was his name?"

"Fred Rose?" I ask.

"Ya, Fred Rose, real sweetheart of a guy, that one!"

All in all, Jonathan describes a delightful little bargain that, of course, would blow up miserably in everyone's face if I surfaced. That's why they were so desperate to eliminate me.

Imagine the Soviets' surprise if, lo and behold, the real Igor Gouzenko shows up very much alive!

Imagine the public's reaction in Canada if the true story, the incredible deceit, is ever revealed!

Imagine the embarrassment and anger of the US Government to learn the role J. Edgar Hoover was playing in all of this.

Now, imagine how hard J. Edgar and his friends in Canada were trying to find me! As long as I am alive I am a major threat to them all.

I have one more question of Jonathan.

"So, if the Soviets, believing I am dead, know all about the grand switch and are fully aware the man everyone thinks is Igor Gouzenko is really some two-bit actor, why bother having Thompson wear that stupid hood over his head?"

"You forget someone here, Igor."

I think for a long moment. "The *Journal* editor?" I venture.

"Yes," replies Jonathan, "the *Journal* editor. Mr. Frowde, I believe his name was. He saw you; saw the real Igor Gouzenko. Without the hood, he would immediately realize that the person claiming to be Igor Gouzenko was a fake—that he wasn't the raving wild man who showed up at the newspaper that night. Thus, the damn hood, and I tell you, it was a real pain that hood. Thompson objected bitterly to it, once made us give him, I think it was $50,000, or he claimed he'd take it off and risk blowing the whole thing.* Matter of fact, he held us up to ransom more than once. It's a wonder Hoover didn't put a hit out on him!"

---

* **FACT:** Records indicate that the Canadian Government gave Igor Gouzenko more than $200,000. That's roughly the equivalent of a million or more dollars in today's terms. It has never been made clear why, since Gouzenko is reported to have authored a best-selling book which would have earned him large sums of money. Was the government money a bribe? And if so, for what?

I have to shake my head in astonishment when I think about all the years I spent in dread of the Soviets tracking me down when in fact, all along, they believed I was dead. "So I was never in any danger from Stalin or Beria, only from you, Jonathan. Do I have that right?"

He has no choice but to agree.

By the time he fills in all those blanks for me, Jonathan is fading fast, but he musters the strength to ask me a question.

"Igor, how come you never came forward to the police? After all our attempts to dump your body in a ditch someplace, why did you never try to tell your story?"

I'm standing now, gathering my notes, preparing to leave, but his question deserves an answer.

"What you people never seemed to understand," I explain, "is that all I ever wanted, the only thing I ever asked for was just to be left alone to live my life. You were never in any danger from me. Your charade worked perfectly, and let's be honest here, Jonathan, if I had gone to the newspapers or the police claiming that I was the real Igor Gouzenko, you would have made damn sure that, in the West at least, I would be viewed as nothing more than a publicity-seeking crank.

"And when it comes to the Soviets, I was more than happy to have them chasing after the man in the hood rather than me. Now I learn that had I told the world I was still alive, Beria and his secret police would have been beside themselves with rage and put enough money on my head to have every bounty hunter on the planet salivating. Any hope I had of staying alive, let alone being allowed to live a normal life would have been destroyed had I surfaced. You had all the weapons, all the ammunition. All I had was my wits!"

In an amazing burst of energy, Jonathan shakes his head until the tubes rattle and he gives a kind of snort of laughter.

"Imagine," he says, "the wit is mightier than the gun!"

As far as I know, those were his last words.

"Goodbye, Jonathan," I say softly.

He just stares at me.

He was dead, they tell me, before I arrived home.

Across the River

BUT, BACK TO 1945 and my flight from Canada. A rooster is crowing just up the road someplace when I finally find the Ivy Lea Marina. Somehow I've managed to avoid any further roadblocks, driving around in the dark until I find Highway 2 and, eventually, the winding dirt road plunging down to the St. Lawrence River and Ivy Lea.

The Hudson's headlights pick out the "Boats for Rent" sign and just beyond I can see several wooden boats tied up to a narrow dock jutting out into the river. The owner, I know from our previous visit, lives almost a mile away and with no nearby houses, I have no fear of being spotted, at least not before daylight.

Before I hide the car somehow, I need to make sure the outboard motors and their gas cans haven't been removed. During the war they almost certainly would have been locked up safely because gasoline was a rationed and very precious commodity, but now gas practically floods the market so they're almost giving the stuff away. As I recall, it was selling at about 21 cents a gallon in 1945. Think of that!

Thank goodness it was so cheap because, yes, only a few steps away from car, I can see there is a gas tank right where it is supposed to be in the nearest boat and the motor is in position. Such trusting folk, these rural Canadians! Reaching down, I heft the tank to make sure there's enough fuel to get me to the far shore and thus assured, I get back behind the wheel of the Hudson. There's a slight glow in the east so I know I don't have much time.

I have to fight my instinct to immediately jump into that boat, crank the motor up to full throttle, and roar off for the American shore. But my mind tells me my chances of escape are better if I can hide this very distinctive looking car that at this point seems to scream "Igor Gouzenko!"

I don't remember heavy woods or even a barn in the immediate area, but then I was hardly looking for hiding places when last I was here, but I do recall exploring this narrow dirt road as it wanders along the shore for a couple of miles before ending up at a tourist resort with several small rustic cabins. It looked deserted at the time and Patsy urged me to break into one of the buildings for, as she suggested, some "sex of the criminal activity kind!" I was tempted, but chickened out.

I decide now that if worst comes to worst, I can pull in behind one of the structures and delay discovery of the car for at least a few hours, although I certainly don't want to have to walk that far back to the boat.

I'm in luck. Only a few hundred yards down the road, I spot what looks like a walking trail through a small clump of trees. I just barely manage to squeeze the Hudson between a pair of massive maples, then down a small embankment. Far from perfect, but at least hidden from the road.

I pat my pockets to make sure the envelope with the money is still secure along with the gun and all three wallets. Mine, Pierre's, and of course, Georgi Zarubin's. Then, reaching into the back seat, I grab the briefcase with its landmine list of spies and traitors and set out jogging back to the marina. It is becoming dangerously light.

As I approach the marina, something wet jams into my hand and I almost jump out of my skin with fright. It's a giant black dog silently trotting alongside me. How he creeps up without my noticing I have no idea. He just seems to mysteriously appear at my side. It's now light enough for me to see that his tail is wagging, his tongue lolling sideways out of his mouth. He's obviously friendly, but is there an owner nearby? What do I do now? What happens when I take the boat? Is this a guard dog of some kind? You can just imagine the thoughts racing through my head. With no sleep or food now for more than 24 hours, my befogged brain is beginning to play tricks.

The dog follows me down to the dock and cocks his head sideways as I reach into Pierre's wallet, pull out two twenty-dollar bills and secure them to the wooden dock with a piece of concrete that apparently serves as an anchor for one of the boats.

To this day I can still see that dog standing there with his head in that funny sideways position as I jump into the boat, yank the cord a few times until the motor thankfully catches, throw off the two ropes from the dock, and head out into the St. Lawrence River. The dog never utters a sound, not a peep. He almost seems to be smiling as I set out for the distant shore.

Many years later I found a pup that looked exactly like a miniature version of the one on the dock. They call it a Newfoundland dog. Perhaps you've heard of them. Very rare. It cost me, what you folks call an arm and a leg, but I brought him home where he lived with us for many years.

I have often wondered if maybe the big black creature that greeted me that morning was really my guardian angel. I am very dubious about angels and things of that nature, but my dear wife has always insisted that the dog was my personal angel, the same one that looked after me during those grim days in Minsk. I always ask her why, if I have a guardian angel, he or she didn't do a better job of keeping me out of trouble in the first place. Just as my mother when confronted with a question she really didn't wish to answer, all I ever get from my wife when I express skepticism is a wicked stare.

Guardian angel or not, I manage to make my way through the very choppy, chilly waters and the maze of islands in the St. Lawrence River and find that same village Patsy and I pulled up to what seems like a lifetime ago.

The sun is doing its best to warm a cold breeze blowing off the river, which may account for the fact there is not a soul at the Alexandria Bay, New York, dock to see North America's most wanted man—which is what I am sure I am—come ashore. No one to watch as I push the boat out into the current and watch it bob away downstream. I then turn and walk up the street to where a ramshackle little restaurant is just now opening its doors, the neon light flashing OPEN—HAMM'S BEER.

Marie

"MY, MY, YOU'RE THE EARLY BIRD NOW, aren't you? Not looking for a worm I hope. We don't serve those here!" One glance at the chuckling woman who greets me and I immediately recognize her. It's Lauren Bacall, rising young star of the movie *To Have and Have Not* that Patsy and I saw only last week and now playing to rave reviews in theatres around the globe. It's Lauren Bacall serving me! That is, if she's aged 20 years and gained maybe 15 pounds!

She's got the hair thing down just about right though, swooped in the famous Bacall curve over her right eye, eyebrows thick and arching, lips full and pouting. Her naked ring finger signals "still looking for my Humphrey Bogart," and her eyes say, "Maybe you'll do!"

She hovers close as I order breakfast, making sure I get a good look at what appears to be a pretty decent figure, even with the extra pounds. When she returns with coffee, the top button of her blouse is open to provide improved observation, and yes, as intended, I observe.

As she bends over, I can't but notice that despite my desperate need for sleep, the sight of her breasts stirs me. My brain perks up too! An idea begins to take shape.

"Hey, did anyone ever tell you that you look very much like Lauren Bacall?" Her hand flutters to her hair and brushes it back from her forehead. She literally beams with a smile that for a moment makes you wonder if maybe there was a time when she was every bit as beautiful as any movie star.

But, oh my God, she is so achingly vulnerable, and I ask myself, "Can I really do this?"

"Thank you," she says, still stroking her hair, "Lauren Bacall is my favourite actress; you flatter me."

"Actually," I say, "Lauren Bacall is a real good-looker, but I really prefer Bogie. Humphrey Bogart, I mean."

An elderly man wanders into the place, but for a moment she ignores him.

"Oh, did you see them together in…what was that movie they did down there in the Caribbean? Weren't they wonderful?"

"*To Have and Have Not*, I think is the movie you're talking about," I tell her. "It was a Hemingway story and, ya, I did see it. Bogie and Bacall were really something in it, I sure agree with you there."

She leaves to serve the older man and a couple of fishermen who have taken a seat at the counter, then returns to my table.

"So, you from around here? Haven't seen you before. Staying long? Just visiting? Can I get you some more toast?"

And so as the morning passes, in between serving other customers, the age-old dance continues.

With cup after cup of coffee keeping me reasonably alert, I drop the hint I'm looking for a place to stay for a few days. Thinking my accent might cause her some concern, I explain that I've driven down from Montreal for a bit of sightseeing along the St. Lawrence and am a little disappointed that my "French Canadian accent" seems to disturb a few of her fellow Americans. She's quick to reassure me that she knows several people from Quebec and thinks they are just wonderful. "Actually," she confides, "my name is Marie, which I think is French, isn't it?" I nod in agreement.

"My car broke down, just up the highway," I lie. "I'll have to go back to it and get my suitcase and my clothes, but I think it's one old Chrysler that's rolled its last mile. I guess I'll have to get myself another car, but in the meantime you wouldn't know of a place I can stay for a few days that's not too expensive would you? By the way my name's Pierre, Pierre Gratton. Pleased to meet you, Marie."

She doesn't reply, but I can see she's intrigued, so to soften her up a bit I gradually spin a story about a rollicking, big, loving family in Montreal, complete with grandparents.

Finally, to seal the deal, I confess in a woefully sad voice that what I'm really doing here in Alexandria Bay is trying to forget a love affair gone bad.

That does it. She gives me a kind of wounded look and I get the definite impression she knows all about love affairs gone bad.

"You look like you didn't get much sleep last night," she says. I give her a deep sigh. "Not a wink; I imagine you've had a few nights like that." Her shoulders slump for a moment. "More than a few," she says and then almost to herself, "more than a few."

Suddenly she reaches into her apron pocket. "Here," she says and hands me a key. "My place is just around the corner." She points out the window. "Look for a little brown-shingled house with a screened-in front porch. Make yourself at home. You look dead on your feet, so feel free to take a nap on the couch if you like. And by the way, pardon the mess, I'm a terrible housekeeper. I'll be home right after lunch. My full name is Marie Welch, so if anybody asks what you're doing at my place you can tell them you're my cousin or something."

I know this kind of thing would never happen today. A woman would be crazy to do it, but this was a different time. The war was finally over; there was euphoria in the air. Crime in small towns like this was negligible. And if I do say so myself, I was a pretty trustworthy-looking kind of guy.

As for loneliness? Well, that's one thing that never changes, does it?

. . .

She cries when we first make love. Puts her head on my chest and cries like a baby. It almost breaks my heart.

"Please," I beg her, "please understand this is not a serious thing. I'll be going home in a few days and we likely won't ever see each other again."

"Do you think I don't know that?" she sniffles. "It's just, well, so nice. So really, really nice, that's all. Sorry. I'll stop this stupid crying. Sorry."

I find myself patting her on the back as I would a child who's stubbed a toe and I manage to resist the temptation to burden her with my tale of woe.

During the next couple of days while I try to decide my next move, I discover that while she seems to enjoy the sex all right, what she really needs is a friendly shoulder to cry on. And Lord only knows she has plenty to cry about.

From what she tells me, it was the usual "wham, bam, thank you ma'm" stuff from a couple of the local louts, followed by four years of living part-time with a trucker who it turns out had two other families stowed away—one in Virginia, another someplace near Chicago, neither of which was aware of the existence of the other.

Then finally, through some sort of "pen pal" club organized by the local American Legion, she meets—via the mail—what sounds like a really wonderful soldier serving with the US Army in Italy.

Believe it or not, this guy survives the entire Italian Campaign without a scratch, writes her a letter almost every day, and even talks about marriage when he gets home. He fights at Monte Cassino and in several other major battles without so much as an ingrown toenail. Then, on either the last day of the war, or maybe even the day after the Armistice is signed, he's joyriding around the countryside on a borrowed motorcycle when a wire strung across the road by a couple of kids just fooling around decapitates him!

And as if all that's not enough to deal with, now she has me! All I can do is make it as easy as possible for her when I leave, but I must confess all the lies I had to tell her bother me to this day.

The lies continue into the second afternoon when, after she returns from her little restaurant I tell her that police must have towed my car away someplace with my suitcase so I'll have to buy a whole new set of clothes in the village. She swallows the story without question and tears flow again when I return from my shopping expedition with a pair of gloves for her similar to the ones Lauren Bacall wears in one of her publicity photos. "That's the nicest thing anyone has ever done for me," she says in a choked voice.

As you can appreciate, the temptation to relax, stop running and just bury myself in Marie's considerable breasts is overwhelming. A strange lethargy overtakes me, even though I know full well the danger this inaction presents. I suspect it won't take long for Jonathan or someone else who's looking for me to put two and two together, maybe even with Patsy's help, and start looking along this side of the St. Lawrence. They must surely have found the Hudson by now and figured out how far a tank of gas would propel a wooden boat that has strangely gone missing. But despite that knowledge, I can't seem to shake myself free from the comfort of Marie's soft, warm thighs and this quiet little village.

Today, I suppose, a big-brained psychologist would describe my malaise as some sort of post-traumatic stress disorder, but whatever it was, it was foolish and almost did me in.

As it turns out, it takes Jonathan and company only three days to deduce that I must have piloted that little wooden boat across the wide St. Lawrence and am hiding out someplace in the United States. I had no way of knowing it at the time, but this suits J. Edgar Hoover just fine. Now that I am on his side of the river, he can turn the heat up full blast on the search for the real Igor Gouzenko and he does just that.

It is Marie who awakens me from my deep and almost fatal lethargy. As I meet her at the door of her home that third afternoon in Alexandria Bay, she greets me with a brisk, "We've got to talk!" She marches grimly past me into the kitchen, and I follow without saying a word, my heart pounding. I have a pretty good idea what's coming, and I'm afraid.

With her stiffened back to me, she clutches the counter with both hands and says between clenched teeth, "A guy came into the restaurant today, a strange guy with a fancy suit and shiny shoes asking if anyone had spotted a tall, light-haired man with a Russian accent."

I try to conceal my panic but have to ask, "What did you say?"

She turns to face me. "I told him no, but if he knew of any tall, good-looking men with or without hair of any colour to send them to my place." She tries to give a tiny chuckle, but it's obvious she's not enjoying any of this.

"What did he say?" I ask. She stares at me for a long time. "What am I mixed up in here?" Her eyes are pleading. "Please—what am I involved with here? That's you he was talking about, isn't it? That's not a French accent you have, that's Russian, isn't it? Please, who are you? Your name really isn't Pierre, is it? What's your real name? What have you done? Are you going to hurt me?" She's trying hard to stifle tears.

I step forward and throw my arms around her, then caress her cheek lovingly. "Marie, Marie, I would never hurt you." And I realize, to my surprise, that I mean it. This poor woman doesn't deserve any of this. This is a heartless thing I have done.

And so with my conscience cruelly flogging me, I apologize for involving her in all of this and do my best to explain what is happening and the danger I am in. I can see she has difficulty understanding everything I am saying, but when I finish she does something that is so wonderfully kind and touching that this time it is my eyes that brim with tears.

Reaching out with both of hers, she takes my hand and gently presses the palm to her lips, looks up into my eyes and says, "Let me help you."

She understands I have to leave right away and, incredibly she insists on coming with me.

In this my conscience is clear. Well, not entirely, but I do take some comfort in knowing I did my best to discourage her.

"Your life is here," I insist. "That's your restaurant just around the corner there. This is your house. You can't come with me; I don't even know where I'm going from here. I have no idea what is going to happen to me and you've got to understand that these are very bad people who are after me. They'll do their best to track me down and kill me and for all I know they won't hesitate to kill anyone who's with me. If you come with me you may be in great danger. Your life is here, Marie!"

The argument rages for nearly half an hour. "My life here, in

Alex Bay!? What life?" she asks. "I have no life here. The restaurant barely puts food on my table and now that the tourist season is over, I'll have to shut it down for the winter and go begging relatives for hamburger to stay alive. I probably won't have enough money to pay the rent on this house in a couple of months. You call that a life? And the men!? Get into bed with one of them and you come out smelling like fish guts!" She shudders for a moment, I guess at the memory of one of those fishy encounters and makes a sound like she's just bitten into something rotten.

"Look," she says, "I've got a car here—it's about the only thing I really own fair and square. Let's load it up with a few things and hightail it out of here so quick that Mr. Hoover and his men won't see anything but a big cloud of dust!" She pauses briefly, then adds, "or fish guts," and giggles nervously.

And so, in the end, she wins. Or maybe I let her. We do exactly as she suggests. That is, throw a few things into the trunk of her little Ford coupe, including, of course, the briefcase with its incriminating evidence still intact, and head for the only city she has ever visited.

The one thing I do not tell her is my real name. She doesn't really believe me when I insist I really am Pierre Gratton but seems to understand that knowing who I really am might further endanger both of us.

It's close to midnight when we finally arrive at a small, "no questions asked" hotel at the edge of Syracuse. Marie and her trucker friend stayed there once and she remembers it well.

"Bringing me here was the only romantic thing the bastard ever did with me," she confides during the drive from Alexandria Bay. "But it was during the World Series, so all he wanted to do when we got here was listen to the game on the radio." Here she smiles in self-deprecation. "But guess what?" Before I can ask "what," she answers her own question. "The radio faded out about halfway through the game and he got so mad he smashed it up against the wall and they billed him five dollars for it the next day. It was the best part of the trip!" She breaks into raucous laughter. I find myself liking this woman more all the time.

It is here, in this dingy little room with its water-stained ceiling and dusty drapes, that I finally open the briefcase I was supposed to have delivered to Mr. Frowde at the *Ottawa Journal*. It seems strange today to think that until that moment I hadn't even opened the briefcase, let alone examined its contents, but I suspect it was because I somehow thought that if I didn't look, the whole nightmare might just go away.

I am astonished to see what is packed inside.

Not just various official-looking documents in Russian and English, but telegrams, handwritten notes, letters, reports of varying kinds and dossiers on Soviet agents working in the United States and Canada. As any student of Cold War history knows, a similar briefcase given to Justice Minister Louis St. Laurent by the man claiming to be Igor Gouzenko is reported to have contained some 109 documents which led to the arrest of 39 suspects in Canada, 18 of whom were eventually convicted of espionage.

The most famous of those caught in Canada was Fred Rose, the only member of the Communist Party ever elected to the Canadian Parliament. His worst crime appears to have been providing information to Moscow concerning a secret wartime session of Parliament. He was sentenced to six years in prison, served four and a half of those years, and then went into self-exile in Poland where he died in 1983.

The information I am rifling through in that Syracuse hotel, which in reality is more like 250 separate pieces of information, also contained evidence of a major espionage ring in the United States.

The man primarily responsible for my predicament, Klaus Fuchs, was among dozens of individuals in the States and Britain eventually caught and convicted of various crimes right up to and including, in the case of the Rosenbergs, conspiracy to commit espionage.*

Some historians claim the so-called "Gouzenko Affair" eventually led to the discovery of notorious Soviet spies operating in Britain, including Donald Maclean, Guy Burgess, HAR (Kim) Philby, Anthony Blunt and John Cairncross. The so-called Cambridge Five.

And then, of course, there was Alger Hiss!

---

* **FACT:** Julius and Ethel Rosenberg (pictured, above) were executed at Sing Sing Prison on June 19, 1953 on charges of conspiracy to commit espionage, following a long and very controversial trial. Julius was recruited as a spy by the KGB on Labour Day 1942, and began providing the Soviet Union with highly classified information concerning the development of the atomic bomb at Los Alamos. David Greenglass, Ethel's brother who was working on the Manhattan Project, spent ten years in jail for his role in supplying the Rosenbergs with the atomic secrets. The Rosenbergs thus became the first civilians in US history to be executed for espionage.

Alger Hiss

IT MUST BE TRUE WHAT THEY SAY about danger heightening the libido! That night in the fleabag Syracuse hotel, Marie is virtually insatiable. Aroused, excited, exciting and experimental far beyond anything I have thus far experienced with her. When we finally fall sweating into each other arms, she begins giggling and exclaims, "Oh my God, can we do that again? That was fun!"

It is a wonderful distraction, but something I have plucked from the briefcase has my head churning with an idea and the adrenaline pumping! Have I discovered an escape hatch in those documents?

As dangerous as it will be, heading right into the lion's den, so to speak, I now know what I must do—go to Washington and find a man named Alger Hiss!

Departure the next morning is delayed somewhat by Marie, who insists on a bit of morning fun. I'm anxious to get going, but what the heck, as they say in the movies, you only live once!

I've decided that before we do anything else, we've got to get rid of Marie's car and buy a new one. It won't take the hunters long to get their bloodhounds sniffing out clues and begin tracking a car and its owner mysteriously gone missing from a border village.

As we drive into Syracuse the first automobile dealership we spot is one with a huge sign proclaiming, "THE 1945 PLYMOUTHS HAVE LANDED!"

And so we purchase one of the 1945 Plymouths that have just landed. According to an earnest young salesman, the new cars are selling so fast they can barely keep any on the lot. Most auto manufacturers in North America stopped making cars in 1942 and plunged into the war effort. The first post-war cars didn't appear until late in 1945 and we have just bought one of the very first. "One thousand dollars plus your 1936 Ford coupe," the salesman tells Marie.

It's essentially take it or leave it, so we take it. The thousand dollars, of course, coming from that fat envelope Jonathan waved beneath my nose back at Harry Sowell's house.

Marie is almost giddy with excitement as we drive away in our new car. She's hugging me so tightly I have to playfully push her away. "You're crazy," I scold her. "You're going to have us in the ditch." But I can feel the excitement, too. I figure, with any luck, I'll be well out of this country before Mr. Hoover is able to follow the paperwork trail involved in the switch of cars.

Today you can easily drive from Syracuse to Washington in a single day, but in 1945, a trip of that length along the patchwork of roads available prior to the construction of the interstate highway system was an adventure of at least two and possibly even three days, depending upon the reliability of your automobile and the density of the burgeoning post-war traffic. It seemed that just about every-one was hitting the roads out of pure joy, and the fact that gas was cheap didn't hurt either.

I forget where we spent the first night after leaving Syracuse, but I do recall that Marie was in a much more sombre mood than the night before. She didn't talk much and finally admitted that the gravity of the situation was beginning to sink in. She seems gen-uinely horrified, however, when I suggest that we buy her another car with which she should turn around and head back to her little house on the St. Lawrence.

"Listen, mister," she says fiercely, "get it through that thick head of yours. I'm not going anywhere without you. In fact, come over here right now! What do you think you're doing standing there with your pants on?" Good question!

She's fast asleep when I open the briefcase again. I want to have another look at the contents to reassure myself that what I saw last night wasn't a figment of my imagination. I also want to make sure I haven't missed anything of significance and I'm hoping I may find a bit of extra inspiration.

What first caught my attention when I sorted through the var-ious documents and notes last night was not Alger Hiss's name. I didn't know him from Adam, as the Americans say. What I did no-tice was a reference to the Dumbarton Oaks Conference and the Yalta Conference. As luck would have it, I was very familiar with both of those events, having done considerable research for articles that ap-peared in *The Soviet Union Today*. As I told you earlier, I was the as-sistant editor of the magazine published monthly by our Ottawa Embassy. Since it was obvious that the Soviet Union had scored major diplomatic victories on both occasions, we were very proud of the role played by Joseph Stalin, and our publication was filled with chest thumping.

It was at the Yalta Conference held in the Crimea February 4 to 11, 1945, that Stalin was deeded territory, which greatly increased the size and scope of the Soviet Union. This, by the way, included what became East Germany. Most historians today agree that during the Yalta Conference most of Eastern Europe was turned over to communist domination, a tremendous victory for Stalin.

It was at the earlier Dumbarton Oaks Conference held in Washington in the fall of 1944 that the first major step toward the formation of the United Nations was taken. It granted the Soviet Union powers equal to those of the United States and the United Kingdom.

Those were some of the facts I knew when I first snapped open that briefcase. What I did not know was that a senior US State Department official named Alger Hiss was one of the chief organizers of both those historic events and much more to the point, Alger Hiss was a Soviet spy!

Alger Hiss, according to a document I now carefully fold into my wallet, is a well-buried mole who provided Stalin with information concerning agendas and strategies first at Dumbarton Oaks and then at Yalta. Some historians today will tell you that Alger Hiss played a major role in the expansion of the Iron Curtain to include most of Eastern Europe.

One of the great mysteries in all of this is the fact that the documents in my briefcase very clearly named Alger Hiss as a spy. I don't know this yet, of course, but the documents that were turned over to Pedro Thompson, posing as me, and given to Justice Minister Louis St. Laurent, only stated that an *unnamed* Soviet spy was operating in the State Department. Despite my efforts, it was only later that Hiss was identified and charged.

Was the failure to name Hiss as the State Department spy in the documents given to the Canadian Government accidental or deliberate? We will probably never know.

I am unaware if there were any other discrepancies between what I was given by Jonathan that fateful night and the information that was finally released to the public, but the briefing documents I received listed some of the secrets Hiss is believed to have turned over to the Soviets, thus greatly assisting Stalin in his negotiations with Winston Churchill and Franklin Roosevelt.

One of the handwritten notes, which I now examine as Marie sleeps beside me, claims Hiss is still in the State Department and as such, is one of the most dangerous spies in the western world!

Dangerous to the western world perhaps. But I am convinced that through Alger Hiss lies my path to freedom.

It shouldn't be difficult to find him. The incriminating document contains not only his home address, but also his telephone number.

Alger Hiss testifies at his first trial, August 1948

Yet Another Mystery

[Here the narrative comes to an abrupt stop,
and there are a few seconds of "dead air," as though
the tape has been rewound and restarted.]

SORRY, I GOT A BIT AHEAD OF MYSELF THERE. I want to take a moment or two here to pose yet another mystery and a possible solution, or answer, if you prefer.

You must admit that it is very strange indeed that while Igor Gouzenko is supposed to have defected with his long list of Soviet spies on September 5, 1945, none of this came to public light until February 3, 1946. That is five months later, almost to the day.

I've tossed you a few other mysteries so far, but how do you like this one?

Think of it please. The Justice Minister of Canada is presented with overwhelming evidence of a huge espionage ring operating in both Canada and the United States and somehow this doesn't come to light for *five full months*. Why would that be? Surely there must be a very good reason why Canadian Prime Minister Mackenzie King didn't confirm the defection, amazingly enough, until February 15. In fact, there is every reason to believe that if American journalist Drew Pearson hadn't broken the story of a "gigantic Russian espionage network" to a nationwide audience when he did, there's a real question as to whether the existence of the spies would ever have been made public.*

While it lends some credence to Jonathan's deathbed claim that part of the deal made with Moscow was that no information would be made public until the Soviets had time to extract some of the agents they wanted to preserve, it doesn't explain why there was a delay of almost five months, does it?

I believe I know the reason why Prime Minister Mackenzie King and Justice Minister St. Laurent, as well as Hoover and the FBI, kept this whole thing quiet for so long. I have come to the conclusion that the delay occurred because they were not convinced that Pedro Thompson could carry off their massive hoodwink. In particular, they were concerned about the consequences if the real Igor Gouzenko—me—showed up somewhere to tell his story while they were trying to pawn off a two-bit actor as the defector.

You've got to understand the dilemma they were in. If, as they expected, I was caught and killed before I had a chance to tell my story, no problem. The public would never know.

---

* **FACT:** The facts concerning Pearson's disclosure and Mackenzie King's admission are a matter of public record.

If I decided to go public with my list of spies before they sprang Thompson on the public, Mackenzie King, St. Laurent and Hoover could plead utter ignorance and leave it to others to try and discredit me. But if I appeared on the scene *after* they presented Pedro Thompson as Igor Gouzenko, well that's going to be a tough one to deal with, isn't it? Especially if I show up with a list of spies that differs from the one they've released to the public.

Thus, it seems obvious to me that what Mackenzie King, St. Laurent and the FBI were doing was stalling for time. Waiting until I was eliminated, as they were assured would happen.

So then comes the final question in all of this. On February 3, 1946, Drew Pearson, a syndicated American radio broadcaster told his audience that a Soviet spy had defected to Canadian authorities with information about a "gigantic Russian espionage network" within both Canada and the United States.

The question is this: From whom did Pearson get his information?

I know the answer to that very well.

[Here, there is a pause on the tape, and then he shouts:]

HE GOT THE INFORMATION FROM ME!

[I jump; he continues in a much calmer voice.]

Why would I blow this whole thing sky high?

Revenge, my friend. Pure revenge and an almost-fatal escape plan!

Let me explain.

The Stonewall Jackson

IF THIS IS INDEED THE AREA in which Alger Hiss lives, he must come from old and very considerable money. I doubt very much if even the rarified salary of a senior advisor in the State Department could underwrite any of these homes. Actually, "estates" is a much more accurate word to describe what I am seeing while scouting his neighbourhood.

My documents say he lives in Washington, DC, but in reality when I track him down, his address turns out to be in Oakton, Virginia, a very affluent suburb about 25 miles west of Washington. This is a place of huge, tree-studded lawns, palatial homes gracefully introduced by long winding driveways, split-rail fences, duck-filled ponds, and white-tailed deer delicately nibbling at carefully mani-cured gardens. All of it shouting money, power, influence. Except in a place like this, they probably have a bylaw against shouting.

As we tour the meandering tree-lined streets, Marie is wide-eyed with awe. "Look at that," she keeps gasping. "I had no idea people lived like this. Oh my God, look over there!" We stop briefly at one address to admire a pair of horses enclosed in a front yard paddock. Only about a block away is a large field that a sign informs us is the Oakton Polo Club.

It is so well hidden behind a small forest of giant oak trees that we can't actually see the house on Palm Drive in which Hiss lives, but the US Postal Service has no reason to lie, so we believe it when the mailbox at the end of the curving driveway states in large capital letters: HISS.

It all certainly makes me wonder how on earth the owner of that mailbox and what is probably a mansion of a home could even contemplate doing something that places all of it at risk. Which, I realize, greatly strengthens the hand I am about to play. Common sense tells me that the more Alger Hiss has the less likely he will be risk losing it.

I need some time to plan my next move, so we've checked into a pleasant place in nearby Manassas called the Stonewall Jackson Hotel. I find the name a little curious until the bartender explains we aren't very far from the famous Civil War battlefield upon which the two battles of Bull Run were fought.

"Ole Stonewall Jackson kicked the living bejesus out of the damn Yankees twice just three miles from here!" To say the least, this is strange-sounding stuff, coming as it does, from a little guy with a broad Scottish accent and whose knobby knees are exposed by a tartan kilt! We're the only late-afternoon customers in the hotel's cozy pub-cum-lobby so after serving us a couple of beers and a plate of sandwiches, our little Scottish friend plunks himself down at our table and insists upon a chat.

"Clive Nichol at your service," he says, holding out his hand. "Refugee from Glasgow's fair city to ole Virginie. Own this place. Rescued it, so to speak, from some damn fool from New York. Where you folks from? Knew at a glance you're nay Yankees!" This he finds so hilarious it requires a good snort of a laugh and a whack on a bare knee.

"Montreal, Canada," I mumble, while Marie gets up to examine a large display of artillery and mortar shell casings that is the main decorative feature of the place. From what I can see, there's everything on display, from old Civil War artifacts to what appears to be shell casings of recent WWII vintage.

When she's out of earshot, Clive shoots his elbow into my ribs and, nodding towards Marie, leans over and whispers into my ear. "I can see you like 'em older. You know what they say?" I shake my head only slightly to indicate that not only do I not know what "they" say, but I'm really not interested in any of this. Undeterred, Clive plunges on. "What they say is, the older ones are best, 'cause they don't yell, don't tell, don't swell and are grateful as hell!" He explodes with laughter, this time slapping my knee instead of his.

I can feel my face flushing with anger. In other circumstances he'd have more than just a breeze up his knees, but crudely or not, he does make a point. A young man travelling with an older woman, especially in 1945, is something people notice and the last thing in the world I want right now is to be noticed. We've got to be more careful.

My gut tells me we're probably safe here for a few days, but time, I sense, is running out. I know it will not be long until Jonathan and his men pick up our trail. And even more urgently, if I have any hope of escaping this nightmare, I must reach Alger Hiss before the espionage-ring story becomes public.

Since I have no way of knowing that our hooded friend, posing as me, has already given the Canadian Justice Minister the duplicate package of information, I begin to suspect that the whole business about a "substitute defector" may be just a lie Jonathan fed me along with everything else. Problem is, I can't be sure.

I listen intently to the radio every day and read every newspaper I can find, but so far, there's not even a hint of a defection or of any espionage ring. Most of the news is euphoric. Troops returning home to flag-waving, joyous crowds. Pictures of wives and children throwing themselves into the arms of returning heroes. Douglas MacArthur getting the Japanese straightened out. New cars pouring off the assembly lines. All happy stuff; no spies. Stalin is still a great friend, no Cold War fears…in fact that term hasn't even been coined yet.

Don't forget I'm the one who is supposed to have launched the Cold War; but in early September of 1945 nobody—well hardly anybody—knows it yet! All the while, I'm trying to contact someone who, I have just learned, is one of the most dangerous spies of the 20th century in hopes he can save my skin!

Haste is vital, but what I am about to do requires careful planning. I need to make sure I won't get lost in the maze of Oakton or Manassas streets. Experience warns me I may need a quick exit strategy, but most of all I need to find a safe meeting place. An open public area would be the best, removed from buildings or trees. I don't anticipate any difficulties, but I have no intention of being ambushed again. And just as important—I need a safe hiding place for a briefcase full of documents so explosive they could blow the world apart!

Something our kilted Scots jokester said intrigues me. We're on the edge of a Civil War battlefield; presumably that means lots of wide-open spaces available to the public.

Marie has gaily set out on a shopping spree to, as she jokes, "brighten up my wardrobe and get some womanly things." Clutching a handful of cash I've given her with instructions to also buy me a good set of binoculars, a few tools and some warmer clothes, she plants a major-sized kiss on my forehead and heads for downtown Manassas while I try to locate this famous battlefield I'm hearing so much about.

Civil-War era cannon

Bull Run

IT'S NOT HARD TO FIND. Almost every traffic sign in town points me towards the "Bull Run Battlefield National Historical Park" or in some cases the "Manassas National Battlefield Park." It's been explained to me that the Yankees, that is northerners, still call them the 1st and 2nd Battles of Bull Run, but in the south they insist that where the Confederacy kicked Union butt twice was at Manassas.

Whatever they call it, I can see that the park is a perfect meeting place. A large gravelled car park; two large Civil War cannons to mark the entrance to a small welcome centre and a walking trail wandering through the battlefield that is comprised largely of a gently sloping valley.

I'm surprised there aren't more visitors as I hike two or three miles along the trail paying special attention to likely places for a meeting. The dense bush that crests the eastern slope concerns me a little. A sniper could easily hide among the trees; in fact, a guide tells us that it was from those very woods that Union troops unleashed volleys of musket and cannon fire at the "rebels" storming up the hill towards them.

As I descend deeper into the valley in the centre of the battlefield, I discover what you can be sure thousands of Confederate soldiers quickly learned—gunfire from the trees can't reach you down here. You are also out of sight of both the parking lot and the welcome centre.

I nod to myself. This is where we will meet. Here, in front of an inscribed plaque which reads:

It was here on July 21, 1861, that the first great battle of the Civil War was fought. More than 50,000 took part. There were more than 5,000 casualties on both sides. More than 1,000 died in this valley and on these hills.

It is as I leave the park that a mischievous boy of about ten solves another major problem for me. I watch as a man, who I assume is his father, yanks what looks like a large wooden cork out of his son's hands and jams it into the gaping barrel of one of the giant cannons guarding the entrance. Since the barrels of both point at an upward angle, they are stoppered with large wooden cork-like plugs to prevent rain from pouring in and perhaps deter boys from trying to insert various body parts. Somehow, this young man managed to work the plug in one of the cannons free and, as boys are wont to do, was trying to stick his head down the barrel to have a good look.

Bless him; he has just located a major piece of the puzzle that confronts me. And while he will never know it, our Scottish friend Clive is going to lend a helping hand, as well.

On the way back to the hotel, I stop at a drug store and buy a package of condoms from a profusely blushing young female clerk.

Yet another piece of the puzzle!

It's lunchtime and the Stonewall Jackson Hotel pub is jammed with office workers from the headquarters of the National Rifle Association located about half a mile away in the town of Fairfax. "My best customers," Clive explains, as I find an empty stool at the bar.

[Here there's a slight pause on the tape, followed by a brief chuckle before he continues.]

Let me leave my story just for a moment here while I tell you that I had no idea what the National Rifle Association was until many years later when there on my television screen is Charleton Heston waving a gun and saying something like "From my cold dead hands!" The announcer explains that Heston is president of the National Rifle Association, headquartered in Fairfax, Virginia, and what he is waving over his head is a ceremonial rifle presented to him during the association's convention in 2000.

It brought back a flood of memories, most of which I would sooner not have.

[There is another long pause on the tape here, followed by a sound that is hard to decipher, but seems to be a low groan. The voice then resumes in its normal tone.]

I remember very well that Clive was still dressed in that crazy kilt of his as he stood behind the bar chatting up customers and occasionally serving up drinks.

I nurse a beer until most of the crowd has paid and left, and then, taking a five-dollar bill from my wallet, I drop it on the bar and point to one of the artillery shell casings that line the pub shelves everywhere. The casing I indicate looks perfect for my purposes—polished brass, about three feet tall and with an opening about four inches in circumference. I have since learned it was probably from a four inch, 50-calibre naval gun of World War I vintage.

"Clive," I say, "we're heading back to Montreal, going home in a couple of days and I'd really like to take back a souvenir for my father, who's a bit of a military buff. I'll give you five dollars for that shell casing there."

He sees the one I'm pointing at; glances at it, and then back to the five-dollar bill.

"Deal," he says, grabs the money, sticks it his pocket, hoists the casing off the shelf and hands me my prize. I get the idea he would have settled for far less. Don't forget, in 1945 five dollars is a lot of money.

As an example of this, when Marie returns about an hour later, she presents me with two new shirts for which she paid $2.50 each, the binoculars and tools I asked for came to only $6, and she found a great "Washington Nationals" jacket for me. I have no idea what a Washington National is, so Marie explains that it is a baseball team. She got a great deal on the wool and leather jacket—just $7—because local fans don't like the name, preferring to call their team the "Washington Senators." I pretend I understand.

For herself, she has bought an entire outfit of skirt, blouse, leather belt and shoes for herself that cost only slightly more than ten bucks.

But it is what she describes as a minor miracle that has her ecstatic: She's been able to buy not one, but two pairs of nylon stockings! As she patiently explains to me, in some cities, women are lining up for hours to buy the nylons that the DuPont Company is turning out as fast as they can. In fact, Marie tells me she's been hearing about "nylon riots" in places like Chicago and New York, where women, so anxious to get a pair of these fantastic stockings, have actually rioted.

The women of Manassas and surrounding Fairfax County apparently aren't quite as desperate because as Marie boasts, "my lineup was only two hours long, and look at this, I got two pairs!"

At first she refuses to tell me how much they cost, but finally admits, rather shame-faced, that she's paid the outrageous sum of $6 a pair. She was told that in 1940 when they first appeared in stores, they'd sold for less than a dollar a pair but women have been deprived of nylons for so long during the war that DuPont just can't keep up with the demand and women are prepared to pay almost any price.

I have to admit, the new stockings do a marvelous job of showing off Marie's fine legs, especially when she rips off all other pieces of clothing and tosses them into a corner.

Right then and there I am convinced. It is the best $12 ever spent!

· · ·

When things cool down a bit in our room, Marie is curious about the shell casing and laughs out loud as I haul out the package of condoms. "A bit late for those I would say," she giggles. "Any damage has already been done. For heaven's sake, don't worry. You know I've already taken care of all that anyway!"

But it isn't sex on my mind now. Opening the briefcase, I remove all the documents except for a small handful I've kept aside, roll them up as best I can, stuff them into the shell casing, and then carefully stretch a condom over the opening. Marie is fascinated. "What are you going to do with that?" she asks. Then as an afterthought she leers up at me, "I never had to stretch one of those things to fit over anything that big, darn it all!" Little does she know that this isn't the first time I've used a condom for something other than that for which it is intended. A chill goes down my spine as I remember Generalkommissar Kube and the hot water bottle.

Marie is sleeping soundly beside me, snoring lightly, as I rise from the bed and check my watch. Almost 2:00 a.m. I dress quickly, tuck the shell casing under my arm and quietly tiptoe down the stairs and out the front door of the hotel to my car. Some 15 minutes later I'm at Battlefield Park, the twin cannons looming just ahead in the dark.

I've brought a screwdriver but find I don't need it to pry the wooden plug out of the cannon's barrel. Instead, it pops out with little effort. The boy's father, earlier that day, obviously hadn't jammed it in very tightly. The shell casing I'm carrying fits easily into the barrel. I drop it and hear a metallic clunk as it slides down and hits bottom. I stick my arm and shoulder down the barrel as far as I can, but my "stash" is out of reach. Good, if I can't reach it then neither can any other curious arm just poking around.

I force the wooden plug into the barrel as tightly as I can, hammering it several times with my fist until I am satisfied it will now take a lot more than a mischievous child to remove it.

If all goes according to plan, the hiding place will only be needed for a few days so I'm not worried about accidental discovery.

Only a few days. If only I had known what lay ahead!

Making test runs several times to ensure I know the shortest route, I have no trouble in the dark finding the exclusive enclave of Oakton. At this hour of the morning, there are only a few curious deer to watch as I drop a small envelope into the mailbox marked HISS.

One more piece of the puzzle in place.

Another ten minutes and I am back in my bed.

My instructions are followed to the letter. Precisely at ten the next morning, the pay phone in the outdoor booth just around the corner from the hotel rings despite a large handwritten sign taped to the door that says "OUT OF ORDER." On the fourth ring, I pick it up. "Stanley speaking," I say gravely. "How may I help you?"

The caller emits a brief snort of derision. "Yes, well I suppose we'll just have to see how helpful you can be, won't we?" His voice is clipped, precise, and while he tries to mask it, arrogant and dismissive. The voice of a man used to power and its application. A man not kindly disposed to being challenged or questioned. Nonetheless I sense he's nervous; the questions come too fast.

"So where did you obtain that information you deposited in my mailbox? Do you really expect me to believe you're some kind of escapee from the Soviet Embassy in Canada? To be perfectly frank, it sounds to me like you're nothing more than a blackmailer. What's the information you claim you have about me? That I'm having an affair with my secretary? That I wear polka dot underwear? What…?"

I interrupt with as firm a voice as I can muster. "Listen carefully because this is going to be a very brief conversation. I know you may be trying to trace this call so I will only say it once.

"I am who my note to you says I am. You saw the documents that you know could put Mr. Fuchs behind bars, maybe even in front of a firing squad. My information about you is even more persuasive and detailed, but please remember you and I are on the same side. I want to help you. I don't want to turn these documents over to the Americans. They're after me right now because I refused to do that, but I need some help and I think you're in a position to provide it. What I need from you is a new passport, a driver's licence and safe passage to a safe place. In return, I give you everything I've got that could get you a change of address from Oakton to Sing Sing!" There's a scornful grunt, "huh," but unfazed I plunge on.

"I've given you my photograph and the personal information and name I want to use. Someone in your position at the State Department will have no trouble having a passport and driver's permit prepared in time for our meeting at four o'clock this afternoon."

There is no reply, so I continue.

"This afternoon, four o'clock, bring a new passport with the information I've given you and a New York or DC driver's permit for me and I will give you half of the evidence I have involving you. We—just you and me—no one else, at Battlefield Park, the bottom of the valley by the plaque announcing a thousand deaths. Do you know where that is? Do we have a deal?"

"What do you mean you'll give me *half* of the documents? I…"

I don't let him finish. "You get it all when I'm safely out of the country. Is it a deal? This afternoon—four?"

There's a slight pause.

"I guess we'll have to see, won't we?"

Time to drop the hammer on him.

"Well, let's just put it this way. Either we have a deal or that radio broadcaster, Drew Pearson, has one hell of a scoop!"

And I hang up.

• • •

Marie is there at noon, circulating around the park with a busload of tourists from Cleveland. Her job is to scout ahead and make sure no one is setting any kind of ambush or trap for me. Her apparently aimless wanderings take her more or less over the entire battlefield but primarily I want her to, as best she can, patrol the outer perimeter from which the bottom of the valley can be seen.

Her eyes widen with alarm when I explain I want her to be on the lookout for any place where a sniper might conceal themselves without being spotted by visitors or me. A dip in the ground, perhaps, or a clump of trees or shrubs. And of course, "If you see anything, anything at all that makes you suspicious, take off your jacket at ten minutes to four and swing it around your head as though you're batting away a bee or something. I'll be watching you closely through the binoculars."

While Marie is thus occupied, I've got the Plymouth cruising slowly along the roads leading to Battlefield Park. I'm doing outside the park exactly what Marie is doing inside—watching for anything the least bit suspicious. In the back of my mind maybe it's Jonathan or maybe even Harry Sowell I expect to see in every car that passes.

Two hours of this and nothing appears out of the ordinary, so at about three o'clock I begin looking for a place to park the car along the western fringe of the Park.

My plan is to surprise Hiss, and anyone he might have with him, by foregoing the front gates in favour of a sneak approach from the side or rear of the Park. I noticed earlier that only a simple cattle fence surrounds the area. Nothing I can't easily climb over. After a few twists and turns I find a small housing development at the western fringe of the battlefield. I park my car in front of a vacant lot, and with growing nervousness, I wait. Timing is very important. I want Hiss to arrive first, but I've got to be within binocular sight of Marie at ten minutes to four so she can give me the all-clear signal. At least I hope it's all clear.

I find myself checking my watch every few seconds until I remember from my boyhood something my mother used to advise when time seemed to barely crawl as I waited for a highly anticipated event. "Now dear," she would say, "you've got to remember, a watched kettle never boils!"

As a child, I could never quite figure out what she meant, but the mere thought of that dear woman, bustling away in her kitchen, calms me.

We Meet!

AT 15 MINUTES TO FOUR, I leave the car, cross the vacant lot, clamber over a rusty fence and land in a hayfield that I recognize as the outer edge of the battlefield. With my binoculars I can see a handful of tourists poking about below me doing what tourists do. It's now almost ten minutes to four.

I hone in on the lowest part of the valley, and suddenly, I see him!

There is no mistaking Alger Hiss. I've seen pictures and read descriptions of him in various newspapers. I focus my binoculars until the image is clear. He's just as advertised: tall, thin, with dark hair; patrician looking. Most accounts describe him as refined and handsome. I recall reading once that his had been voted the best handshake at Harvard Law School.

He's checking his watch and looking intently toward the front entrance. I watch carefully to see if he glances around to check on an accomplice who may be hidden someplace. I detect nothing untoward. He looks restless, out of place; his finely tailored suit clashes noticeably with the informal dress favoured by the holidayers milling about.

Leaving the image of Alger Hiss for a moment, I scan the battlefield carefully and finally spot Marie on the eastern slope in front of the woods on the far side of the valley, her jacket still firmly buttoned up.

Satisfied, I walk through the hayfield, stuff my binoculars in the left pocket of my Washington Nationals jacket, check the gun in my right pocket once again, pat the inside pocket that holds the documents I kept apart, take a deep breath and descend into the valley where only 84 years ago more than a thousand soldiers were slaughtered.

"Mr. Hiss," and despite myself I add the deferential, "Sir."

He whirls about in surprise but makes no movement toward a weapon.

I'm about 20 feet up the slope behind him with the setting sun at my back. I have no intention of approaching any closer. If there's a sniper out there someplace with his sights already aimed at the area now occupied by Hiss, at the very least I'm going to force him to move and thus create a slightly more difficult shot. The changed angle might even force a shooter to expose himself.

For a moment or two, there is a standoff. Neither one of us moves, each carefully observing the other.

I break the silence. "It's a lovely evening, Mr. Hiss. Would you care to take a little walk with me? There are some very interesting gravesites just up ahead."

Slowly, he approaches to within a couple of feet until I can see the hate—and yes, it's there as well—the fear in his eyes. There are dark hollows under those eyes. I get the impression he slept very little last night.

I'm not trying to be funny here, but it is a fact that Hiss actually hisses at me. "All right, let's get this over with, I abhor blackmailers."

I'm a little taken aback by all this, since I thought I had explained to him that it is my intent to save his neck, not put a noose around it.

I try to reassure him of this again, but he's not buying any of it.

"I've got a passport and DC driver's permit here," he says. "You will see I have followed all your instructions. Now where are those papers you claim to have? Let's have them."

He glances around, but no one is paying us the least bit of attention, so he hands me a small package and once again demands the incriminating documents. "Here's your damn ransom," he snarls, "now let's see those papers you have."

This is the moment I fear the most. If there is going to be some kind of sting or a bullet through the head, this is the most likely time. What worries me is that Hiss may have tipped off the FBI, or maybe even Beria's secret police, and made a deal that the moment he receives the documents from me they can take me down. It would be a foolish thing to do perhaps, in that I still have additional incriminating information, but I don't believe he is aware of Marie's existence and may believe that I've hidden all the documents in a safe place, which with me dead, will never come to light.

It's an unlikely scenario, but at this point, in light of all that has happened, I am paranoid. Can you blame me? The rules are all different in the spy game. Nothing is as it seems. Everyone is a suspect. No one can be trusted.

Even though I can clearly see that Marie is not signalling any danger, my heart is racing. But I've thought this through very carefully. Reaching into my pants pocket for the documents, I take two quick steps towards Hiss, then to confuse anyone lining up a shot, without warning I squat down almost at his feet.

The sudden move spooks Hiss. "What the hell?" he exclaims.

The documents are in my hand. " Here," I say, "if you want this stuff here it is." He's forced to squat down beside me and gives me a look that says he believes he's dealing with a lunatic.

At first, for some reason I don't understand, he seems reluctant to take the papers from me, and when I place them in his hand he holds the package as he would a smouldering dog turd.

We're both standing now and I find myself ducking my head into my shoulders in anticipation of a bullet taking out my kidneys. Hiss gingerly opens the envelope and glances briefly at one of the papers. There's a sharp intake of breath and he flinches and turns pale. "My God" he exclaims, "where the hell did these come from?" He takes another look and his hand begins to tremble. "How much more of this is there?" The arrogance is gone. He's almost pleading. "How do I get the rest of it? What more do you want? Money, is that what you want? How much?"

I almost feel sorry for him. Foolishly, I let my guard down, my shoulders straighten and my fear dissolves.

I now know, only too well, that I should have known better— should have known that, like a wild animal, a man like Alger Hiss is most dangerous when cornered and it's obvious he believes he's cornered.

I shake my head. "I don't want your money." I find myself getting angry. "Look, damn it, I told you before I don't want to turn you in. I know you don't believe me, but I'm risking my life to protect you. I'm helping you and now that I have a passport and driver's permit, all I need is for you to tell the Kremlin I have not defected, that I am not a traitor and want to go home. When I'm safely back in Belarus, I'll let you know where the rest of the documents are hidden—all of them—not just the ones that concern you personally. Tell Stalin or Beria or whomever you report to that

I'm protecting the identity of Soviet spies here. That's all I want. I just want to go home."

Hiss is incredulous. "What kind of influence do you think I have over there? What makes you think they'll buy your story? What happens if they arrest you the moment you set foot in the Soviet Union?"

I lean into him so we are almost nose-to-nose. "Tell them," I say in as threatening a voice as I can muster, "that the moment anything happens to me, anything at all, that whole list—the whole thing—all the spies, including the ones in the State Department," here I glare at him, "everything—every one of you—is on the front page of every newspaper in the country!"

Hiss flinches and steps back. "Okay, okay, I'll do what I can, but good God, why on earth do you want to go back there?"

My reply is quick and I hope convincing. "I just want to go home!"

It's a giant lie, of course, intended to confuse my pursuers. I have no illusions about what would happen if I were to set foot back in the Soviet Union, no matter what promises might be made. I have a far different destination in mind.

I try to sample his famous Harvard award-winning handshake, but Hiss only stares at my outstretched palm for a moment, mutters an oath under his breath, turns on his heel and strides away. I get the feeling he'd like nothing more than to spit on it.

Half an hour later, Marie and I are back in our hotel room packing to leave. I, trying hard to conceal my excitement, anticipating a chance to escape this nightmare. Marie, however, is bravely managing to hold back the tears.

"This means goodbye doesn't it?" she says in a faint whisper. "If you go back to Belarus, you can't take me with you can you? I'll never see you again, will I?" Now the tears come and I find myself wishing there was another way to do this. I may not be in love with this woman, but I am surprised to find that the thought of leaving her makes me very sad. I feel like crying myself and am barely able to resist telling her the truth.

I don't have to respond to her questions. We both know this is the end for us, but I understand myself well enough to know that I cannot just abandon her.

I take her gently in my arms and when the sobs abate I tilt that dear sweet face up and tell her that we are going together to New York. "Yes you know I will have to catch a ship to Europe but first, you, my little movie star," I say softly, "are going to live like a princess in New York. We're going to find you a nice little apartment some-place downtown. I'll pay the rent for a year in advance and leave you with enough money to keep you in fine nylons for at least that long, even if you don't want to get a job, and of course, this car is yours." I try a lame joke in an effort to lighten the mood, "And you can be pretty sure New York men don't smell like fish guts! You'll have to fight them off!"

She tries to smile through the tears. "Don't be so damn silly, you're going to need every cent of that money you have, I'll be just fine." She brightens a bit. "Hey, maybe I can stay in Manassas and ask old Clive here for a job waiting tables, I see the tilt in his kilt every time I walk by!"

Oh, how I wish she had won the argument.

Murder

JUST TO BE ON THE SAFE SIDE I'm taking some back roads north out of Manassas as we head for, as they say, the bright lights of New York City. Marie has a map spread out on her lap, the tears have dried, the idea of life in the big city seems to have her cheered up a little, although she still insists that she doesn't need any of my money. "I'll sell the car," she tries to convince me, "they say it's just a pain to have a car in New York anyway, and that will give me plenty of money until I get a job." I don't argue but my mind is made up. Where I'm going, the four or five thousand dollars I'll be left with will be more than enough for what I have in mind.

We are driving through beautiful wooded, rolling countryside headed north towards the small town of Leesburg, Virginia, where we intend to stay the night before continuing next morning for New York.

It's unusually warm; traffic along this gravel road is almost non-existent, the odd car that passes sends up huge billows of yellowish dust. In the distance, to our left, silhouetted against the setting sun are the gently undulating crests of the Blue Ridge Mountains.

Someone somewhere is burning leaves and I roll the window down to better enjoy that wonderful smell with its memories of home and boyhood. Raking fall leaves into giant piles was something my father loved to do, sometimes frolicking in them with me. He claimed he hated setting fire to his handiwork but would throw open all the windows and doors of our little house to let the pungent smoke pour in. As part of the yearly ritual, my mother would playfully chase him about the yard with her broom charging him with "stinking up my house!" We would all laugh and sometimes get even sillier. It's one of my happiest memories of growing up.

Darkness descends suddenly as we enter a thick pine forest; a light mist begins to fill the hollows and dips in the road. We take a wrong turn and Marie admits she's "terrible at reading maps" so we stop at the side of the road and switch roles. She drives while I try to decipher the map and keep us on course.

Marie has tuned the radio into some of her favourite songs and contentedly taps the steering wheel in time to Glenn Miller's "String of Pearls," when a low slung Ford appears seemingly out of nowhere, swiftly pulls up beside us and a shotgun blast blows away most of that beautiful little face!

The Plymouth, with Marie's body slumped over the steering wheel, plows through a flimsy wooden railing and plunges down a steep cliff, careening wildly off trees and rocks. I am being tossed about like a cork on an angry sea, when the passenger door is ripped from its hinges and with the car flipping end over end, I am hurled free, landing violently in a clump of juniper bushes. The Plymouth, with, I presume the shattered body of Marie still inside, continues pinballing to the bottom of the ravine.

The side of my face feels like it has been hacked off. My exploring hand discovers that much of my left ear lobe is missing, my clothes are blood-soaked, every bone in my body cries out in pain, but amazingly enough, nothing seems broken. I reach inside my jacket. The wallet is still there. So is the gun that I fear I may soon have to use.

I know Marie must be dead, and in shock and confusion I am determined to find her in the dark, but as I painfully try to get to my feet, the sound of a car braking to a stop in the gravel just above me and two male voices warns me to lie still. A moment later a cone of light flicks on and probes the path of destruction gouged out of the hillside by the plummeting car.

"Christ," I can hear one of the men say, "we'll fucking well have to go down there and make sure both of them are dead!" The observation is greeted with a string of curses from the second voice and mumbled concern about breaking a leg on the way down.

Thus alerted, I pull my gun, slippery with blood, from my pocket and release the safety. I am trying to clean it as best I can with a part of my shirt that is still relatively dry when the light begins a bobbing descent in my direction. Obviously they have no idea that one of their intended victims is very much alive, armed and lodged halfway down the cliff, directly in their downward path.

The footing is treacherous and steep, so the flashlight's descent is slow and cautious. One of the men skids on loose gravel or rocks and utters a brief curse as the light tilts momentarily skyward. I can't see the men, but taking a chance that the one with the flashlight is holding it about belt high in his right hand, I take aim, as best I can in the dark, and fire at a spot about a foot to the right of the light and a couple of inches higher, and then quickly pump five more bullets at the same height in a tight pattern slightly to the right, then left, in hopes of striking the second man.

The light bounces crazily; what I presume is the flashlight crashes to the ground and for a brief moment the only sound is that of something ricocheting down the cliff ending with a faint "clunk" as it smashes into a rock or tree. Then something much more ominous. From just above and to my right there's a groan, guttural cursing and what sounds like panting. At least one of the killers is still alive and probably still holding that deadly shotgun.

He won't have any idea where I am until I talk, so I flatten myself against the bushes as best I can. As the groans, and now moaning, grow louder I take a chance he's wounded badly enough not to try killing the only person able to help him.

"Can you hear me?" I ask.

"Jesus Christ, help me," he groans.

"Where did I get you? How badly are you hit?"

There's a brief pause followed by hoarse heavy breathing and deep groaning.

"My hip, you got me in the hip, Jesus, can you call an ambulance or somethin'? Holy Christ, the pain is killing me, I think it must be broke or somethin'."

"What about the other guy, your partner, where is he?"

I can hear some movement.

"Don't move an inch, you son of a bitch, or I'll finish you off for sure," I shout.

There's more groaning in the darkness.

"He's dead, you got him square in the chest, I was just checkin' him to be sure. He's dead all right. You got him good."

"Where's the shotgun?"

The reply is eager. "Up in the car, we left it in the car."

"You must have a gun. I heard one of you say if there was anyone alive down in the car you were going to finish them off. Who's got that gun? Where is it?"

He replies reluctantly amid more groaning, "Gary's got a 45, I don't have nothin'."

"Can you reach it? His gun I mean?"

I hear some more movement, then a loud scream of pain. "Jesus, God, you've got to help me. Get me a doctor, I can't move, aghhh! I'm bleedin' like a stuck pig!"

He's not going to get sympathy from me! "Which one of you fired that shotgun? You killed an innocent woman, for God's sake! Why? Who the hell are you working for?"

The voice sounds frightened this time. "I swear to God it weren't me pulled the trigger. That was Gary. I swear we didn't know nothin' about no woman with you. When we saw it was a woman drivin' I yelled at Gary not to shoot but he don't listen. I didn't want to kill no woman."

I don't believe him for a moment. "Who are you working for? Are you FBI? Did Hoover put you up to this?"

He sounds a little puzzled. "Please, I'm bleeding here. Christ Almighty, I'm dyin', ya gotta get me a doctor or somethin'." There's another series of groans and little yelps of pain. I'm not sure if he's faking most of it, but from the strength of his voice it doesn't sound like he's in any danger of dying.

I repeat my question. "Are you FBI?"

"The FBI? Naw, never did nothin' for them. That guy Hoover is too cheap a son of a bitch."

I sense he's stalling but what he's just signalled is that someone has paid these two for their dirty work this evening and probably paid them well. Murder for hire, but who did the hiring?

I'm still lying on my stomach in the midst of the junipers, holding my head to the side so the blood from my damaged ear doesn't run down my neck, but a rock or a branch is jammed into my ribs and I need to shift position. As I push myself onto my knees, a branch beneath me snaps with a loud crack.

"Don't shoot, don't shoot me again," cries the wounded man, "here's my gun. Here I'm throwin' it down the hill." There's a grunt, a cry of pain and sure enough I hear the sound of metal hitting a rock well below me.

"You lying bastard," I shout, "you lied to me, said you didn't have a gun. What else are you lying about? You're probably the one who fired that shotgun. I'm coming up there now to put a bullet into your guts and leave you here for the vultures!" I roll completely off the junipers with a loud cracking sound and am rewarded with sobs of anguish.

"No, no, please," he moans and begins begging for his life. It's a sickening sound, coming as it does from this slug of a human being.

My initial shock is being overtaken by rage and I want him to know it. "You've got exactly ten seconds to tell me who you're working for; come up with the right answer or you're a dead man. Are you working for Hoover? Are you FBI?" I start to count. "One…two…three."

"Gary made the deal," he moans. "I just come along as a helper, honest to God." I continue counting. "Four…five."

He starts snivelling again. "All right, all right. Geeze, I'm a dying man here. All I know is that Gary sometimes done some work for the State Department, up there to Washington; he had a contact there with some guy high up. Some big mucky-muck is all I know. Ya gotta believe me, I don't know nothin' else."

So there it is: The State Department can mean only one thing— Alger Hiss! Dear God, I should have known. Marie! Marie! Oh my God, Marie, I should have known! I'm sorry, I'm so sorry.

Filled with remorse, grief and anger, I abandon the wounded man and blindly stumble and slide down the rest of the hill to the wrecked Plymouth that rests on its side against the base of a large oak tree. The moon casts enough light for me to see both the gaping hole where the door should be, and the body that sprawls halfway out of it.

I want to reach out and touch her, but for the first time in my life, my body betrays me. I begin to tremble so violently I have to clutch the car's twisted frame for support.

Thinking back on it now, I realize I must have blacked out for a moment, either from some sort of delayed shock, or more probably a minor concussion, because the next thing I know I'm on my hands and knees puking my guts out.

How long I'm like this, I'm not sure, but it must have been some time, because when the trembling and dizziness finally recede enough for me to stand, the almost full moon is high in the sky. I almost wish it wasn't so bright because I now very clearly can see the shotgun's carnage.

A car speeds past on the road above, its driver deaf to the screams for help from the wounded killer and oblivious to the tragedy just below him. It drives the last of the fuzziness from my head.

Stumbling about in the deep shadows cast by the trees, I manage to somehow get my arms around Marie's poor shattered body and pull her free of the car.

I know that when you hear this you may think what I did next was very strange—a little crazy perhaps. All I can tell you is that at the time it seemed to be the right thing to do. Until now, only my dear wife knows what I did next and it is she who insists that my actions that terrible night be included in this account. She insists what I did was beautiful. Others may not agree.

I have heard what sounds like a swiftly flowing stream at the bottom of this cliff and knowing how much Marie loved the water; I am determined to find a spot beside it where, alive, she would be happy. Perhaps in some confused way I believe it will help atone for what I have done to her.

The stream is not far and I find a spot, soft with fallen leaves and moss, upon which I lay her body. Out of the shadows the moonlight is sufficient for me to notice that the nylons she had so joyfully donned that morning are torn and blood-stained. I am not ashamed to admit it; the sight of those nylons tears my heart apart. I break down and cry like a baby, so loudly that the wounded killer high above me stills his moans and pleadings. I suppose he is astonished at the sounds I am making.

With tears still pouring down my face and without fully realizing what I am doing, I make my way back up the steep slope, find the wrecked car and manage to pry the trunk open. Pulling out our suitcase, I rifle through our clothes she so carefully packed only hours ago and find her second pair of nylons stowed away in a side pocket.

This is what I suspect some people may find distasteful.

Returning to her body, I strip her torn nylons from her legs, and with water from the stream, manage to wash the blood from them. Then, with some difficulty, I roll on the new nylons and throw the torn ones as far away as possible. Kneeling down beside her, I utter a short prayer. "Dear God, bless this poor woman and forgive me for what I have done to her." I kiss what is left of her face and say goodbye.

On the Run!

THE REST OF THAT NIGHT REMAINS FUZZY. Later I find a lump the size of a walnut on the side of my head which doctors now tell me probably indicates I was suffering from post-concussion syndrome. I do recall stripping nearly naked in the stream and washing the blood from my body, pulling on another pair of pants and a shirt from the suitcase, and then realizing I have forgotten my shoes, returning to the stream and finally locating them. I don't remember doing it, but thank goodness I transferred my wallet with its bundle of cash into the pocket of the clean pants.

On my way back up the cliff, I vaguely remember hovering over the wounded man and thinking seriously about finishing him off but instead reaching down and extracting his partner's wallet from an inside coat pocket and a revolver from his shoulder holster.

I promise the wounded man I'll phone for help at the next gas station, which I'm pretty sure I can remember doing. And although I have no clear memory of it, I obviously drove away in the car the pair had left idling on the side of the road.

My next clear memory is almost two days later when I pull into a gas station with the killer's car that I am foolishly still driving and see a road sign indicating that Lexington, Kentucky is only 12 miles ahead. I must have been driving day and night! I have no idea how or why I am in Kentucky and more importantly how I am going to get rid of this car and find another. I can't remember where I have stopped to sleep, if at all, on my journey thus far. Likewise I have no idea where I got the piece of adhesive tape that covers half my ear. All I know is I am now on the run, with quite possibly every police force including, for all I know, the US Marines, in hot pursuit!

Something about bluegrass country, or perhaps the cool crisp Kentucky air, must have cleared my brain, because as I'm driving past the world-famous Keeneland Racetrack it suddenly strikes me. All I've got to do is pull into the track's vast parking lot, already jammed with vehicles of every conceivable kind, leave the Ford there, walk to the nearest dealership, buy another car and then just drive away.

Sooner or later someone will recognize this sedan I am driving as the car they've been looking for all over hell's half acre, but if anything it will just help throw them off my track.

Kentucky is well west of where they shot Marie, so when they find the killer's car in the Keeneland parking lot, they will automatically assume I'm headed west, when, in fact, my destination is in an entirely different direction.

So I wheel the Ford into the parking lot, pull in beside a giant horse trailer, toss the keys into the glove compartment, check my pockets to make sure my wallet and new gun are in place and start walking.

As luck would have it, I'm hardly half a mile up the road heading into town when some old geezer with a jacket boasting "I TRAINED SEABISCUIT" pulls his truck over and asks if I want a ride.

"What's a seabiscuit?" I ask as I climb aboard. He gives me a strange, questioning look. "Only the finest racehorse ever rode. You never hear of Seabiscuit!?" I quickly realize my mistake and vaguely recall a famous horse that raced back before the war. "Oh ya, sure; you really train him?"

"Naw," he admits, "wish I had though. Won this here jacket off a fella last year up in Louisville. He claimed he had once helped train Seabiscuit, doubt it though; guy couldn't pick winners worth one sweet damn. Where you headed?"

He drops me off in downtown Lexington; I spot a Chrysler dealership, walk in, lay down $950, then about an hour later drive out with a pretty nice looking, only slightly used maroon-coloured 1942 Imperial. In response to my question, the salesman assures me "This little dandy will treat you fine all the way to California." He even gives me a free map showing me the best route to Los Angeles.

Kentucky is so beautiful, so similar to Belarus with its wooded hills, vast rolling meadows and piney forests that I am tempted to stop at one of the grand horse ranches I keep driving past and try to pawn myself off as some kind of horse trainer. Hell, if Hoover and the rest of them would just leave me alone, cleaning out stables the rest of my life would suit me just fine.

I know that can't be, of course, but more than that, there is a letter carefully folded away in my wallet whose siren song keeps pulling me south.

I really have no firm idea how best to get to the Bahamas, other than I'll have to find a port along the eastern seaboard from which ships depart for Nassau. I have Miami in mind, but in a rundown little coffee shop on the outskirts of Nashville I happen to overhear a woman telling the waitress she's on her way to Charleston to meet her boyfriend who docks there tomorrow on a ship from Lisbon. "Hasn't seen a woman in a month," she laughs, "so load me up with the strongest stuff you've got, 'cause I'm going to need lots of energy!"

"A month?" queries the waitress, "that must be one slow ship." "Nope," comes the reply, "just one mighty slow man!" They both begin to giggle.

Charleston! If ships are docking there from Lisbon, surely they must have something going to the Bahamas. I'd better track down a map and find out how to get there.

Island Wanderer

Two days later, I'm driving along Meeting Street in downtown Charleston when a cop pulls me over and I almost die of fright. In true southern fashion, however, he's extremely polite and apologetic as he hands me a traffic ticket for not stopping at one of their pedestrian crosswalks. "We'd really all like to keep our people alive down here," he drawls, "you can pay me the dollar fine right now if ya'all want to."

Believe me, I don't argue. Who gets to keep the dollar I have no idea, but I do have my suspicions. The money isn't wasted though, because the officer, believing I am, as my driver's permit indicates, an out-of-state visitor, recommends a little hotel down near the harbour which turns out to be a terrific place to stay. Six dollars a night is the rate and that includes a breakfast large enough to last me most of the day. Chickens that poke, peck and cackle around the front steps and backyard of the hotel provide the eggs that, the owner assures me, and I believe him, are still warm when he cracks them into the pan.

I am a little concerned about the traffic ticket since Hoover and whoever else may be looking for me will probably have alerted some police departments to be on the lookout for a Gilles Trudeau, born October 11, 1919, in Ogdensburg, New York, and now a resident of Washington DC. That's my new identity, courtesy of Alger Hiss.

My concern about being tracked down this soon is somewhat mitigated, by the knowledge that contacting every police department in the United States will probably take several days or even weeks. And, if the "hunters" have taken my bait, they will be concentrating their search along the west coast. They should have absolutely no reason to be in any kind of hurry to alert a sleepy southern town like Charleston.

As I think all of this through, it dawns on me that I'm getting better all the time at this running from the law game. Or running from outlaws, for that matter. At least, so I hope!

There is no question, however, that I cannot, as they say in the south, "dawdle" here. It will be only a matter of time until word gets around that this tall stranger with the funny accent, hanging around the Charleston harbour is on the FBI's, or somebody's, most wanted list.

As much as I try to put her out of my mind, I cannot help but think how much Marie would have loved this stately yet bustling little city and in particular its magnificent, colourful Georgian style homes with their free-flying staircases and high, arched doorways and windows.

Just to assure myself that, indeed, no "most wanted" posters of me have yet made their way to Charleston, I walk several blocks in the shade of tree-canopied streets to Meeting and Broad Streets where I am told I'll find the post office. I am so dumbfounded by the magnificence of the building I almost forget to look for "wanted" posters. When I finally stop gaping at the opulence surrounding me in the main lobby, I discover there are no posters of any kind. Small wonder! After all, who would allow posters to be attached to the solid mahogany that lines the walls or to the beautifully rich marble wainscoting?

And I cannot help but close my eyes and just for a moment imagine how thrilled Marie would have been, if like Scarlet O'Hara, she was able to swoop down the historic winding "Grand Staircase" which, with its solid brass risers and railings, is the centrepiece of what is surely one of the most beautiful rooms in the world.

"How great it would be if I could live and work here," I tell myself, knowing full well it's an impossible dream. The truth of the matter is, I've got to find a boat leaving for the Bahamas as soon as possible. If not, I'll have to drive further down the coast, perhaps even to Miami as I'd originally planned. I give myself three more days in Charleston, but it doesn't look hopeful. As I poke along the docks pretending to be a tourist looking for a way to Nassau, I am warned repeatedly that my chances are very slim. "This is hurricane season," one dockworker points out. "Only fools head to the Caribbean at this time of year. Unless it's a navy ship of course. Hurricanes don't bother them one little bit, but you probably won't be able to find anything heading to the Bahamas at least till the end of November." That's more than two months from now.

I've almost given up my search late afternoon of the third day in Charleston, and am reluctantly preparing to leave this delightful town for a more fertile hunting ground, when the hotel owner knocks on my door, sending my heart hammering my chest. But it's good news he bears.

"An older British couple in a 42-foot Chris-Craft stayed with us here at the hotel last night," he says. "From what I understand, they're heading out tomorrow for West End on Grand Bahama Island and they led me to believe they wouldn't mind having a third person on board to help out. If you're interested, they're down at their boat right now—not sure what slip but you can't miss it, beautiful looking craft I understand—the *Island Wanderer*. Pretty nice couple from what I could see," he adds.

I have no idea where Grand Bahama Island is, let alone West End, but if it's the Bahamas, that's fine with me. I thank the owner and head for the docks, only about a block away.

With at least a dozen people hanging around admiring her, there is certainly no problem locating *Island Wanderer*. She's a beauty all right, with what I'm told a bit later is a highly polished mahogany hull, spotless teak decks, and nickel-plated bright work. A huge Union Jack flutters in a light breeze from her stern, a much smaller Stars and Stripes courtesy flag, as per custom, has been hoisted on the bow. Her home port, according to the inscription beneath her name, is Bristol, England. The owners are nowhere to be seen,

I don't know the protocol, so to the amusement of some of the spectators admiring her fine lines, I knock on the side of the hull. Nothing, so I knock louder. From inside I hear a shout, "Who the hell's that? What do you want? Bugger off!" The accent is decidedly British upper class, the words decidedly not!

I return the shout. "What I want is to go to the Bahamas. Mr. Chilton up at the hotel said you might be looking for a strong back!"

"That so?" And onto the deck steps a man, who I swear, looks so much like the pictures of Charles Darwin I've seen, that I'm tempted to check the name of his boat again to make sure it's not the *HMS Beagle*! Mostly bald pate, save for a raggedy fringe but with a gloriously wild white beard cascading down from well above and in front of his ears, engulfing huge mutton chops, joined about halfway down its plunge by the twin streams of a swiftly flowing moustache before the whole thing comes to a hesitant halt about where his belly button should be. The eyebrows that complement all of this are so overgrown and unruly that his eyesight must surely be impeded.

It's hard to gauge his age behind all that hair; somewhere in his late fifties I would guess, he is at least as tall as I, lean, wiry, and tanned nut-brown. Buried well behind those eyebrows, I detect the sparkle of humor and intelligence.

His tattered and paint-stained white shorts and T-shirt belies the fact that this must be a wealthy man. So too, his gnarled and calloused bare feet. Or perhaps in the circles he inhabits, this is a sign of wealth.

"And who the hell are you?" he asks, "Here, come on board. Take your shoes off, no marking my decks, you see." He extends his hand to assist me, shoes in hand, with the short hop from dock to deck.

"Christopher Hollingsworth, but everyone just calls me Chris," he says, still holding my hand which he now shakes. "Or you can call me Captain since that's what I am when aboard, chief cook and bottle washer too." He smiles.

"Gilles Trudeau," I reply. "Sorry to bother you like this, sir, but I'm trying to get to the Bahamas and they told me up at the hotel you were headed there and might need a helper of some kind."

He cocks his head to one side, I swear just like that dog back in Ivy Lea, and gives me the strangest look. It scares me a bit. Does he know something and just isn't saying? I shake the feeling off as he invites me down below where a large woman, I presume is his wife, is sprawled on the carpeted floor listening to music pouring from a small radio propped against her ear. Some kind of jazz, as far as I can tell.

"Rebecca, meet Mr. Trudeau. He'd like to join us on our little jaunt to West End." Without looking up, Rebecca gives us a little behind the shoulder flip of a hand and a cheerful, "Hi there," and goes back to her radio, head bouncing, in time either to some kind of inner beat, or that being pounded out by what sounds to me like a badly out-of-tune saxophone.

Her two words give her away. Not from "old blighty" this one, more like what I was hearing in Kentucky. Pure Appalachian for sure. Interesting couple!

We leave Rebecca and go back on deck where Chris offers me a beer.

Men judge each other by the jobs they hold, so I'm ready for his question. "So Gilles, what kind of work do you do?"

"I'm a writer and editor," I only half lie. "Done some work for newspapers up in the New York area, thought I'd like to do a feature on cruising around the Bahamian Islands, hoping maybe *National Geographic* might be interested."

Chris gives me that strange look again. "I thought *National Geographic* usually does photo features. You got a camera?" I try to hem and haw my way out of this one, but my deck mate is far too smart.

He watches me in silence for a moment or two as I twist uncomfortably, and then he leans forward on his chair until his woolly face is only inches away.

"Look," he says, "I'm a good judge of men. Have been all my life. It's what got me where I am today. I think you're a pretty decent sort of a chap, but if you want to spend another minute on this boat you'd better come up with the truth."

As Jack Nicholson said in that famous movie I saw a couple of years ago, I don't think Christopher Hollingsworth can handle the truth, at least not all of it, so I give him an abbreviated version.

As he listens intently, never taking his eyes off me, I tell him about the Minsk Ghetto, my escape, the rescue of Yelena Mazanik, my trip to the Soviet Embassy in Canada, and then I skip pretty well everything else, explaining that after receiving a letter from Yelena, which I take out of my wallet to show him, I decided to leave the embassy and find Yelena in the Bahamas. If I do say so myself, it makes a very moving and believable story.

The captain's eyes are sparkling. "Rebecca," he shouts into the cabin below, "come up here my dear. We're going to help write a beautiful love story."

And so, at first light the next day, under dark and threatening skies, we leave Charleston, sail past famous Fort Sumter where the American Civil War started, and head for Grand Bahama Island and the little fishing village of West End.

Deadman's reef view from the beach

West End, Grand Bahama Island

ONE THING I QUICKLY LEARN aboard *Island Wanderer* is that you aren't much use to anyone when, in abject agony, you are spending most of the time hanging over a railing, as my bemused shipmates describe it, "feeding the fish." The captain and his first mate, Rebecca, don't seem to mind at all. In fact, both seem to think it quite hilarious. I get the idea they've been through this kind of experience with other novice sailors in the past. They seem to revel in inside jokes and rib pokings as I turn green. They chuckle as I moan in misery, offer snide references to sea legs, tossing cookies, and especially, from Rebecca, suggestions that maybe what I am really suffering from is lovesickness.

The weather is miserable all the first day and night. The wind picks up to what seems to me gale force during the afternoon, and by nightfall, waves and foam are spilling over the bow and crashing into the enclosed bridge where the captain is humming to himself at the helm. "Not a hurricane, just the aftermath, which, as any sailor knows is the safest time to travel," claims Chris, "nothing to worry about; this old girl has handled plenty worse than this!" and affectionately he pats the hull.

Rebecca, perched beside him, doesn't seem any more concerned than her husband, but has at least given up her jazz concert and instead firmly grasps a large brass lever that operates a windshield wiper whose sweeping strokes every minute or so clear the windshield of that portion of the Atlantic Ocean that hurls itself against our cozy little refuge. "Never did get that thing hooked up to the battery," explains Chris, who gives Rebecca's chubby knee a suggestive rub, "but it keeps my little sweetie next to me now, doesn't it?" His "little sweetie" responds with a leering smile and gives the windshield wiper another vigorous swipe.*

I try going below to ride out the storm on the bed they've assigned me, but that just seems to make me sicker than ever, so I stagger back up top and join my cruising companions on the bridge. I'm still feeling terrible but at least not ready to pull the gun from the waistband of my pants and end it all.

---

* **FACT:** Hurricane # 9 (the current practice of naming hurricanes didn't start until 1951) sprang up in the southern Caribbean on September 12, 1945, and for the next several days created havoc along a path which took it from the Island of Antigua to south of Grand Turk Island where it developed into a category 3. On September 15, it made landfall on the south end of Andros Island in the Bahamas with winds of more than 150 mph. It strengthened to a category 4 hurricane over Key Largo, then turned north up through Florida, finally heading out into the North Atlantic. Damage is estimated at more than $54 million in 1945 dollars. There were 26 fatalities. From approximately September 14 to 21, it would have resulted in strong winds and heavy seas between Charleston and Grand Bahama Island.

At about two in the morning as the storm begins to abate and I begin to believe maybe I'll be able to eat again some day, Chris gives Rebecca a raised eyebrow look. She responds with a little nod, then both give me an appraising glance.

"So, feeling better are we?" asks Rebecca. I'm more than a little embarrassed by my performance so I try to give a little laugh, but it comes out more like a choking sound. "I think I may live, after all."

Chris throws his "sweetie" another sideways look and turns to me. "Do you think you can take over the captain's chair here for a while and hold this course while Rebecca and I go down for a bit of a nap?" The suggestion alarms me greatly. Other than my brief sojourn aboard the *Queen Mary* and the little wooden rowboat expeditions on the St. Lawrence, I've never been on the water in my life, let alone piloted a boat in a storm like this. These two must be crazy if they think I'm going to get behind that wheel or do anything other than try to stop the dry heaves.

"Me? Take over running this boat, in a storm like this? You can't be serious!" I protest. " I wouldn't have the faintest idea what to do. What happens if we meet another boat or hit a rock or something? How do I even know where to go?"

"Oh now," replies our captain very calmly, "any rocks out here are at least a mile or so down I should think. And as for keeping her on course, there's nothing much to it actually. See the compass here? Just keep our bearing dead-ahead south; don't touch any of these levers or anything like that. Hands on the wheel only. Keep her steady as she goes, due south. And as for other ships, I doubt very much if there's another boat crazy enough to be out in this stuff within a 100 miles, but keep an eye out and if you happen to see lights just holler loud and we'll come right up. Here take the wheel for a minute, I'll show you how easy it is. Like I say, nothing to it, an imbecile can steer this thing. Here, take the wheel!"

And so after about a ten-minute course—I hesitate to describe it as a crash course—on how to keep our bow headed south, the randy couple hurries off below for, I suspect, more than just a nap. "Come to think of it," I say to myself, "forget Darwin, this bugger looks much more like an old billy goat, and a horny one at that!"

There are a few streaks of gray to our left and only a slightly wrinkled sea when I see a light in the distance. The "old goat" bounces up the stairs at my first yell and peers ahead. "Rebecca, my dear," he shouts, "bring us some coffee, we'll be pulling into West End shortly."

He takes the wheel and begins to whistle a bar or two of "Oklahoma!" through clenched teeth as he turns the *Island Wanderer* slightly to the east.

"That, my friend," he points, "is the light Bahamian fishermen have very kindly placed to warn us poor boaters of the dangers of Deadman's Reef. Well, actually I'm not sure if it was the fishermen who erected the light, or the U.S. Coast Guard. Many a Coast Guard cutter met its "Waterloo" on Deadman's Reef while chasing a rum-runner!"

I don't want to appear as stupid as I did back in Lexington with the Seabiscuit thing, but I've got to ask. "What's a rum-runner?"

And so, as the sandy beach of what Chris tells me is Bootle Bay looms larger in the dawning light, I get a condensed lesson on the fascinating history of the village of West End, Grand Bahama Island.

"See," explains Chris, "we're only about 50, maybe 55, miles off the Florida coast here. West Palm Beach is pretty much just behind us across the Gulf Stream. So during Prohibition—you know about Prohibition?" I nod and tell him that in Belarus we were amazed at the idea of not being able to buy vodka, wine or beer. "It pretty well confirmed our belief that Americans were a little crazy."

"Well," says a grinning Chris, "they *were* crazy, but what happened is that this little fishing village just ahead of us hit boom times for a while because people they called rum-runners found that the West End of Grand Bahama Island was the perfect distribution point for booze of every description.

"It was shipped into West End from places like Canada, Nassau and even Britain. Then, every night, half the population of the village over the age of five was busy loading the stuff aboard small but powerful boats they called go-fast boats that dashed the few miles across the Gulf Stream to distribution points all along the Florida coast. Huge fortunes were made, but as you might suspect, I don't think the villagers got particularly rich, although they were certainly far better off then than you'll find them today. They claim that even Al Capone visited here a couple times, I guess to check on his investment."

At this point, Chris heads *Island Wanderer* north. "We're going to skirt around West End and come into a little harbour on the other side of the island," he says, "well away from Deadman's Reef. The sea will be a lot calmer over there too. But let me tell you about Deadman's Reef. What a story that is!

"What happened," he continues, "is the US Coast Guard pretty soon got wise to what was going on in the Bahamas, so they'd lie in wait off the coast here with their patrol boats and try to chase down some of the rum-runners. Very often the smugglers, knowing the Bahamian waters very well, would lure the Coast Guard onto Deadman's Reef. They'd head, full throttle, directly for the reef with the Coast Guard in hot pursuit. Then at the last minute, the rum-runner, knowing exactly where he was, would suddenly veer away, leaving the unsuspecting pursuit boat to tear its bottom out on the rocks. It worked so well that very often not only would the rum-runners get away scot-free, but there was a good chance they could loot some of the items from the crashed boats, in particular, the guns.

By the way, " he adds, "there was a good deal of gun-running going on too. It's pretty quiet around here these days, though. Nowadays, it's mostly bonefishing, conching and a few boaters like us. And they still do a bit of logging. Before rum-running, logging the big pine trees that covered Grand Bahama and Abaco Island to the east of us here, was the number one industry, but you'll see when we get ashore that most of the big trees are long gone."*

By this time, we're too busy tying up to a semi-falling-down wooden wharf for me to ask what conching is.

The process of docking is considerably complicated by the fact that more than a dozen young men are fiercely arguing amongst themselves over who is best suited to take our ropes and fasten them to the posts that jut up from the seabed at various angles. Both Chris and Rebecca, who obviously are no strangers to this island and have gone through this before, are laughing and joking with members of the growing and curious throng gathering along the shore and pouring onto the dock. There's some good-natured bantering from those on shore about "goin' for de swim" if the rickety wharf collapses from all their weight.

---

* **FACT:** This account of rum-running in the Bahamas is accurate. So too is the role that Deadman's Reef played in the sometimes deadly game played out between the smugglers and the US Coast Guard. Ever since the travels of Columbus in 1492, the Bahamas' strategic location between Europe, the Caribbean and North America have made it a magnet for the outlaws of the high seas. In the 1920s, during Prohibition, the islands once again served as a base for modern pirates known as "rum-runners." That's also when Deadman's Reef most likely earned its name for the perilous task of putting ashore. Today, the picturesque resort of Paradise Cove sits directly across from Deadman's Reef, tempting snorkelers to explore its underwater treasures.

Believe me, there is nothing I want more than to set foot on solid land again, but this dock looks anything but solid so I wait until the boat is firmly attached and most of the crowd is back on shore before taking that first blessed step onto something that's only slightly swaying rather than briskly rocking.

After instructing someone in the crowd to send for some cans of gasoline to refuel our boat, the three of us set out for the heart of the village to a place called Aunt Lucy's for what Rebecca promises will be the best breakfast of my life. Strangely enough, I find myself ravenously hungry. Not so strange, I suppose, when you consider that my stomach has, for all intents and purposes, been pumped clean.

Aunt Lucy's turns out to be a typical West End two-room house, riotous with colour. Blue, red, yellow, and I think I recall green shutters. Breakfast is served in her backyard by Aunt Lucy herself, a large and affable native woman of about 40. We're shaded by a giant banyan tree and seated around what looks like it might be a chunk of floorboard from one of those wrecked Coast Guard patrol boats. A pair of badly scarred sawhorses serves as precarious supporting legs. The table surface and chairs are covered with red, white and black checkered oilcloth firmly affixed with large roofing nails. Entertainment is provided by a family of six pink piglets constantly squealing with delight as they scurry back and forth along a trench they have rooted out beneath the wooden fence separating Aunt Lucy's backyard from that of her neighbours. For no apparent reason, one minute they favour Aunt Lucy's side of the fence, the next moment they scurry back to the other side. Their apparent indecision ends the instant the first plate of food arrives. All the little piggies flock to our side and circle beneath the table, snouts skyward, in anxious anticipation of "cleanup privileges."

Rebecca is perfectly correct—the food is delicious. Something called Chicken Souse, grits so thick you almost have to cut them, boiled fish, oranges from a tree just up the street and tomatoes from her own little fenced-in garden. And even though, as Chris says, the sun is far from being over the yardarm—in fact it's not quite 9:00 a.m.—Aunt Lucy plunks down a large bottle of locally made and very powerful rum and a huge jug of orange juice.

About halfway through the bottle, Aunt Lucy plops herself down and begins to regale us with stories of the village, in particular revelations about her husband who she claims has fathered three children with her and as far as she knows, another five or so with various other women on Grand Bahama and elsewhere. She doesn't seem overly disturbed by this. "I gits smart bout him las year," she says, "I gits me some o dat birth control!" Rebecca's ears pick up at this. "Birth control? You have some kind of native birth control method? What do you do? How does it work?"

Aunt Lucy begins to laugh. "It work good. I sends dat man to Abaco!"

By the time we polish off the bottle, not only do I know that Abaco is the closest island to Grand Bahama, but Chris informs me that both he and Rebecca have taken such a liking to me that if I can wait a few days until they are sure about the weather and they can do a bit of fishing and conching, they'll take me to Nassau on New Providence Island, about 120 miles to the south.

My heart leaps at this. Nassau—Yelena!

There's something bothering me about all of this, however. "What about customs, immigration?" I inquire. "Don't we have to check in with somebody or something?"

What worries me is my new-found friends discovering that while I have been honest and told them my name is Igor Gouzenko born in Belarus, my passport, of course, tells a far different story, identifying me as Gilles Trudeau, born in New York State. I'm fearful that if my deceit is discovered, not only will I no longer have a ride to Nassau, because my friends will be in trouble, but a panicked phone call will be made to someone and before you know it there will be a real dead man floating out there on the reef.

Chris, who's consumed the bulk of the rum, gives me a reassuring pat on the arm and slurring his words only slightly, says, "don't worry old chap, we're in the British Empire here and when *Sir Hollingsworth* arrives in one of our far-flung colonies, the authorities report to him, not the other way around. Isn't that right, Lady Becky?" Rebecca, who appears about ready to nod off in the mounting heat, gives a bit of a start. "Yes, love."

Did I hear this right, or is this just the rum talking?

"You're a 'Sir'?" I ask. "Sir Hollingsworth?"

"At your service, my dear fellow!"

I shake my head. "Why didn't you say so before?"

Aunt Lucy leans in closer to hear this, apparently as astonished as I. Lady Becky appears fast asleep, her head resting on the table.

"Miss Lucy, my dear, would you have another one of those?" Chris points to the empty rum bottle.

Our hostess laughs until I'm concerned her ample bosom will spill from her blouse. "Yes, me lord, but thas another dolla!"

"Ho, ho," shouts Chris, "this is the British Empire, you treasonous wench. American dollars are outlawed, you will have to settle for good old British pounds."

Aunt Lucy is clearly delighted. "Das fine, me lord, one moah pound be fine!"

As she heaves herself to her feet in search of another bottle, Chris turns to me and explains.

"The peerage thing isn't something I'm particularly proud of. I didn't do a thing, you know, to deserve it. I earned every shilling I've got now, and to be honest I've got a few of those, but the title? Got that from my daddy, who, in truth was a scoundrel, and he got it from his daddy who from all reports was an even worse scoundrel, so there you go. I seldom use the title and would appreciate it very much if you just keep calling me Chris or Captain Chris as I'm known here in the Islands. Probably wouldn't have mentioned any of this were it not for the demon rum!"

Duke, or Baron or Knight or whatever he may be, I can't believe it relieves us of having to file some sort of immigration report, so I ask, "And because you have a title, we don't have to report to customs?"

"Oh," he says, as Aunt Lucy appears with a second bottle, "we'll stop in and pay our respects and a few good old British pounds to our friend the constable just up the road a piece, Miss Lucy's cousin, I believe, and that should pretty well do it."

I can't believe my good fortune. For a moment I forget all about the time not that long ago when all hell broke loose just as I thought I had the world by the tail.

Conch Cracking

THEY TELL ME THAT TODAY CONCH ARE BECOMING so scarce that fishermen must venture into deeper and deeper waters to find them, and that some jurisdictions, Florida for example, have banned their capture outright. But there was a time, not so long ago, when the shallow waters off West End, Grand Bahama, were so thick with these huge sea snails and other marine life, you could simply walk a few steps out into the water and pick as many as you wanted, literally from under your feet.

Which is why in 1945, even with few means of employment and virtually no income, Bahamians in West End, despite the collapse of the smuggling and rum-running business, are not starving. Cast a line baited with a piece of shrimp or crab into the water and within a few minutes you are likely to reel in enough fish to feed the largest family.

And if you tire of fish, pry a few conch out of their colourful shells, grind them up like hamburger, let them simmer in a fish broth for an hour or two on a hot stove along with some potatoes, carrots, tomatoes, onions and spices and you have some of the world's best-tasting chowder. If you prefer, chop the conch up into tiny pieces and eat it raw with a bit of lime juice, lettuce and tomatoes in a salad or, what has become a staple diet in the Islands—an entire meal of cracked conch with pigeon peas and rice.

My introduction to this native delight is a memory I cherish to this day.

By the time the two-rum-bottle breakfast is complete, even the piglets are seeking snoozing space beneath the banyan tree, their "under the fence" exploits stilled in surrender to a blazing mid-morning sun.

Captain Chris, as he is now referring to himself with obvious delight, has to be propped up on either side for the walk back to the boat. I support one side, a constantly laughing Aunt Lucy the other. Miss Becky, as her husband now addresses her, doesn't require propping up, but has to be constantly supervised and prevented from lying down on the side of the road for the nap she keeps insisting she requires. I fear she may lie down on the road itself, which may not actually be all that serious since the pitted pavement, bordering the ocean so closely that stray waves threaten to wash it away, is almost devoid of traffic other than idle strollers.

The villagers, it's obvious, are getting a terrific kick out of all of this, offering good natured advice from their front porches and yards as we weave unsteadily by. Despite their laughter, you get the sense that Captain Chris and Miss Becky are highly regarded and respected by the native villagers.

As we manoeuvre both onto their boat and into their beds, Aunt Lucy, still laughing, turns to me and says, " I tink dis two, out for de night. You come to Aunt Lucy fo dinner, I'm goan make you cracked conch, peas and rice so good, you goan fall in love wid me!"And breaks into even more joyful laughter.

As predicted, Sir Hollingsworth and his lady are still noisily sawing it off as I leave *Island Wanderer* for my dinner engagement. Uncertain as to Bahamian custom, I am a little concerned whether the invitation from Aunt Lucy is for something other than just dinner, but the three very polite and shy young children who greet me at her door that night dispel any doubts about her intentions. Aunt Lucy does the introductions. "Percy, he five, Duncan he six and a half, and my li'l angel Tanganyika, de boss da gang, she nine."

During our breakfast earlier that day I confessed I had never seen a conch, let alone eaten one, so Aunt Lucy, who now insists I drop the aunt and just call her Lucy, takes me out into her backyard once again and points to a large wooden tub into which she has dumped what I now know are three large queen conch.

I recognize the shells immediately, having at some point in my childhood, seen a picture book where one of them was used as a trumpet-like horn to rally the troops, or maybe slaves or something. I just remember some big muscled movie star blowing into one of these things and being rewarded with a sound that reverberated off distant mountains.

"Ah, of course," I say, "these are the shells you can use as a kind of bugle or hold to your ear to hear the ocean's roar," and I reach down to pluck one from the tub.

Lucy waves me off. "Hold on, dats you dinner—lemme."

The three children crowd around, excitedly shouting "me, me, no lemme!"

Lucy bends down, plucks a conch from the tub and hands it to five-year-old Percy. She watches proudly as he picks up a second shell and with a quick thrust, uses the spiked end of the first shell to punch a small round hole into the base of the second, thus releasing the vacuum created when the conch draws itself back into its shell. This makes extracting the meat very easy, so with a small knife Percy reaches into the lip of the shell and slowly slides out two frantically waving dark brown antennae attached to what looks very much like a piece of flat, cream coloured leather. He holds his prize up in a victory salute over his head and then, to my astonishment, takes a quick bite out of it! "Lemme, lemme," cry the other two children, who in turn repeat the performance, including the chomping!

"Now den, we gots to crack dat conch. Who fust?" All three eagerly throw up their hands. In a game obviously played many times before, Lucy pretends to shut her eyes tightly, whirls around three times and points directly at Tanganyika. "Who dat?" she asks, eyes apparently still closed. The beautiful little girl bounces up and down, sending pigtails flying. "Me, me!"

The game over, Lucy watches carefully as the conch meat is placed on a flat board spread over the table and the little girl begins to use a large metal mallet to vigorously whack what obviously is going to be our dinner.

This, it is explained to me, is cracking the conch. Beating it, not into submission, but into tenderness. The conch-cracking procedure is repeated twice more with equal skill and eagerness by the other two children. Lucy carefully examines each piece when the pounding is completed and passes equal and enthusiastic judgment. "Das good!"

The children revel in her approval, and I cannot help but marvel at what a wonderful mother this woman is. For a moment I recall happy times with my own mother and am struck by a pang of sadness, but it soon passes. I am just grateful to be a part, even briefly, of such a loving, giving and gentle family, but once again I cannot stop myself from thinking how fascinated Marie would be with all of this.

The cracking now completed, the tenderized conch is taken into the tiny kitchen where Lucy cuts it into small pieces, then carefully rolls each piece in a special "secret," she says, mixture of coconut flour and various spices. Shooing the children away to safety, she drops it all into a pot of boiling oil.

Cracked conch, a special Bahamian version of pigeon peas and rice, boiled grouper—a tasty fish plucked only an hour ago from the ocean just outside her front door—deep fried plantain and fried bananas covered in brown sugar have all disappeared from the table when I turn to Lucy and give her the news. "Miss Lucy, I admit it, you were absolutely right, I am in love with you!"

I will never forget it!

This poor little house in this poor little village rocks with laughter. For a moment at least, my cares fall away. Better even than the food is the love and joy served up at this table. I allow myself to hope!

At the time, I have no way of knowing it, but it is a joy that will change my life.

Nassau

EXTRACTING CAPTAIN CHRIS AND MISS BECKY from West End is almost as difficult as separating them from a rum bottle. It's ten days before we finally cast off *Island Wanderer's* lines, and then slowly back away from the wharf that miraculously still stands, and wave goodbye to what appears to be at least half the village gathered to bid farewell.

As we pull away with much merry tooting of the ship's horn, I am still marvelling at something that happened just before boarding. As I am shaking hands and thanking several young men who had earlier introduced me to the fine art of bonefishing, I see Lucy gently nudging a shyly giggling Tanganyika toward me. The little girl is concealing something behind her back, trying to work up the courage to approach me on her own. Curious, I bend down and she darts forward, hands me a small package carefully wrapped in brown paper, and then retreats behind her mother's skirts.

Lucy signals me to open it and I am delighted to see a beautifully and very intricately carved wooden figure of a little boy. I see immediately it is the perfect likeness of five-year-old Percy, right down to his much-too-large-for-him, hand-me-down running shoes.

It is very skilful work done by an artist of considerable talent. As I give Lucy an inquiring look, she points at Tanganyika. For a moment I don't get it. Is she indicating that her daughter carved this? This is not the work of a nine-year-old! This can't be, yet Lucy keeps pointing at her daughter, smiling broadly and nodding yes. I say a final thank you and goodbye to my fishing friends and work my way through what now almost looks like a reception line of the friendly and curious and grab Lucy by the arm.

"Are you trying to tell me that Tanganyika did this? This is all her work? You didn't help her at all? This is very, very good, you know," and shade my eyes from the sun in order to examine the figure even more closely.

"I knows dat," says Lucy, "Lord knows it real good, but it ain't me; my li'l angel been doin' it since she dis high." She holds her palm at her knees.

Almost overcome with astonishment, I bend down, put my arms around this "li'l angel," give her a hug and thank her profusely for her wonderful gift then I kiss her on the cheek, which prompts more giggles.

Right then and there, I realize I have to do something. I can't just walk away from this kind of raw talent without somehow helping. This is a very beautiful, peaceful part of the world, but this kind of potential deserves a chance to flourish beyond the confines of a little village.

It suddenly strikes me that here is an opportunity for something good to come out of all of this misery and death.

"Wait here," I tell Lucy, "I'll be right back."

Back on board *Island Wanderer* I retrieve my wallet from its hiding place beneath my mattress, count out some bills and hurry back. Chris has started the engines and finally seems anxious to cast off.

I shove the wad of bills into Lucy's startled hand. "Here, please, I think your little angel has a talent the world needs to see. Promise me that you'll use this money to take her to Miami or someplace in the States, an art gallery maybe, or no, you know what? Take her and some of her work to the University of Miami; they must have an art department or art experts. See what they say, but don't let anyone discourage you or her. Promise me."

There are tears in her eyes. "Dis he-ya five hunner dolla—you crazy!"

There's an impatient blast from *Island Wanderer*'s horn.

I bend down and pick up Tanganyika so I can look directly into her eyes.

"Little angel," I say quietly, "someday when you become rich and famous, I want you to dedicate one of your sculptures to a very special woman named Marie." Even though I doubt if she understands what I mean, the little girl, not appearing to be the least bit puzzled, nods gravely.

Our cruise to New Providence Island and Nassau is uneventful. The sea is relatively calm, the winds light. Chris figures the run will take us about 8 hours without pushing the motors very hard and he's right.

After their rum-soaked adventures on Grand Bahama, I am somewhat relieved and greatly surprised to see that at sea, both Captain Chris and Miss Becky are proselytizing teetotallers, disdainful of anything harder than mango juice. Having witnessed their considerable ability to find the inside bottom of bottles while on land, I thought I'd provide a little treat while serving up lunch about an hour out of West End. "How do you like this?" I ask, whipping out a 40-ounce bottle of 151 proof "Ass Kicker" Jamaican dark rum I've gone to great lengths to acquire back on Grand Bahama. Instead of the surprise and delight I expected, both throw up their hands in offended horror.

"Good Lord, old chap," says Chris, "what are you doing with that?" Miss Becky musters sufficient energy to provide a little shriek. "Eeeekkkkk! Get that away from me!"

Sobriety must be an aphrodisiac for this couple, because on several occasions during our voyage I find myself in the captain's chair, holding a "steady as she goes" course south, while my shipmates are below "napping." I'm beginning to suspect that it's not really her fault that Miss Becky is half asleep most of the time, but rather it's because of that randy old billy goat of a man she's hooked up with who keeps her completely worn out!

Just before dusk, the coastline of New Providence Island begins to gradually appear off our starboard bow. As the thin dark line slowly grows more distinct, Chris glances at me and with some concern asks, "Getting nervous lad?" I hate to admit it, but I am: Nervous and excited.

During the day, while not "pinch hitting" at the helm for the "nappers," I read Yelena's letter over and over again until I have it almost memorized. No matter how I parse the words, the invitation seems very clear, in particular her closing words. "*Still with thank you in my heart and thinking of you often.*" Then there is the sentence where she suggests meeting me again would make her happy. I churn those phrases around and around in my mind. Is it only gratitude she is expressing or is she suggesting the possibility of something else? Then I am struck with a very disturbing thought, "What if she's already met someone else? It's almost a year since she sent me that letter; she's a beautiful woman, looking to settle down, what if she's already married? What then?"

I know I must sound to you like a virgin school boy here, but you've got to remember, sex was one thing, but when it came to affairs of the heart I had no experience at that point in my life. I was very fond of Marie and still missed her, and Patsy certainly was fun before I knew the truth about her, but I knew it wasn't love in either case. I knew that very well; so if all of this sounds a bit like teenaged mooning over the cute little blond girl in math class, please forgive me. Lust I knew about, love was foreign territory for me then.

As we throttle back and slowly pull into the bustling Nassau harbour my eyes are busy scanning the shoreline in the faint hope I might spot Yelena strolling along what I soon learn is Woodes Rogers Walk, a broad path that runs parallel to the concrete seawall of the harbor. My eyes are so busy, in fact, I almost miss the sleek, low slung, high-powered motorboat moored to one of the docks we are idling past. It's not the bright red flag that hangs from its bow that sends my heart into my throat. It's what's in the upper left-hand corner of that flag. A red star, hammer and sickle!

"Goddamn Ruskies," murmurs Chris who then looks furtively at me. "Sorry," he says.

"Don't worry," I tell him. "I'm Belarusian!"

What I don't tell him is that I am a Belarusian who right now is wondering if I've made a huge mistake in coming here. I really have no idea how Yelena will greet me. In the back of mind, as well, is the fear that I may plunge Yelena into the same kind of danger that led to Marie's death.

In thinking back on it today, I have concluded that because of the trauma I had endured I wasn't thinking clearly and was nursing some kind of crazy idea that Yelena and I would instantly fall into love and escape together to some distant Shangri-La where we would live out our lives in permanent bliss.

Whatever the reason, there can be no question my expectations were totally unrealistic. Fantasies really. I realize that now.

Yelena had no magic wand, which when waved would make my problems disappear, but in my troubled mind I gave her that wand and was desperately afraid she would refuse to wave it.

When we arrived in West End I couldn't wait for the feel of solid earth beneath my feet again, but here in Nassau I am experiencing a strange reluctance to abandon the familiarity and security of *Island Wanderer* for the vagaries of a strange city's streets and the mysterious pathways of a woman's heart.

Apparently exhausted from an excess of "napping," both Captain Chris and Miss Becky announce they'll forego an evening foray into the city in favour of "a good solid sleep aboard ship."

They may be sleeping well but I do not. My dreams are filled with visions of wild, raging seas smashing into menacing reefs; somewhere in the distance a beautiful woman clutching a wind whipped coat or carved figure cries out in distress. Try as I might, I cannot reach her.

It is Chris's voice that awakens me. "Having a nightmare, are we? Are you all right then? Anything I can get you? Sorry for knocking you up but we were afraid your cries might summon the local constabulary and we don't want that now do we?"

When I don't move, he gives my shoulder a little shake and says, "Come along then, we'll have some breakfast and then have a look-see at what our former King Eddie and his lovely bride Miss Simpson have left for us here in Nassau."*

---

* **FACT:** This, of course, refers to the fact that Edward VIII abdicated the Throne of England to marry "the woman I love," Wallis Simpson, and was subsequently shipped off to serve as Governor of the Bahamas from 1940 until July 28, 1945.

It is an absolutely gorgeous morning. A few wispy clouds, as though from an artist's brush, accentuate the deep blue of the Bahamian sky. The air is sweet and polished. A soft trade wind toys with the Atlantic, sending little clusters of diamonds dancing across the harbour. The water is so crystal clear I see a school of brightly coloured triggerfish examining the keel of a nearby sailboat. High overhead a squadron of seagulls rides a thermal; soaring, dipping and diving for what appears to be nothing but pure joy.

Their cries are drowned out by metal-on-metal shrieks emanating from the tortured front wheel of a large wheelbarrow which, as far as I can see, is the only transport available to unload a rusty old tramp steamer jammed almost to the sinking point with bananas. According to a notation scratched on her rusted stern the ship's name is *The Goerge*. Her home port, St. Lucia.

I watch fascinated as a reed-thin man, dark skin glistening with sweat, attacks the pile of green bananas that threaten to spill over *The Goerge*'s sides. One by one he hauls long stems out of the pile, each weighted down with between 80 and 120 pounds of bananas, and then dumps three of the stems into the wheelbarrow. With apparent ease he wheels the load down a springy, narrow plank leading from the ship to the wharf where two white men gently place the stems with their unripened fruit into a waiting truck.

Back and forth he trudges with his piles of three, the wheel protesting more loudly each time. Guessing at the number of banana stems on board *The Goerge*, I figure if this one poor fellow doesn't recruit some help he'll be unloading non-stop for the next two days.

Chris is watching all of this as well and says wryly, "If that rusty old bucket made the trip all the way from St. Lucia loaded down like that, they should change its name to *Bloody Miracle*!"

Perhaps it is just the beauty of the day or the harbour theatre. It could be the adrenaline I feel pumping through my veins at the prospect of a romantic adventure. Whatever it is, I am starting to feel much more optimistic. Anxious, even, to see what fate has in store for me onshore. Surely nothing can go wrong on a day like this… Even my fear of Hoover or Jonathan's "hunters" is alleviated somewhat by the fact that the news media still has apparently never heard of Igor Gouzenko.

Miss Becky's radio emitted little more than static and jazz for most of our voyage from West End, but from time to time, when she dozed off, I managed to furtively change stations and pick up a newscast out of Miami.

Actually, I'm not sure if I should be relieved or concerned that there is still not a whisper about a defection from the Soviet Embassy in Canada or even a hint of a giant espionage ring.

Relieved because it means that no one in the Bahamas, including Yelena, will have knowledge of the search for me that is underway, but at the same time I am concerned that the apparent absence of an "understudy" defector means that search is still very much alive. If an imposter comes forward claiming to be Igor Gouzenko with a list of Soviet spies, I am of the belief they'll stop trying to chase me down.

I now know, of course, that I was either very naive, or delusional—probably both.

For a brief moment as we step ashore onto Prince George Wharf in the heart of downtown Nassau, some of last night's foreboding returns and I am side-swiped by a horrible thought. "My God! Suppose that letter from Yelena was a trap? Suppose they've threatened her or her family, made her write a letter to lure me to this place?" I quickly put the idea out of my mind, but it gives you an idea of the stress I was living with at the time.

I am still jittery from seeing the Soviet flag on the bow of that speed boat in the harbour, but I assure myself that a woman brave enough to place a bomb in the bed of "The Murderer of Minsk" could never be induced to betray the man who saved her.

Now that we are on land again, my shipmates are anxious to locate the closest rum shop, obviously convinced my Jamaican over-proof contribution will have far too short a lifespan. I, on the other hand, want to find the Soviet Consulate, so we agree to part company. Surprisingly it is Rebecca who grasps my hand, stares into my eyes and says, "Good luck; I hope you find her and that she is everything you want her to be." I am so taken aback hearing this from this vague and dreamy woman who has hardly said five words to me since we met, that the best I can do is mumble, "Thank you." For the first time I catch a glimpse of the sensuality concealed beneath those half-closed eyes.

Unlike the sleepy little village of West End, the city of Nassau, as the capital of the Bahamas, is a thriving, bustling, colourful, crowded and very noisy city with ancient and late-model automobiles jockeying with horse-drawn carts and buggies for space on the narrow roads.

Despite the rising heat, self-important-looking white men, most in surprisingly formal business suits, some even with bowler hats and furled umbrellas, share the sidewalks with those of much darker skin, many of whom are dressed as though they just arrived from the fields or fishing boats. There's a riot of enterprise at every street corner—crates of live chickens, mangoes heaped upon upturned buckets, ramshackle wooden stands piled high with oranges, lemons and limes, and large bunches of plantain and bananas are for sale everywhere. One young boy sits astride a huge sea turtle shell, at least I hope it's just the shell.

In Nassau, it seems, if you are white you work for the white government or one of its agencies including the courts and the banks. If you are black most probably you are a farmer, fisherman, street vendor or servant. Lots of black waiters too, just now setting up tables for the lunch crowd in a multitude of outdoor cafés, bars and restaurants.

The Bahamas did not gain full independence from Britain until 1973. In 1945 the colony was firmly under the iron thumb of what many called the "Bay Street Boys", a despotic group of wealthy white merchants, bankers, and government officials whose pillaging of the islands surpassed even that of earlier visitors, such as Woodes Rogers and other assorted pirates.

As I pass what a sign claims is the world's largest straw market, all of us within earshot are besieged by laughing, colourfully dressed women vendors shouting lewd jokes and inducements of varying kinds. It all reinforces my impression that the Bahamian dialect may be difficult to understand for someone like me, but their universal language of laughter cannot be misunderstood.

While I am anxious to locate the Soviet Consulate and somehow make contact with Yelena, I cannot help but stop to admire some of the wares on display. Everything from tiny dolls to entire floor mats; hats of every size and description, handbags, baskets and large fans, all painstakingly woven from straw or palm fronds, some with intricate and colourful designs stitched in with wool. I pay special attention to the woodcarvings on display at several of the stalls and quickly see that the artistry falls far short of that created by a little nine-year-old girl in West End Village.

Each time I stop to examine something, a woman immediately sidles up to whisper, "Doan worry bout de price, I'm goan give big man like you very special deal." And if I make the mistake of picking something up for close examination, the question is always the same. "How much you wanna pay for dat?"

It's a game I've played many times before at markets in Belarus, but I'm no match for the woman who sells me a very stylish Panama hat. She swears up and down she made it herself, "wid dees hands." I don't believe it for a moment, in fact I can see where someone has ripped out the small "made in" label, but in the end I'm sure I pay at least double what I could have if I were concentrating better.

Yelena, I know, must be very close and it's time for me to, as I am sure John Wayne would say, buck up my courage and find her. I am determined not to come this far only to succumb to timidity.

"Where's the Soviet Consulate?" I inquire of the Panama hat woman. She gives me a quizzical look. "What you wan dem for?" She's not laughing anymore, not even smiling.

" Well," I say rather hesitantly, "I know a woman who works there. I haven't seen her in several years." This admission prompts the reappearance of a smile. "So de fox chase da chicken!" I laugh and shake my head.

"Jess up dere," she points to my left. " Jess pass Bay Street, on Parliament Street cross from de Rawson Square where de white boys run tings." As I turn to leave, she grabs my arm. "Is you a Rooskie?" I shake my head no. "Well den," she warns, "you be careful now. Days not nice peoples dem Rooskie peoples!"

The red flag with its hammer and sickle announces the presence of "Rooskie peoples" the moment I turn off Bay Street onto Parliament. Despite everything I am trying to tell myself about her wanting to meet me and having nothing to worry about, I feel my heart beating faster and a light sweat breaks out on my forehead that has nothing to do with the sun.

The Consulate appears to be housed along with several other offices in a large pink building with green hurricane shutters about half a block south of the Nassau Public Library. Only the flag and a small brass plaque announcing, CONSULATE OF THE USSR identify it as anything other than one of the legal offices that seem to dominate the street.

Pulling my new Panama hat down over my forehead, I stroll past the building in the off chance I might see her through one of the windows. As I suppose I should have known, official Soviet offices do not have windows through which those on the outside can see.

Across the street is a small park whose wooden benches are shaded by one of the largest banyan trees I have ever seen. I can easily see the front entrance of the Consulate from there, although I will be partially screened by a hedge of flowering hibiscus. The perfect observation spot.

I cross the busy street, accept the open invitation from a shady bench, set myself down, pull my Panama hat down even further over my eyes, watch the passing parade, and with no small amount of trepidation, wait. It's shortly after 11:00 a.m. Hopefully she'll emerge alone and seek out one of the nearby restaurants for lunch, or barring that I'm quite prepared to wait until closing time.

I don't have long to wait. Like good public servants everywhere, those working for Stalin are very punctual, at least when it comes to lunch. At the stroke of noon the front door to the Consulate bursts open and a handful of people spring briskly out in a hurry presumably to claim choice tables at favourite restaurants.

I recognize her immediately. Jet black hair tucked neatly beneath a large white floppy hat. Even from here I can see the piercing black eyes that observed me so carefully in that little Minsk bakery. It's obvious she is eating much better now than she was before our wild ride to freedom, but the prominent cheek bones are still there. Her figure is fuller but still shapely beneath the frilly white blouse and the almost knee length flowered skirt she is wearing, but as she crosses the street only a few yards in front of me I see that there is nothing changed with that determined, no-nonsense stride I remember so well.

I am relieved to see she is alone, but as I slip in behind her, I remain well back, observing her every move, watching carefully to see if she is being followed or if anyone appears to be paying her an inordinate amount of attention. I am taking no chances.

The restaurant she chooses is tucked well back from the street, comprised of only a dozen or so small tables circled beneath a wooden awning. Two large, slowly turning overhead fans stir the skirts of three very pretty young women seated at one of the tables, several men in business suits occupy another, and more customers are just now arriving. A waiter, who obviously knows Yelena, smiles as she approaches and tilts his head in such a fashion that seems to indicate that, yes, he's saved her favourite table, the one nearest the street.

Pulling my Panama down until it almost covers my eyes, I stroll casually past. She pays me no heed. Nothing appears out of the ordinary. I cross the street, Charlotte Street as I recall, and watch to see if anyone is following me or observing her. It is all so innocuous I'm beginning to feel a little silly. "Time to stop stalling, Igor," I tell myself. "Buck up your courage and take the plunge." Crossing the street again, I stroll with feigned casualness into the restaurant, and as she bends her head to examine the menu, I take a deep breath and sit down across from her.

"Hello, Yelena!" She looks up, startled, and throws her hand to her mouth. "Oh my God! Igor! Igor! Is that really you? Oh my God! I thought you were in Canada. How did you get here? Oh my God, Igor, I can't believe it's really you!"

She is making such a fuss that a concerned waiter comes over to ask if there is a problem and gives me a strange, inquiring look.

"No, no, oh goodness knows, no, no," she laughs, "this is just an old friend I haven't seen in years. Oh Igor it is so good to see you! What in the world are you doing here? Oh this is so wonderful, I can't believe it!"

So far I haven't had a chance to say a word. I just stare at her as though dumbstruck. To be honest I'm probably as surprised as she that I am actually here and she is there across the table from me!

The food arrives, but in her excitement she doesn't touch her plate. I lie that I am on holiday from the Embassy in Ottawa and decided to visit the Bahamas and look her up. I tell her about Captain Chris and Miss Becky but don't feel comfortable enough with her yet to relate any of the details of my flight from danger.

She fills me in on her life since her letter. She hasn't heard anything from Urie Labonak and sadly admits she believes he is probably dead. She cheers up quickly though, obviously thrilled to see me.

"It's been really fun and interesting here in Nassau," she says breaking into Belarusian, then leans over to whisper, "although I didn't have much luck with the Duke and Duchess when they were here. As a matter of fact," she laughs, "I didn't get invited to a single one of their parties. Apparently they aren't too crazy about Communists! And," she confides with a wry grin, "we haven't been able to spot a single escaped Nazi hiding in a palm tree either. I think they've all headed further south to Argentina and Brazil, the Nazis I mean; we've got plenty of palm trees here, although as I'm sure you know the Duke and Duchess have left us for greener pastures or maybe better wine or something. I don't think they were up to anything bad here in Nassau, but I can't be sure. I guess I'm not much of a spy." she confesses, but doesn't seem too disturbed about it.

She leans back in her chair as though to study me more closely, and then begins to bombard me with questions about life in Canada, some of which I answer truthfully.

I ask about her sister.

"Oh," she says, "Valentina will be so glad to see you again, and you won't believe how she has changed, how she has flowered since we arrived here. She was so serious before, so unhappy most of the time. Well, not any more, I am pleased to say. In fact, what a social butterfly my little sister has become, she's got every single male and more than a few married ones on the island in a tizzy, that's for sure. We had some poor love-besotted soul show up at our apartment door last week in the middle of the night, believe it or not, with a guitar. His singing and playing were so terrible the neighbours reported him to the police!"

We are both laughing, beginning to feel more comfortable with each other.

An hour later, she glances at her watch, gives a little gasp, "Oh, oh," she exclaims, "they'll be jumping all over me if I don't get back to work. You must come for dinner tonight. It won't be anything fancy but we have so much more to talk about. Here's our address; it's not far." She jots down the information on the back of the bill for the meal I have been too befuddled to even offer to pay.

Leaning over the table she gives me a peck on the cheek. "It is so wonderful to see you again, especially not riding a motorcycle!"

Her laughter is contagious, but as she waves goodbye and launches into that brisk walk again, I feel strangely deflated. No magic wand was waved. No magic anything.

Valentina

IT COMES AS A TOTAL SURPRISE to both of us. We neither expected it, nor did we necessarily want it, but that night Valentina and
I fall in love. Total, absolute, glorious and oh-so-joyful love. The love
of my life and hers.

Yelena is right, her sister has indeed blossomed into a beautiful *woman*! She is no longer the frightened, sweet teenager I met in
Belarus.

It has never been easy for me to talk about my emotions, and I
understand what I am about to say may sound kind of Hollywood
soppy to some, but all I know is that the moment Valentina opens
their apartment door and throws her arms around me in welcome I
become a raving lunatic!

I want to bury my face in her neck, in her hair, between her breasts, between her legs. I want to taste her, to inhale her. I am in love with her earlobes, her eyelashes, the way she holds her glass, I am in love with her knees, her elbows, her smell, her laugh, the way she glances shyly at me. I want to take her toes in my mouth and devour them. The delightful nipples I see hardening beneath her blouse I want to take in my teeth and nibble and bite until she cries out in pleasure. I adore the mole on her shoulder, I want to caress the little cold sore at the corner of her mouth. My heart races, I walk on air, I am quite mad!

It is exhilarating and terrifying. It is a night of magic!

Even Yelena, who begins to watch us closely very early in the evening, realizes there is something, as she admits later, "going on." "There was so much electricity in the room," she says, grinning broadly, "I could almost see the sparks flying each time you even came close to each other."

Far wiser people than I, virtually from the dawn of recorded history, have attempted to explain what happens when two people fall in love as quickly as Valentina and I did. Libraries the world over are filled with books about the phenomenon. Many a movie mogul's fortune has been made exploring the possibilities and consequences.

I see where even neurobiologists in England have analyzed the brain activity of people experiencing what they describe as early romantic love and found that, "when falling in love the skin flushes, breathing is heavier and palms become sweaty because the brain is experiencing a biochemical rush of dopamine, norepinephrine and phenylethylamine that are chemically similar to amphetamines."

That's science for you! My explanation, achieved not through the use of an MRI, but rather from personal experience, is that essentially love strikes suddenly and without warning when two people find they are just absolutely crazy for each other for no apparent reason.

I don't recall skin flushes, heavy breathing or sweaty palms,

266

(well maybe a bit of heavy breathing and certainly heart racing) but I certainly remember being crazy about this beautiful woman. And according to her, that pretty well sums up her reaction to what she describes as opening the door to "this really good looking man."

All those men in Nassau weren't mistaken. The woman who opens that door is very attractive with her long, shining black hair, flashing dark brown eyes, olive skin, full breasts and with what I tell her repeatedly in later days is an absolutely "gorgeous bum!" In fact, to be totally accurate, there comes a time when I inform her she has undoubtedly the most perfectly formed, beautiful and, yes, I admit it, sexiest bum in all the Caribbean. "The most beautiful bum in all of Christendom," is how I once describe it during close examination. She is delighted with the assessment!

And yet—and yet, there is something far beyond mere physical attraction that strikes both of us. It is that mysterious thing called love, for which there is no rational explanation, scientific or otherwise. Only those who have experienced it will understand what I am saying.

Valentina quits her job as a clerk in a local bank so we can spend every day together, exploring the city and each other.

We manage to avoid sex for the first few days. We both seem to understand that this is a relationship that needs to be savoured and nurtured before we succumb to the lust we freely admit we feel for each other.

Incredibly she is a virgin, something she shyly confesses, so the sex when it does begin is hesitant and very tender, becoming much more uninhibited and passionate as our exploration of each other takes us down new pathways of pleasure and desire. I do bury my face in the crook of her neck, between her breasts, between her legs and my teeth do tease her nipples until she cries out in ecstasy!

She is intensely curious to see the reaction of my body to her stimulation. She loves to stare deeply into my eyes as she performs various experiments. "Oh my goodness," she will say with mock surprise "look at this," or, "well, well, I'm getting the idea you kind of like me doing this!"

I rent a lovely little apartment overlooking the harbour and every night we fall asleep in each other's arms and awaken holding hands.

At first I am worried about Yelena's reaction to all of this. What fantasies might she have had about me? It is a concern that is unwarranted. She is thrilled to see her sister so happy and any reservations she may have had about our relationship seem to dissolve. She jokingly takes me aside one day and with faked anger shakes her finger in my face and says, "If you ever cause my sister one moment of grief so help me I will have to kill you with my bare hands!" I, of course, dutifully promise that I will bring nothing but joy, wealth and infinite happiness to the entire planet and we both laugh uproariously.

At times I lie in bed thinking how strange it is that all the fantasies I had spun around Yelena are now coming true with Valentina. I push aside all nagging fears and doubts.

The three of us spend one lovely afternoon with Captain Chris and Miss Becky cruising around New Providence aboard *Island Wanderer*. Once, as Valentina delightedly watches two dolphins playing leapfrog—or would you say "leapdolphin"—in our wake, Chris gives me an exaggerated wink and a thumbs-up signal.

Sadly though, as we tie up back at our wharf this truly wonderful, if eccentric, couple announces that they will be leaving for the Azores in the morning, on their way back to Britain.

Before we say goodbye, Chris pulls me aside and hands me a small business card. "Listen, old chap," he says gravely, "I have this feeling that you may be in a bit more spot of trouble than you are admitting. If ever I can help in any way, here is my address and private phone number." I try to refuse it. "You've done enough already for me," I insist, "we'll be just fine." Chris pushes the card back into my hand and rather gruffly says, "Don't be so damn silly, I am not without influence, and hear me now, you should never say no to a man who wants to be your friend." Rather reluctantly I accept his card and thank him and Miss Becky again for all that they have done. We all shed a few tears before finally saying goodbye.

At the time, of course, with everything brightly glowing in a new and perfect light, I imagine all my troubles are over. In bed that night, we both roar with laughter when Valentina turns to me and very seriously says, "You know something? That Captain Chris reminds me of an old billy goat my father used to have!"

As with people everywhere who are truly in love, we delight in each other's idiosyncrasies. She does her best to deny it, but finally admits that she is not a morning person. In fact we both agree she is a "miserable old bear" before she has her first coffee of the day. I, on the other hand, am wide awake at dawn's first light, ready to take on the world. Thus it is that my first task each morning is to hike around the corner to a little restaurant and return with a large mug of coffee that within an hour has the desired effect of converting her from an "old bear" to her usual sunny self.

She, on the other hand, learns how to tease and humour me out of my dark moods.

It is Yelena who brings us back down to earth.

Grim-faced, she gives us the terrible news. "Moscow is recalling us," she announces. "With the Duke and Duchess gone from the Bahamas, they claim there is no need for us to remain here." She's almost in tears, waving her hand in front of her face as though to brush the thoughts away, then attempting a dismissive laugh. "Either that or they've finally discovered that we are rotten spies."

I am thunderstruck. Valentina turns pale, clutches her throat and groans with dismay.

"That can't be," she protests. "The assignment here was for five years, we've barely been here a year!" Angrily, Yelena holds out a formal-looking letter and shakes it in her sister's face. "Here, damn it, look for yourself. We've got exactly two weeks to get our things together and get back to Moscow."

A moment later they are in each other's arms sobbing bitterly.

Somewhat composed but with tears still in her eyes, Valentina turns to me and asks the question I have been dreading: "Can you come with us?" Then, with surprising resolve and determination, she adds, "because I am not going anywhere without you!"

"Please," I say sadly, "there is something I must tell you."

And so, as you would say in North America, I lay it all out there on the line. I tell them everything, from start to finish. "White Gloves'" death, cigar-smoking Jonathan, the traitorous ambassador, the flight across the St. Lawrence, Marie, Alger Hiss, the trip to West End, even Miss Lucy and her pigs; everything. Aside from a few gasps of shock when I describe the tragedy involving Marie, Yelena and Valentina don't utter a sound. When I finish, we all sit silent, transfixed for the moment. They, attempting to absorb it all, I in fear of their reaction. Valentina stares at me unblinking and wide-eyed. Is this the end for us? I cannot bear the thought of that.

It is Yelena who finally breaks the silence. I fear recrimination for not telling the truth earlier, but receive only concern. "Are you in any danger here?" she asks. She doesn't inquire if she and her sister are in any danger. Her only concern is for me. Her unspoken message very clearly is, "We faced death together before without flinching and I am prepared to do it again!" An incredibly brave and loyal woman.

I don't believe I am in any immediate danger here and tell her so. "I feel guilty for not telling you the truth before this," I admit. "I didn't want to involve either of you in my troubles, but if I had thought even for one moment that there was any real danger, I would never have come here or contacted you and Valentina in any way."

Valentina surprises me with the forcefulness of her response.

Switching into Belarusian, she spits out the words. "Stalin and that bloody murderer Beria can go straight to hell. I am not going back. Never! " She turns to me and says fiercely. "Igor, you know I love you. I loved you the moment I first saw you and I will always love you. I will never leave you, and neither you nor Yelena can make me change my mind. We will leave here and find some place where we will be safe from all the bastard dogs that either Hoover or Stalin can send!" Her eyes are flashing.

I am terribly torn. I would follow this woman to my death, but cannot bear the thought of leading her to her death and I tell her so. "Bah," is her disdainful reply. "I've faced far worse than this before and so have you." She turns to Yelena. "And so have you my sister. We both watched, helpless, as they hanged our brother. That was far worse than death. And we have all seen things that are worse than death; cowardice for one. Love is all that matters, and no threat of death will turn me away from that."

The force and eloquence of her outburst momentarily stuns Yelena and me. We are both seeing something in this young woman we have not seen before nor even suspected.

"Let's all calm down now and think this through," says Yelena, who turns to me with a question. "Does anyone other than the Hollingsworths know you are here, Igor? What about immigration in West End? Did you report in there? Can anyone track you here through official sources?"

I shake my head and tell her about the five British pounds Chris had paid the lone village police officer. Chris didn't even mention the fact that he had a passenger with him and clearly the officer couldn't have cared less. "The answer to your question is, no. For all intents and purposes I never arrived in the Bahamas." I then add, "Why?"

Valentina is watching her sister very closely but says nothing.

"Well," replies Yelena thoughtfully, "there are something like 700 islands in the Bahamian archipelago, many of them very remote, I suppose it would be possible to hide out for years on any number of them, but life there would be very primitive, I am afraid."

An idea is bubbling away in my head, but I don't say anything. I want to hear exactly what Yelena is thinking.

After a brief pause during which she seems to be gathering courage, Yelena says sadly, "We must all understand one thing: If you two decide to defect—to run away and hide someplace—I can't join you. In fact, I have no choice, I will have to return to Moscow."

Valentina cries out in protest, but with a wave of her hand Yelena quiets her. I think I know what she is going to say, yet clearly it has not as yet dawned on Valentina that a decision to flee with me may very well mean she will never see her sister again.

Yelena explains. "If the younger sister of a 'Hero of The Soviet Union' defects with an unknown suitor, the romantic Russian mind can understand and accept that, but if the 'hero' herself turns her back on the Motherland, that is quite another thing. The Kremlin would consider that a terrible insult and cause them to unleash their entire pack of wolves on us all. They would track us to the ends of the earth, drag us all back to Red Square, stage a huge show-trial for all the world to see, then ship us all off to one of their lovely gulags. I have no choice—we have no choice. I must return and present a false face that is sad and angry because my little sister has fallen in love with a young man from America who has spirited her away for a decadent, miserable, capitalist life in California!"

We debate the possibilities and ramifications for several hours. It is clear Valentina is still trying to digest and accept the fact she and her sister will have to part company. I will not say *if* she comes with me, because Valentina makes it very clear her fate lies with me. Any attempt at asking her to reconsider is met with absolute rejection.

Valentina and I spend a mostly sleepless night, tossing and turning and talking. I finally fall into a fitful sleep, but awake with a start shortly after dawn to realize that my lover has left our bed. I panic for a moment until I spot a brief note in large block lettering, which she has left on the kitchen table: "GONE TO FIND A BOAT."

Shortly before noon, Valentina bursts into our apartment, triumphant. "Can we afford fifteen hundred dollars?" she asks, "because if we can, I've found the perfect boat that will take us almost any place in the Bahamas, or for that matter to the United States. With a couple of extra cans of gasoline we could even make it to Cuba, for all I know!"

This woman never ceases to amaze me. Nothing will do but we must immediately set out to examine her "prize".

And a prize it certainly appears to be. According to the owner, a tiny crab-like fellow who is missing most of his left arm, the *Linda* was at one time one of the best rum-runners in the Islands. Built in 1931 by the Indian Lake Boat Company, she is 26 feet long, has a top speed of about 30 knots, which is about 35 miles per hour, "that's fully loaded now" he grins, "with just the two a ya probably hit close to 40, although if I was you I wouldn't open her up full tilt like that, unless of course ya got the whole of the US Coast Guard a-chasin' ya!"

The light is poor inside the boathouse that has been her home for nearly 15 years, but it is easy to see that the *Linda* is indeed a classy lady with clean lines, and a highly polished mahogany hull. What seems strange by today's standards, is that she is fitted with two cockpits. When I inquire about this, the owner gives me a conspiratorial look. "The front cockpit was for me," he says, "the back part is where I kept the money. Ha! Ha!"

The boat has obviously been well cared for over the years. The powerful engine, which occupies the centre section, roars to life at the first push of the starter button as we prepare to take her for a test run. "Don't need this beautiful old girl anymore," says our host rather sadly, "them rum-runnin' days is over." Then, as an after thought, "Kinda wish they wasn't."

Clear of the harbour, he turns the wheel over to me, gives me a few instructions, we push the throttle forward and whip across the waves. Valentina, who has been quiet until now, begins to laugh with the excitement and the possibilities.

I offer him a thousand American dollars. We settle for twelve hundred and he throws in two ten-gallon cans of gasoline and a marine chart of the Bahamian Islands. "A full tank on *Linda* will take you about 100 miles if you keep the speed down to maybe round 12 knots or thereabouts," he says. "Where you headed?" I don't really give him an answer. "Just around, nowhere special." Obviously not a curious man, he's satisfied.

We shake hands, no papers are exchanged, no ownership is handed over. A deal is a deal and a handshake will seal it just fine. Those were vastly different days indeed!

We still have a week before Moscow expects the Mazaniks to return, but now that her mind is made up to defect, Valentina is in a rush to leave.

"The longer we wait, the more chance there is of something going wrong or someone at the Consulate getting wise," she argues. She doesn't seem concerned about our eventual destination, only that we leave Nassau as soon as possible. She has questioned me several times about the destination I have in mind, but when I am vague with an answer she drops the matter. I, on the other hand, understand only too well that the haven I have chosen will require a long and dangerous voyage in a small boat over open water.

As we have been warned several times, this is hurricane season, something that provides additional concern. In fact, our planned departure has to be postponed four days as a vicious hurricane churns up from the Caribbean, crosses through central Cuba and passes only a few miles to the south of New Providence Island. There is very little damage in the Bahamas, but the sea is whipped into a fury that doesn't begin to abate until the storm is well out into the North Atlantic.*

The storm convinces me we need to be very well prepared, so I load the *Linda*'s rear cockpit with two additional ten-gallon cans of gasoline, two life preservers, enough food and water to last us at least four or five days, some blankets, several knives, a large flashlight, two large paddles, a coil of rope, a tool kit and several fishing lines with lures and hooks. I carefully examine all the motor's hoses and belts, and while they seem sound, I manage to track down several feet of replacement hose and two standby belts. At the last minute I locate a chunk of sailcloth large enough to cover the supplies, figuring that if the motor breaks down we can use it to rig up a makeshift sail with the paddles as masts.

My final act of preparation is to carefully tape my gun and a box of ammunition I have been able to buy to the underside of the dashboard, out of sight but within easy reach of anyone at the wheel.

---

* **FACT:** Hurricane #11 started as a tropical storm off the coast of Panama on October 10, 1945, strengthened to a category 2 hurricane (150 km/h) as it crossed Cuba, then veered northeasterly, passing about 62 miles south of New Providence Island before petering out mid-Atlantic on October 16.

The hurricane has dragged a large area of high pressure behind it, bringing clear skies, calm seas, and light winds. The morning of October 17 dawns perfect for anyone courageous, or dumb, enough to take to the high seas in a small boat.

We have all said our goodbyes. Yelena and Valentina spent most of yesterday together, talking, laughing and sometimes crying. Both understood perfectly when I told Yelena I was keeping our destination secret. "That way," I explained, "when they ask you where we went, you can look them square in the eye and truthfully say you don't know."

What I did do was give her Chris Hollingsworth's mailing address and private phone number, with instructions to commit them to memory. "When you can do so safely, write Chris at that address and let him know how he can get in touch with you; if you are really fortunate you may even be able to telephone him at that number, and since by then I will have informed him of our whereabouts he will tell you where we are in such a way that only you and he will understand. Through Chris," I explain, "we can at least keep in contact until a day comes when saner heads take over in both the United States and the Soviet Union."

Both Yelena and Valentina seem a little puzzled by this, but I tell them not to worry, I know how to convey our location to Chris, so he can pass the information on to Yelena in such a way that anyone reading the letters or listening in on a phone conversations won't have the faintest clue what they are writing or talking about. What I have in mind is very simple. Chris and Yelena would understand a destination described as "the island of six pigs!"

And so with dawn just a faint idea in the east, on a glassy sea with the Miami weather station promising light winds and a cloudless sky, we set out for the almost 130 miles of open Atlantic Ocean between Nassau and West End on Grand Bahama Island.

It's too dark for us to see her so we have no way of knowing she is there at the time, but as we pull out of the harbour, Yelena stands on shore with tears pouring down her face watching our lights disappear to the north. For the first time in her life, she drops to her knees and prays. "It was a prayer," she admits years later, "begging God to protect us all from the storms that surely lay ahead!"

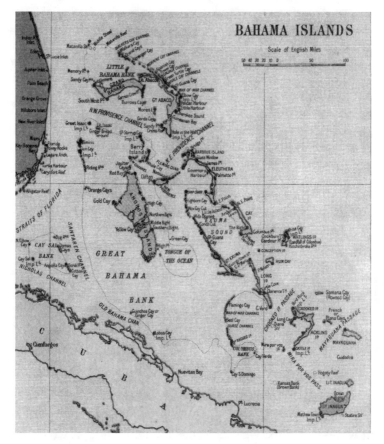

Map of the Bahama Islands

Heaven on Earth

Now, IF I WERE WRITING A SCRIPT for Hollywood, I would paint a picture of a perilous journey through wind and rain and crashing waves. It would include motor failure, being lost in dense fog, maybe even sea monsters or days adrift under a blazing sun.

In fact, our trip is totally lacking in drama. Just as promised, the weather is perfect, virtually no wind, no rain, no fog; instead of giant waves the worst we experience is a light chop as we enter the Gulf Stream; the engine keeps pumping out 12 knots with nary a whimper of protest, the hoses all hold firm and we don't get lost. Well actually that's not quite accurate.

About nine hours out of Nassau, we spot a small rocky island that I immediately suspect from checking our chart is either the southern tip of Abaco Island, well to the east of our destination, or hopefully it is the far eastern end of Grand Bahama. In other words, either our compass is slightly off or the current has pushed us further east than I had factored and instead of coming ashore at the western end of Grand Bahama we are well to the east. Slowing to a crawl and, with the aid of binoculars, examining the distant shoreline of a large island that looms ahead, I determine from the chart that indeed we were at the far eastern end of Grand Bahama.

Valentina is ecstatic. "You mean we've actually made it?" she cries. "This is Grand Bahama? We're safe?" I abandon the wheel for a moment and clasp my hands over my head in a cheer. Together we do the best imitation of a victory dance that our confined quarters allow.

I turn the *Linda*'s nose west, open the throttle, and in a little more than two hours I see Deadman's Reef off our starboard bow as we approach West End. Carefully threading through the reef as I have seen Chris do, we sail around the western tip of the island and before you know it we have pulled into the same tumbledown wharf that provided safe harbour for *Island Wanderer* only a few weeks ago.

News travels fast in West End, and within minutes Lucy comes puffing up, hair and apron flying in all directions, throws her arms around me and almost lifts me off my feet.

Everyone is full of questions and intensely curious about Valentina. "You see," I tell them, "when I told Valentina that West End was heaven on earth, she insisted I drop everything and rush right back here with her!" The claim elicits a few snorts of skepticism but for the most part it's broad smiles all around.

And you know what? It *was* heaven on earth.

For the first few days, we board with one of Lucy's cousins until we locate an abandoned rundown shack overlooking the ocean at the eastern edge of the village. With half of West End's population pitching in to help, during the first weekend we scrub the place from floor to ceiling, and by Sunday night there emerges what Valentina delightedly calls "a little love nest."

Emphasis please on the "little." One small bedroom, one small living room-kitchen combined—but the roof doesn't leak, the floorboards hold our weight, the water pours when we turn on the tap, even if it is only cold, and wonder of wonders, a few days after we move in, a big yellow truck pulls up outside and they hook us up to electricity. Please notice I haven't mentioned a bathroom. In 1945, West End has no sewer system, and outdoor privies are state-of-the-art! Cooking is done outside on a small stove previous tenants have rigged up, utilizing an old oil drum.

Within weeks of our arrival, someone from the nearby native village of Eight Mile Rock begins erecting the island's first hotel to accommodate the increasing number of boaters and fishermen showing up on our shores. I earn a few American dollars, the currency that is far more popular than the British pound, as a carpenter. The hotel, by the way, was later named The Star, and became one of the most famous landmarks on the island, attracting people from all over the world, including movie stars and politicians.*

[There is a brief pause here on the tape, indicating that Igor has rewound it, before he continues.]

Valentina, whose English is letter perfect, spends most mornings volunteering as an English teacher in West End's only school.

---

* **FACT:** Many years later, the Star Hotel was torn down and later replaced by a luxury development called Old Bahama Bay that today is a vacation spot for many celebrities, including movie star John Travolta, whose son Jett tragically died there January 2, 2009.

Afternoons are usually spent riding off on the bicycles we bought, discovering and roaming the multitude of deserted beaches that rim the island. It's our goal to make love on every beach we can find, and during those first happy months we certainly do find a lot! Sometimes two or three in an afternoon!

We learn to fish, gather conch and catch lobster, occasionally from the *Linda*, but mostly we use smaller local fishing boats. The villagers vie for the "honour" of taking us out in their boats and demonstrating some of their fishing techniques. As you can imagine, every man firmly believes that not only are his skills the best but his knowledge of the waters, the reefs, channels and sandbars around the island is superior to all others. As a result we get a kind of crash course in local oceanography.

I'm not sure who started it, but I know why. The natives have great difficulty in pronouncing my first name. No one even attempts Gouzenko, so somewhere along the line Igor starts coming out as Eager and before you know it, because I have a boat of my own, to everyone in West End and beyond I soon become "Captain Eager." Valentina has a boatload of jokes over that one, believe me, and she too begins using the term. She shouldn't have laughed so hard because it's not long until she becomes "Miss Valentine!"

While boating, we soon learn where the safe channels are, along with the sandbars, the rocks and the reefs. Fishing is especially good just off Deadman's Reef and lobsters are so plentiful there in the coral you can often dive a few feet beneath the surface and poke dinner out of a hole with a sharpened stick. Valentina becomes especially adept at this, often catching enough lobsters in two or three dives to supply Aunt Lucy's little restaurant for a week.

Valentina plants a small garden just outside our front step and grows tomatoes, onions, sweet potatoes and peppers, which supplements the pigeon peas, oranges and bananas already on the property. If our money ever runs out, we figure we can survive very well off the land and the ocean.

It is an intensely happy time.

The old fear of being hunted down nags me from time to time. Now that we have electricity, we listen to Miami radio stations, but even by the time the New Year's giant Junkanoo parades and celebrations, with their spectacular papier mâché costumes, cow bells and whistles take over the island, there is still not a peep on the news about either a defection from the Soviet Embassy in Canada, or an espionage ring. It continues to puzzle me, but I become more and more convinced that Jonathan was lying through his teeth when he talked about an "understudy."

The safer and more secure we feel, the more Valentina begins to insist that we somehow get a message to Chris back in Britain, so that if and when Yelena contacts him he can pass along the good news that we are comfortably settled on the "island of six pigs"!

The problem, which I had not anticipated, is that there is not a single telephone as yet on all of Grand Bahama Island. The only outside contact, other than by mail, is via police radio in the communities of West End and Eight Mile Rock. The nearest public phone, we are informed, is in Marsh Harbour on Abaco Island, a good three- to four-hour boat dash from Grand Bahama.

The obvious answer is the mail boat that stops briefly at West End every Tuesday, dropping off supplies, parcels and mail and picking up whatever needs to be shipped to the United States, including mail.

The boat's arrival always creates considerable excitement; sometimes it appears as though half the village descends to the wharf as a welcoming committee, everyone anxious to see what surprises may have arrived. Even advertising flyers or posters are met with great enthusiasm.

Perhaps because the mail boat represents a link with the outside world, the visits begin to make me confront the reality that, as idyllic as this life may be, Valentina and I cannot spend the rest of our lives here. As much as I may try to deny it, we are in effect stranded here, trapped. Each time the mail boat pulls away from the dock, I am left with a growing sense of isolation. One night I dream that Valentina and I are wrapped into a large parcel and mailed to some distant land.

Just as occurred in the Minsk Opera House slave camp, I become determined to somehow escape, not only from this little island, but also from the fate that has turned both of us into fugitives. I am tired of the dark cloud that looms over our heads no matter where we go, and when I finally broach the subject with her, I am surprised to learn that Valentina agrees. "I love it here with you," she says, "but if we can come up with a plan that will put an end to all this hiding then I will be even happier!"

And so together we begin to work out just such a plan.

It takes us two sleepless days and nights to create something we both believe may work. Finally, with Valentina pouring the coffee to keep me awake, I sit down and begin to write.

I don't stop, except for bathroom breaks and food, until I have written virtually everything I have told you in this recording up to that point. It is one of the reasons why today I can recall so many past events with such clarity. Everything that happened to me prior to January 21, 1946, was committed to paper, sometimes by candlelight, in that little house by the ocean. As I write, I firmly believe that in order for our plan to work I must go into great detail, almost as much as I am providing you. If the recipient of these pages is going to help, I'm going to need all the persuasive powers I can muster.

It takes me almost two full days to get it all down; at one point we raid the school for additional writing paper.

Valentina copies many notes for our own records. Notes that assisted me greatly now as I relate my story on tape. Valentina and I have spent many hours comparing memories. She has been a wonderful help to me to make sure my recollections are accurate.

When I finally finish, I write out a short list of instructions, sign it, and then place everything in a small cardboard box, along with an envelope containing most of the information I still have concerning Alger Hiss. We carefully wrap it all, pay the mail boat captain two pounds to affix the proper stamps and address it to Sir Christopher Hollingsworth, House of Lords, Saint Margaret Street, London, England.

Valentina and I stand on shore, clinging in hope to each other as the boat with its precious cargo gradually disappears. Then in contemplative silence we mount our bicycles and pedal home.

We awaken after almost 24 straight hours of sleep and begin preparations for all hell to break loose!

The Chase

RAPID POUNDING ON THE DOOR and a loud whisper rouses us from deep sleep. "Cap'n Eager, Cap'n Eager, Miss Valentine, open de door quick!" It's a frantic Lucy. Heart leaping, I throw open the door and she bursts in, breathless.

"Deys two men lookin' for you," she gasps. "Deys got guns and fancy suits on, pounden on de doors sayin' you bad peoples goin' be arrest! I don like da look a dem. I axe em what you done wrong an deys jist give me de evil eye. One o dem he call me a nigger! Get out o de way nigger, he say!"

It's only eight days since we mailed our plan and our hopes to Chris; has he betrayed us? Oh, dear God, please; not Chris!

"How far away are they?" I ask, "how much time do we have?"

"Bout ten—maybe fifteen—minute. Deys pounden on doors

axeing peoples where you is at but no ones tellin'. Cap'n Eager you gots to git Miss Valentine on yo *Linda* boat and git quick to Abaco, axe fo Hector Bridgewater. Dat my husband. He in Green Turtle Key now. He goan help when you say you a friend ob Lucy."

Quickly, we dress, gather my wallet, our passports and other papers, and kiss Lucy thank you as we race out the door, leap on our bicycles and make a dash for the docks and our boat.

We throw off the *Linda*'s lines as quietly as possible but there is no muffling the sound of our engine as it roars to life and we slowly back away from the wharf and turn east towards Little Abaco. I reach beneath the dashboard, grope for the gun, rip it from its tape fastening and place it on the seat next to me.

There is no warning. The gunboat comes out of nowhere. From its darkened lair the predator springs at its helpless prey. Full throttle, aimed directly at us. Looming huge and black and deadly!

The *Linda* almost leaps out of the water as I ram the throttle forward and spin the wheel left. I don't see enemy faces, only a steel hull tearing past less than a yard away.

I aim for the narrow channel leading out of the harbour swerving hard left to avoid a jagged coral rock that guards the entrance. I'm running without lights, hoping against hope that our pursuer will lose us in the dark, or better yet, run aground on the coral or one of the sandbars that pepper the area.

I've taken this route many times in the past months, but in the dark at full speed I hold our lives in my hands and my memory. One wrong turn, one forgotten obstacle and at this speed we are surely shark food.

By the time our attacker spins around and its captain gets his bearings, we are safely out of the harbour, two or three hundred yards in the lead, but my heart sinks as I realize we don't stand a chance.

A powerful searchlight snaps on, roams the ocean and picks

out our mahogany hull whose reflection shines like a beacon in the night.

As we round the northwestern-most tip of the island gunfire rakes the ocean just to our right. "Get down," I scream! "Hang on!" Desperately I jerk *Linda* to the right, then the left, trying to confuse the gunman who draws ever closer.

The searchlight loses us for a moment or two and the gunfire ceases. I am now well away from shore, headed directly west, towards the Florida coast, but I know we have no hope of reaching it alive. From time to time, by veering suddenly left and then right, I am able to escape for moments the searchlight's beam, but steadily the gunboat gains on us. Death is closing in.

The *Linda* may have been able to outrun patrol boats made 20 years ago, but it's no match for the post-war engines that obviously power this sleek stalking machine moving in for the kill. There's another hail of bullets, several of which I feel thudding into our stern. We're in the ghostly finger of light for a moment, then out, but we cannot escape it.

We have only one chance. Without warning, I suddenly spin the *Linda* 180 degrees and head directly back towards Grand Bahama Island. The attacker is confused at first and the gap between us once again widens to several hundred yards.

The other captain obviously knows his business well, because it takes only a few seconds for the spotlight to find us again. I am now weaving wildly to avoid the gunfire, but a burst sends splinters off the bow just to my left. Valentina, who has been silent to this point, screams.

"Are you all right?" I yell at the top of my voice. But the high-pitched roar of the engines—ours and those from the boat that is now perilously close behind—makes it impossible for me to hear her reply. I can only hope and pray.

And then, I see it. There! Off our port bow. The light guarding Deadman's Reef. I try pushing the throttle even further forward, urging every last ounce of power from *Linda*'s aging pistons and take dead aim at the light.

Like a shark closing in for the kill, the gunboat follows ever closer on our tail. They've stopped shooting. Their intent is clear. They are going to run us down!

Can we make it? Closer…closer…closer. I suddenly realize I am screaming at the top of my lungs. "No! No! Not this time, you bastards! You're not going to get us this time!"

Closer…closer…NOW!!

With the deadly reef less than ten yards away I yank *Linda*'s wheel hard right. Have I gauged it correctly? The stern swings completely around, our propeller pops out of the water, only inches from destruction.

Too late, the gunboat captain realizes his mistake and pays for it with his life.

He probably would have been wiser to throttle back as best he could in the few seconds before the crash, and take the reef head on, but he tries to follow me with a hard right turn. It's a terrible mistake. His boat slams into the reef broadside; caving in the entire left side of the hull and sending him head first onto the jagged rocks.

I throttle back and bring the *Linda* around hard, approach to within a few yards of the crash site, retrieve my gun from the floor where it has fallen, lift a badly shaken, but otherwise unhurt, Valentina back up onto her seat, give her a quick hug and kiss, turn our engine off and listen. The only sound at first is the waves crashing onto Deadman's Reef.

Then we both hear it. A faint cry for help somewhere off to our left. Under different circumstances I would be tempted to let the sharks deal with whoever is out there crying for help, but I desperately need information that only this would-be killer can provide.

The prey is now the hunter!

By the time the dim glow from our flashlight picks him out in the choppy waters, he's almost done. His cries for help are growing weak. "Show me your hands," I shout to him. Slowly his left hand appears above the waves. "Let me see the other hand, or I'm leaving you to the sharks." He's floundering badly by now, the weight of his clothes and boots dragging him down. "I can't lift my right hand," he manages to gasp, "I think my shoulder is broken."

I hand my gun to Valentina. "Here, climb into the rear cockpit," I tell her, "take the gun and if this son of a bitch makes any move—shows any kind of weapon—shoot him in the face!" "Huh," she says, "with pleasure!" She may not know it, but that is exactly what her sister replied when asked if she would help kill Wilhelm Kube: "With pleasure!"

I reach down, grab the drowning man by the front of his jacket and haul him into the cockpit with me. He doesn't appear to be armed, but still Valentina keeps the gun trained on him, inches from his face. He's clutching his right shoulder gasping and moaning.

"What's your name?" I demand.

"Go fuck yourself," he groans.

"Well, Mr. Go Fuck Yourself, it looks to me like you've got a separated shoulder. Tell me your name and I'll fix it for you." There's another groan. "Ray." he says.

Having watched Babunia perform this operation several times back in the Kurapaty forest zimlanka, I think I know what to do. I plant my foot firmly against his ribs, I grasp his right wrist and pull hard. There's a click, a scream, and then silence. Our friend has fainted. I reach inside his sodden jack and extract his wallet and a badge. Ray Douglass it says, FBI Special Investigations, which obviously means "licence to kill."

A splash of water to his face quickly brings him around. His pain has been reduced to a point that he attempts to sit up. I push him down to the floor again as Valentina keeps the gun pointed at his nose.

The incoming tide has the *Linda* rocking vigorously so I have to brace myself as I stand over his sprawled body. Barely controlling my anger, I reach down, grab him by the throat and squeeze hard. "You murdering son of a bitch," I scream in his face, "you didn't come here to make an arrest, you came to kill us just like those other thugs who killed Marie Welch back in Virginia." I squeeze harder. He's gasping now, feebly trying to knock my hands away.

"Tell me who sent you, or by God I will strangle you with my bare hands. Who sent you here? If you're the FBI, then someone must have ordered a kill operation. Who sent you? How did you find us?"

He's on the verge of blacking out so I release my grip on his throat.

"Tell me, you piece of dog shit, or you're a dead man."

"Fuck you," he manages to gasp.

The incongruity of his response almost makes me laugh despite myself but it does serve to calm me down.

"Back to that, are we? I'm going to ask you this one more time or we'll turn you over to the sharks. Whose orders are you following and how did you track us here?"

There's a brief pause as he thinks it over, but it's the same answer that comes back.

"Fuck you!"

I'm tempted to dump him overboard, but I need answers to questions a dead man can't provide.

I have a better idea.

Using fishing line stowed away on board, we tie his hands and feet and with Valentina still holding a gun to Ray's head, I power the

Linda up again and head back to our dock on the other side of the island.

Once into the harbour, we stop at our dock only long enough for Valentina to hand me the gun and hop onto the wharf. I've instructed her to pedal back to our house on her bicycle, which we'd left there after our mad dash to the boat, and grab the shovel from her garden and bring it Bootle Bay Beach, which is about five miles east.

She's a little puzzled at this, but nods her agreement.

The Captive

WITH RAY DOUGLASS TRUSSED UP like a Thanksgiving turkey at my feet, I weave my way, carefully this time, out of the harbour, around the tip of the island where only a few minutes ago we'd been dodging bullets. I swing well out, away from Deadman's Reef, its wreckage and dead man, and in a few minutes I pull into a secluded bay once frequented by a pirate named Bootle.

I know the beach very well—sloping fine sand that allows the beaching of smaller boats like this one.

Our bow safely captured by the sand, I kill the motor and with some effort, manage to drag Ray out of the cockpit and onto the deserted beach.

"What the hell do you think you're doing?" he growls.

Rather pleasantly, I reply, "I'm going to bury you alive!"

"Jesus Christ," he shouts, "you're fucking crazy. You're dealing with the FBI here for Christ's sake; do anything to me and they'll hunt you down like a dog!"

I chuckle for a moment. "Well, Mr. Douglass, exactly how would that be different from what you're doing right now?"

He yells a stream of oaths, even though I point out that there's not a living soul within at least five miles.

Nevertheless, I am worried that perhaps a night stroller might hear something and come to investigate. "Mr. Douglass, if you don't shut up, rather than bury you alive, I'll tie you down on the beach and let the crabs tear you apart."

"Christ," he says, "you're fucking crazy." But he pipes down.

I hear a sound coming down the footpath towards the beach and jam my gun into the side of his head and hiss a warning to keep quiet.

I recognize the distinctive clanking of Valentina's ramshackle bicycle. She's here with the shovel.

I pick a spot beside Ray's head and begin to dig in the wet sand.

I've got a pretty good start on a sizable hole when I pause and tell Ray, "Now, if I were a Nazi, I'd make you dig your own grave before shooting you. But in your case Ray, I've decided a bullet to the back of the head is too easy." I scoop out several more shovelfuls before continuing.

"What I'm doing here Ray, is digging a hole deep enough to bury you up to your neck. Then we'll plop you in there, still tied up nice and neat so you can't wiggle and let the crabs and the tide finish the job. I figure it should only take a couple of hours before you're sucking salt water up your nose, but come to think of it you won't have to worry about that because the crabs will likely have your nose chewed off. Pretty well the rest of your face too! I don't know if you've ever seen Bahamian hermit crabs. They only come out at night. Some of them are almost as big as your head!"

Ray doesn't respond, so I add, "of course we're going to have to get a fair amount of blood from you to leave a trail for the crabs." I turn to Valentina. "Did you bring the knife with you?"

"The sharpest one I could find," she says, playing along.

Ray wriggles a bit on the ground trying to get some circulation back into his legs. "Fuck you both," he says. But by the waver in his voice you can tell the bravado is waning fast.

Another half hour, and the hole is deep enough. Ray tries to struggle and continues to curse us but we have no trouble rolling him over twice and dropping him in. I've guessed very well. He's in up to his Adam's apple.

As I start to shovel the sand back in around him, he starts to shriek. "All right, all right, Jesus Christ, what do you want from me? Stop it! Stop!" he shouts as I continue to dump the sand on him. He's wedged tight up to his belly by now.

I dribble some sand on his head and he starts to sob hysterically. His teeth are chattering.

"Please," he sobs, "I've got two kids, please, what do you want from me?"

I sense Valentina has had almost all of this she can stand, so before she steps in, I drop the shovel and sit down beside this pride of the FBI.

"Who sent you?" I ask. "Who's issuing the orders to kill us?" Ray stops his hysterics. In a defeated voice, he finally says, "Beatty. He's head of special projects."

The name doesn't ring a bell with me. "First name?"

"Jonathan, Jonathan Beatty."

Bingo! The guy I knew as Jonathan Walters!

Just to make sure, I ask, "What's this guy, Beatty, look like?" Ray pauses for a moment and tries to shake some of the sand out of his face. I reach over to help him. "I only actually met him once. Fat guy, smokes terrible cigars." I nod. Ah yes, how well I remember those "special" cigars!

Now comes the crucial question. The question that could decide our fate. "How did you track us down here in the Bahamas?"

Ray is gaining back a bit of confidence and snorts. "That was easy. You left a trail a mile wide. We found the Ford at Keeneland Racetrack, and then checked out local car dealerships. The salesman at the Chrysler dealership remembered you—it was your accent—so we knew about the Imperial. The car was spotted in Charleston, where you made quite an impression on the docks. A tall, blond man with an accent, obviously a landlubber, wanting to venture out in hurricane season was memorable. And, you were seen boarding the *Island Wanderer* by lots of people."

It is the best possible news we could get under the circumstances. Sir Christopher Hollingsworth has not betrayed us! Our plan may still work; in fact, this night's dirty work could very well help us.

A new idea begins to dance in my head!

The Messenger

WE EXTRACT A SUBDUED RAY DOUGLASS from the sand of Bootle Bay and load him aboard the *Linda*. The rising tide has by now almost freed our bullet-pocked boat from the sandy grip of the beach, so slowly I back out a few yards, turn around and head to the other side of the island and our wharf. There we untie his feet and, at gunpoint, frogmarch him through the darkened village to our house where we attach him snuggly to a chair.

He starts to curse at us again, but a good rap on his sore shoulder with the butt of my gun shuts him up.

" Hit the bastard again," suggests Valentina. "He tried to kill us in cold blood. I wonder how many others he's murdered? Probably women and children too!"

Far from being traumatized or cowed by our terrifying brush

with death, Valentina is angry and defiant. Courage is obviously a family trait.

I pull up a chair directly in front of our captive so that we are eye to eye. "Do you have access to Jonathan Beatty?" I ask. Ray nods, "I can contact him, yes."

"All right then, let's get down to business. Here's what you are going to do." I spell it out for him, point by point.

"We are going to send you back to Florida, where you will immediately contact your Mr. Beatty and inform him that within a few days all hell is going to break loose. An American journalist is going to tell the world about a defection from the Soviet Embassy in Ottawa, Canada, and a major espionage ring threatening the national security of both the United States and Canada. There's nothing I can do to stop that now. I'm letting your people know this as a goodwill gesture; a sign of my good intentions if you like, so they can have their actor friend primed and ready to start his performance."

Ray gives a derisive snort that I ignore.

"Then, you tell your friend Mr. Beatty, that he or Mr. Hoover himself had better show up here in West End for a face to face meeting in the next ten days or the whole sorry mess will blow up in their faces."

Ray stares at me through narrowed suspicious eyes and asks, "Who the hell are you anyway? I thought you were Igor Gouzenko!"

I lean my face into his. "Jonathan Beatty and J. Edgar Hoover know bloody well who I am and they also know the grief I can cause them. You tell them both I don't want to reveal their nasty little scheme, but if I have to, I will. You also tell them that if anything happens to me, an accident of any sort, there are others, including a member of the House of Lords in London, who know all about their rotten scheme. More importantly, these friends of mine know where the documents are hidden and they won't hesitate to tell the world exactly what's going on." I wait for him to respond, but he just continues to stare at me as though I'm some kind of madman.

"All right then," I continue, "you tell Jonathan or J. Edgar that they either meet me here without their hired killers or the whole filthy mess will blow up in their faces. Truman seems to me like a guy who will go berserk if any of this hits the newspapers."

Ray still seems to have trouble understanding it all and starts to ask a question. I cut him off.

"By the way," I tell him, "just in case you 'forget' to pass this message along, you should know that Mr. Hoover is going to get a little note from England saying pretty much what I've just told you. But if you wait till they receive that message, everyone will already know about the defection and the spy ring. So you could be in big trouble for not warning them in advance."

It's amazing to see how a man's perspective changes when a death sentence is commuted to mere message conveyer. "That's it?" asks a surprised Ray Douglass. "You're going to let me go? All you want me to do is deliver a message?" There's almost a sneer in his voice.

I stare him down. "Delivering that message may be the only decent thing you've done in your miserable life," I tell him, "it can set two innocent people free, or do you prefer shooting innocent women? Let me tell you something, you rotten excuse for a human being, I know a woman who risked her life to kill a man like you. Blew him up in his bed. That man, just like you, had innocent blood on his hands. He was a Nazi who killed out of hate and ignorance. You—you kill for money and, I suspect, for the fun of it! For the sport!"

Ray knows enough not to reply. Valentina hovers over him with a knife, but rather than plunge it into his black heart, which is what I suspect she wants to do, she severs the cords binding him to the chair.

There's a promise of dawn in the east when we roust Lucy from her bed. To avoid waking the children, we beckon her outside, still in her nightgown.

She's shocked and taken aback when she sees Ray, whose hands are still tied. "Dat de man who call me nigger," she says and spits at his feet.

Valentina calms her down and explains that we want to get this man back to Florida as quickly as possible. "We need someone with a go-fast boat and..." She reaches into Ray's wallet, searches for a moment and pulls out two twenty-dollar bills, a five and three two's. "We can pay, let's see, fifty-one dollars for the trip."

"Geeze," protests Ray, "that's my money, I..." I tell him to shut up and give his shoulder another whack.

Lucy seems delighted to hear the sharp cry of pain.

"For fifty-one dollar," she exclaims, "ole Henry Rolle, he take dis white boy to Cuba!"

Valentina laughs, "No Lucy, we don't want to take him to Cuba, just Florida. How soon can you get Mr. Rolle and his boat going?" Lucy, who has no idea what has preceded all of this, laughs loudly. "We gots light in de sky—fifty one dollah—ole Henry Rolle, he fly!"

And fly old Henry Rolle does. In less than twenty minutes, we see the last of one sorry human being named Ray Douglass.

Half an hour later, after big hugs from Lucy, we're on the way to the boat to get Valentina off the Island, in case anyone else is after me. I am confident that I can stay strong myself, but if anyone was hurting Valentina...well, that would be another story.

All Hell Breaks Loose!

LUCY COMES FLYING OUT OF HER HOUSE, yelling. The soccer ball I ordered almost a month ago has finally arrived with today's mail boat, so I'm in the street kicking it around with a bunch of kids, including all three of hers, when the sound of her voice scares me half to death. "Cap'n Eager, Cap'n Eager, come quick—come, come, come—quick," and she dashes back inside the house. The soccer game comes to a screeching halt as I sprint up the stairs and through the open door. "Listen—quiet—listen!" Lucy bubbles with excitement as she turns up the radio.

I hear only the last part of the story. It's Drew Pearson, the American journalist talking about a giant Soviet espionage ring stealing nuclear secrets from the Manhattan project and the White House. I've missed the part about the defecting cipher clerk in

Canada, but it doesn't matter. We've hit pay dirt! Captain Chris believes our story and has done his job splendidly.

Drew Pearson obviously has all the information we want him to have. The documents concerning Alger Hiss and my notes have done what I hoped and prayed they would do, convince Chris and Mr. Pearson that the defection and espionage story is true.

It is February 3, 1946,* only three days since Jonathan sent a gunboat and its crew out to kill us, eleven days since a mail boat left West End with precious cargo addressed to the House of Lords.

Pearson's concerned voice continues on at length explaining how the defection may have occurred, and he speculates on the possible ramifications. Pearson interviews several military and nuclear experts asking, among other things, if this means the Soviets can now make an atomic bomb. What does this mean for the United States?

"Churchill talked about an iron curtain coming down around the Soviet Union. What risks does this now pose for world peace?" he asks. The experts agree on only one thing—that all hell is likely to break loose.

Even though I've tried to explain the situation to her, Lucy doesn't fully understand what this is all about, but she does know the broadcast is wonderful news for Valentina and me, so she gladly joins in my victory dance around her living room. Actually, I'm

---

* **FACT:** Even though the Gouzenko defection occurred on September 5, 1945, it wasn't until February 3, 1946, that American broadcaster Drew Pearson first broke the story to the public. Two days later, February 5, Canadian Prime Minister Mackenzie King informed his Cabinet that a Soviet espionage ring had been uncovered, but it was not until February 15 that arrests began and the public was officially notified of the Soviet perfidy. There has never been a satisfactory explanation for the more than five-month delay, nor did Drew Pearson ever reveal the source of his information!

laughing, crying and dancing all at the same time, totally unaware of the astonished giggles from the little soccer players gathered around the open door.

Sir Hollingsworth has wasted no time coming to our rescue. Bless him and that wonderful new service—transatlantic airmail!

Wheezing a bit from her exertions, Lucy plunks her generous bottom down in a chair, laughing at our silliness. "Miss Valentine goan be trilled too, Cap'n Eager?" I squat down beside this lovely woman so I can look directly into her eyes. "Yes, Miss Lucy, Miss Valentine is going to be thrilled at this news." Lucy's weathered hands reach out and grasp both of mine as she pulls me closer. "Is your troubles over den? Can Miss Valentine come home from Abaco?" I shake my head no. "Not yet, Miss Lucy, but soon I hope."

I'm feeling a little guilty, though, because I've misled Lucy and everyone in West End, for that matter. Valentina is not in Abaco. We told everyone we were taking her there for a few days' visit, and to further the deceit we pulled out of the harbour heading east towards Abaco, but once out of sight of West End, we swung completely around and headed southwest for Bimini. The reason for our deception is fairly simple. I cannot risk that word of Valentina's real hiding place may leak out, accidentally or otherwise. We must keep it secret, even from Lucy.

Valentina objects strenuously to the idea of leaving West End, demanding to stay with me, but in the end I persuade her that if she was taken hostage she could be used as a weapon against both of us. "Nothing could make me tell them where those documents are hidden," I explain, "except the thought of harm coming to you. I can withstand anything but that!"

Hemmingway Country

NEITHER VALENTINA NOR I KNOW MUCH about the two tiny islands of Bimini southwest of Grand Bahama, just off the southern tip of Florida, but I remember once telling Marie that Ernest Hemmingway wrote parts of his famous novel, *To Have and Have Not* while staying at the Compleat Angler Hotel on North Bimini. The conversation took place shortly after Marie had seen the movie starring Lauren Bacall and Humphrey Bogart and when I told her what I knew about North Bimini and its famous hotel she got a little dreamy and begged me to take her there.

I don't tell Valentina this, of course, only the part about Hemmingway and his favourite hotel.

It turns out to be a pretty modest three-storey building in the heart of Alice Town, on North Bimini, but despite lobby walls plastered with pictures of Ernest Hemmingway hefting giant fish in various poses, the Compleat Angler is only half full. They're delighted to accommodate Valentina for as long as she wishes.

We haven't made it halfway across the lobby on the way to her room when we are accosted by a magnificent specimen of bronzed, heavily muscled manhood, who, with flashing teeth, offers his services as a fishing guide. We decline, but climbing the stairs, Valentina on the step above, gives a delicious little wiggle of that wonderful behind of hers, leers down at me and says, "Now this looks like it could be a really fun place!" I give the wiggle a playful pat of appreciation, and am rewarded with a repeat performance.

There's no time to go beyond the playful patting stage unfortunately. I want to get back to West End before dark. Valentina clings to me as we kiss goodbye. "Promise me you will be safe," she whispers. I hold her tightly and tell her again how sorry I am that she's involved in this, but she won't let me finish. "Damn it," she explodes, "how many times do I have to tell you that the decision to come with you was mine and mine alone? I understood all the risks then and I understand them now, along with all the problems and all the dangers. I don't want to hear this sorry stuff anymore. Hear me? No more sorry stuff!"

I give her my best imitation of a chagrined look. "Sorry!" and I laugh.

She chases me out of the room shouting, "Just for that I'm going fishing tomorrow and I need a guide!"

I have never loved her more, but even as we try to make light of it, we both ask ourselves the same terrible question: "Will we ever see each other again?"

The Rescue

THE EXPERTS WERE CERTAINLY CORRECT. All hell has broken loose. This morning, radio stations up and down the dial are talking about nothing other than the "giant espionage ring" exposed last night by syndicated radio commentator, Drew Pearson. Music programs and daytime "soaps" are pre-empted for the latest news concerning the revelations. Other regular programming is interrupted for a special statement from the White House announcing a complete investigation into reports that spies are operating even within its walls and that of the US Treasury.

Drew Pearson makes another syndicated broadcast claiming he has additional information that he will reveal shortly. I'm not sure what that information might be, since he already has everything I plan to provide. Has he done some independent research? Is he going to tell us what a dirty little weasel Alger Hiss is? That would certainly be nice! Revenge at its best.

The FBI and J. Edgar Hoover are strangely silent, which leads me to speculate they may already be on their way toward West End to meet me and—hopefully—offer a truce.

I keep hoping that somehow the good news has filtered through to Valentina down there in North Bimini. I can just imagine how excited she will be at the prospect of finally being able to lead a normal life and perhaps even see her sister again.

I can tell you now; I had no idea how naive I was! How absolutely, stupidly naive!

Thank God someone knew! Otherwise by the time Hoover and his boys did show up and were through with me, there probably would not have been enough left of my hide and vital organs to provide a decent meal for a shark!

God only knows what they would have done with Valentina. I still shudder to think of what could have happened.

In the Minsk Opera House, heavenly intervention arrived in the form of a broken thorn from a statue of Christ.

In West End, Grand Bahama, salvation again descends from the heavens—this time literally!

I recognize the roar of an airplane immediately. For a brief moment my instinct is to run for cover, but though it passes closely overhead, there are no bombs, no strafing, just two huge pontoons. A seaplane is coming to visit. I've never seen one before.

My heart starts to pound, but I am once again able to summon something from within that has served me well in the past. I pull a curtain of calmness over myself. My heart slows, my breathing is normal. I see and hear things with an almost eerie kind of clarity. All my senses seem heightened. If this is Jonathan or J. Edgar who have just arrived in the plane, it means one of two things: a beginning or an end, the start of a new life for Valentina and me or the end of any kind of life worth living.

As I slowly pedal through the centre of this ragged but delightful little seaside village, towards the harbour where the plane is just now tying up, I notice some things for the first time. Brightly polished conch shells with their deep red lips lined up along Romeo Higgs' porch railing; beautifully flowering bougainvillea running right up to the roof of Carleton's little shed; I forget his last name. And I see where waves have washed away most of the cement block foundation of Jimmy Folly's "Seaside Fish Market". How soon will it tumble into the sea? Am I seeing these things now because I subconsciously sense I will never pass this way again?

I'm about halfway to the harbour when a very excited Tanganyika and two of her little friends come racing up to greet me. Our budding artist is overjoyed to be the one to give me the news. "Captain Eager, there's a man in dat airplane who want to see you. He in one big hurry!"

Only one man? That's strange! Has Jonathan come alone? Would he really have the courage to face me by himself? I doubt it.

I pedal faster.

And there he is waiting anxiously on the wharf. Woolly face and all—Sir Christopher Hollingsworth—as large as life and twice as welcome!

He's got a big smile and an outstretched hand. "Cap'n Eager?" he chuckles, "they call you Cap'n' Eager here? Old boy, how in THEE hell did you get that moniker?"

I laugh with relief as we embrace and I begin to explain, but Chris interrupts, patting me on the shoulder. "Sorry, dear chap, but we don't have a lot of time. Where is Valentina? We need her right now. If you've got any goodbyes to say, better say them now. I wouldn't be surprised if Mr. Hoover isn't already on his way here with a small army with shoot-to-kill orders!"

My face must register shock because Chris gives me a quizzical look.

"You didn't really think that Hoover would be frightened off by your threats of exposure, did you? They want you badly, my boy. You know where the skeletons are hidden and, believe me, they'll get that information out of you so fast your head will spin—that's if you have much of your head left. By the time they finish the first few minutes of their "interrogation," not only will you be begging to tell them where those incriminating documents are hidden, but you'll offer to go get them—that's if you're still able to walk—which I very much doubt! What the FBI and Hoover know about getting people to sing their hearts out would make the Gestapo blush with envy."

He becomes grave, almost sad. "You wouldn't last an hour in their little room of horrors." There's a long pause. "I've heard some of the stories. My information is that Hoover wants both you and Valentina dead. They'll torture you until you tell them where the documents are hidden, at which point the world will never hear of you again.

I've got to be honest with you," he adds, "at first I didn't want anything to do with any of this, too risky, not my business I told my-self, but Rebecca, you remember Miss Becky? Well, when she heard what was going to happen to you and Valentina, she told me flat out, either I come to your rescue or she would never speak to me again, let alone sleep with me. For sure that settled the matter!"

He shakes his head as though trying to dismiss the thought, then adds rather grimly, "I admit to being ashamed of myself for even con-templating washing my hands of the whole affair, pulling a Pontius Pilate so to speak, knowing that they were going to butcher you."

He quickly cheers up. "But that's not going to happen, is it? Here's ole Captain Chris flying off to rescue young Cap'n Eager. Where's Valentina? Let's jump on aboard old Betsy and get the hell out of here."

He's only slightly surprised, but not concerned, about having to drop in on North Bimini to pick up Valentina, but before we leave I have one final task to perform.

Lucy must be out with some fishermen this morning, but Tanganyika is standing on shore, bug-eyed with fascination. She's obviously never seen an airplane before and isn't too sure how safe it is. Don't forget, we are talking about children who not only have never seen a plane up close, but since this is long before television hits the Bahamian airwaves, they have probably never even seen a picture of one.

When she makes it clear she's not going to approach any closer, I jog the length of the wharf to her side and pick her up in my arms.

"Tanganyika," I say, "you tell your momma that I want her to have this boat," and I point towards the *Linda* tied up at a nearby dock. "Tell her Captain Eager wants her to sell the boat to somebody and add it to the other money I gave her to take you to the States. Do you understand that? Maybe it will be enough that she can even take you to Europe some day." She nods gravely and says, "You tole my Momma I goan be a famous artist when I grows up!" I hug her and place her back on shore.

"You *will* be a famous artist when you grow up," I assure her, "but first you must go to school. Do you understand that? You've got to go to school in the United States first."

Her face lights up with a brilliant smile. "I knows dat!"

Chris is anxiously calling me and in a few minutes we taxi out and then, as we bank left and soar over West End, I look down for the last time at our little bit of heaven down here on earth, and see a lovely pigtailed little angel waving goodbye.

Some thirty minutes later, we splash down onto the shining turquoise waters off the coast of North Bimini, taxi in to a small hotel wharf and in a few minutes take off again, this time with the most beautiful and happiest woman in the world on board, still dressed in a damp bathing suit. Chris refuses to give her time to return to the hotel to pick up her clothes. "If Hoover gets wind of what we're doing here," he warns, "I wouldn't put it past that son of a viper to order the navy to shoot us down! We've got to clear out of here *tout de suite!*"

We've paid in advance, so at least we don't—to use American slang—"stiff" Hemmingway's favourite hotel.

The rest, as they say, is history. On February 15, Canadian Prime Minister Mackenzie King and the FBI's J. Edgar Hoover are forced to finally raise the curtain on their sorry little one-act play with the hooded wonder they claim is Igor Gouzenko. Arrests are made, careers are destroyed and, in the case of the Rosenbergs, lives are lost. The Cold War drags on, half the world is building bomb shelters in their backyards. In Ottawa, Prime Minister John Diefenbaker orders construction of an entire underground bunker, dubbed "The Diefenbunker" by the media, to house the government and other key personnel in the event of nuclear war. You can be sure the Americans had something similar, so too the Soviets, but in the end it is the threat of mutually assured destruction, also known as MAD, that probably prevents the world from blowing up. So who knows, maybe all those spies actually did us all a favour.

Chris, bless him, flies us from North Bimini to Jacksonville, Florida. From there, we fly to New York where we catch a new DC-4 transatlantic flight to Gander, Newfoundland, and then across to Shannon, Ireland.

A few weeks and a boat trip later we settle into a lovely little cliffside cottage Chris has located for us. I will refrain from telling you where for several reasons, chief among them being our neighbours' peace of mind. You can imagine that even today some people might not be thrilled to learn that the really nice old couple just up the road a bit was actually spying for the Ruskies or some such thing. "Just think, Alice, we once had them babysit our kids!"

I discover a talent for painting, and find work editing a local newspaper. Valentina gardens and teaches school for nearly thirty years. We marry shortly after our arrival, but never manage to have children. Not that we don't try, mind you.

We sometimes worry that Hoover or Jonathan or even the Ruskies might find us but Chris, bless him again, assures us that he has covered our tracks exceeding well and we learn a bit later that he's also pulled a few strings to help keep the wolves at bay.

Following Glasnost, and in particular after the fall of the Berlin Wall, Yelena visits us frequently. She is appointed to a senior post with the Minsk Public Library* and lives a very quiet but fulfilling life. As the history books will tell you, she passed on a few years ago.

Tanganyika did become a very accomplished sculptor. I was very moved four years ago when I read in the *Times* that one of her creations entitled "Marie" won a major prize at the Paris Arts Festival. That certainly made me smile.

Lucy was appointed one of the chefs at the new Jack Tar Hotel complex they built in West End and lived to a ripe old age. In later years we talked several times on the telephone and she told me that

---

* **FACT:** Yelena Mazanik, or Elena Mazanek as some history books identify her, spent the later part of her life as a Director of the Library of the Belarusian Academy of Sciences in Minsk. I can find no record of her private life and have been unable to determine if she ever married. Other than a brief mention of the fact that Yelena and her younger sister lived together in a bombed-out apartment building in Minsk prior to Kube's death, the history books remain silent concerning the fate of Valentina. There is a reference to the fact that before Yelena would agree to place that water-bottle bomb in Wilhelm Kube's bed, she insisted that Valentina be rescued from Minsk and be kept safe from the Nazis whose retaliation would have been horrific.

only hours after we flew away with Chris, a patrol boat with at least a dozen armed men came looking for me. "Dey was some mad when you was gone," she said. "I invite dem all fo lunch but dat jes make em madder." To this day I remember that beautiful belly laugh of hers when she tells me. "I was goan feed dem bad fish, make dem trow up der guts!"

Chris died 14 years ago, a good friend till the end, and here I must confess something.

In order to protect his children, one of whom has political aspirations, in this narrative I have changed the name of a well-known member of the House of Lords. You may recognize him from the apt description I have painted for you, but the man who rescued us was not named Chris Hollingsworth. This is the only instance in all I have told you here where I have concealed the true identity of someone. I hope you will forgive me. If you have figured out the true identity of the Good Samaritan who saved us, I would ask that you refrain from making it public.

All the Proof You Need!

So THAT IS MY STORY. If you still have doubts as to whether it could be true, let me present final proof that you have all been hoodwinked.

Proof that, incredibly, comes from none other than the man you have been told is Igor Gouzenko himself. A man who put his foot in his mouth on one occasion and as much as admitted to the world he was a faker. Not only did this great imposter slip up, but he did so in print for all to read.

All you doubters please read the autobiographical book authored by the man calling himself Igor Gouzenko. It is entitled *This Was My Choice* and was, from all reports, a best seller. Let me quote, verbatim, the paragraph that almost screams LIAR! LIAR! LIAR!

"I am no hero. Nature seems to allow very few to don the heroic mantle. I was born a very ordinary little man of Russia."

Please, please, listen again!

"I was born a very ordinary little man of Russia."

Those are the exact words of the man claiming to be Igor Gouzenko!

But wait a minute! Igor Gouzenko was not born in Russia! He is not Russian! Igor Gouzenko was born in Belarus. He is Byelorussian! All the history books agree on that. Igor Gouzenko was born January 13, 1919, in Rahachow, about thirty kilometres from Minsk, the capital of Belarus.

Let me assure you, no bona fide citizen of Belarus would ever mistake Belarus for Russia. Russia, under Stalin, treated Byelorussians so brutally, murdering more than a million of my countrymen, that at first many of us welcomed the German invasion.

For anyone who is supposed to have been born in Belarus to maintain he is an "ordinary Russian man," seems to me to be proof positive that he is a liar.

For anyone to make that assertion is tantamount to a Roman Catholic born in Belfast, Ireland, claiming to be British during the 1960s, or a man born in Paris claiming to be German in the 1940s.

Only someone totally unfamiliar with the hatred and distrust between the two countries would possibly make the mistake of calling himself Russian after having been born in Belarus!* It is, however, the kind of mistake that someone born in Montreal without intimate knowledge of Eastern European politics could easily make.

---

* **FACT:** Amazingly, Igor Gouzenko (or the man claiming to be him) does say in his book *This Was My Choice* that he is Russian.

To me, that one paragraph should be all the proof anyone needs to know that either the man you know as Igor Gouzenko was not born in Belarus or he wasn't Igor Gouzenko! What further proof do you need?

And Finally

As I TELL YOU ALL OF THIS, I feel compelled to inform you that Valentina and I are still very much in love, and even though these days she walks with the aid of a cane, she still has the most beautiful little bum in all of Christendom and occasionally I am compelled to pat it. Playfully, of course.

Signing off I am your faithful servant, Igor Gouzenko.

Goodbye

AS I WAS PREPARING THIS BOOK FOR PUBLICATION, I received in the mail an envelope postmarked Glasgow, Scotland, containing the following clipping from *The Scotsman* newspaper, dated October 12, 2009.

> *The West Highlands town of Oban lost one of its most venerable citizens on Monday when well-known local artist Gilles Trudeau died in hospital at the age of 90 after a short illness. Mr. Trudeau, who came to Scotland from the United States shortly after WWII, was highly regarded for his brilliant watercolour portrayals of local scenes, in particular the islands of the Inner Hebrides and the granite mountains of the Morvern peninsula. He is survived by his wife of 63 years, Valentina, who taught school for 27 years in Oban's*

primary system. Funeral services will be held at 2:00 p.m. on
Thursday, October 15, 2009, in St. Columba's Cathedral, Oban.

The accompanying note in a scrawled handwriting says simply,
"I loved him dearly!"

It is signed: Tanganyika

Follow-up

I N AN EFFORT TO VERIFY THE TRUTH of this story, I have made serious efforts to locate two cannons that at one point may have guarded the entrance to the Bull Run National Park in Manassas, Virginia. The park, of course, is still there, exactly as Igor described, but when I visited this historic site recently there was no sign of large cannons at or near the entrance—plenty of cannons but none at the entrance. When I inquired as to their existence, one elderly gentleman who claimed he had lived in nearby Fairfax for the past 52 years told me he remembered at least one such cannon, but had no idea where it might be now.

Requests to various officials concerning the whereabouts or even the existence of two large cannons have been less than helpful.

As well, I have researched the House of Lords membership

during the post-war years and I believe I have discovered the true identity of Sir Christopher Hollingsworth, but in keeping with the wishes of the narrator I will keep silent in that regard. Let me just say, if I am correct concerning Sir Christopher Hollingsworth's true identity, I believe it was not just about keeping him safe from the Russians—or anyone else who may have been after Igor. I suspect Miss Becky was someone other than his wife!

Epilogue

EXPERIENCE HAS TAUGHT ME to be cautious when walking the streets near my downtown office. You never know when the stoned, the drunk, or the just plain loony will consider a guy like me fair game. Always be aware of your surroundings the police warn, it's a dangerous world!

So as I step outside I notice the well dressed man in black slacks and a grey shirt standing there in front of our building, middle-aged—fifty-five, maybe sixty—heavy-set, balding with just a fringe of grey hair, about my height. No alarm bells though until he suddenly steps forward and grabs my arm.

What the hell! But before I can yank my arm free or yell, he stops me cold.

"Gouzenko," he whispers, leaning into my face, still holding my arm. "I know what he told you. It's all true, but he didn't tell you the full story. He doesn't know it. I do." He releases my arm and steps back, waiting for my reaction. I'm so stunned I just stand there speechless for a moment.

I'm finally able to muster up a question. A whole barrage of questions, actually.

"Who the hell are you? What do you mean you know the full story? What full story? How do you know who I've been talking to? What...?"

He interrupts. "Can we go inside? Is there a place where we can talk privately?"

And so there in my office only one day before this book is scheduled to be printed ready to be distributed to bookstores across the country he tells me that for one million dollars he will provide me with the missing part of the Gouzenko story and the documents proving it is all true.

I start to laugh. This guy must take me for a fool! "Sure, sure, a million bucks, what the hell, why not two million? Why not go for three? Let me get my chequebook!"

I stand up to signal goodbye to this bozo.

"I've got the missing Mackenzie King diaries," he says calmly. "They confirm what Gouzenko told you, but that's only a small part of it."

He leans forward, takes my hand and gently pulls me down into my chair again. "The real bombshell in the diaries is the story about the deal they cooked up with Lavrenti Beria."

Now he's really got me intrigued.

"What deal are you talking about?"

He stares at me for a moment without speaking.

I'm about to stand to signal an end to our conversation when he finally replies. "It's all there in those missing pages of the Mackenzie King diaries—the plan to assassinate Stalin!" I give him the raised eyebrows, head snapped back, disbelieving look, but he plunges on.

"What you've got to understand," he explains, "is that the real purpose of the Gouzenko defection, with his list of nuclear spies, was to scare Truman, Churchill and, yes, Mackenzie King enough to get them agree to Hoover's assassination scheme.

"'See,' Hoover told them, 'we warned you Stalin was no friend of ours. Look how he's spying on us. He now knows how to build an atomic bomb and gives every indication he's more than willing to use it. We have no choice. We've got to take care of him. Let's not make the mistake we made with Hitler!'

"Truman and Churchill are finally persuaded largely thanks to the so-called 'Gouzenko defection,' and agree to the assassination. The fact that Mackenzie King is opposed really doesn't matter. The whole thing almost falls apart when Clement Attlee defeats Churchill in the July 1945 British election, but surprisingly it is easier to convince Attlee of the urgency of the matter than it is Churchill."

It's all so fantastic that I start to laugh again.

"And for a million dollars, you'll show me these missing pages and all will be made perfectly clear!" I'm doing my best not to keep laughing but it doesn't seem to disturb him in the least.

"Yes," he says, nodding slightly. "Yes, that's exactly what I am saying."

I decide to play along for a bit. What the heck!

"And just where do you think I'll be able to find a million dollars to hand over to you?"

Now it's his turn to smile. "That's easy. When you include the missing diary pages that confirm Gouzenko's story, as well as documentation proving the plot to kill Stalin, your book will outsell anything Dan Brown ever dreamed up. The millions will come pouring in. All I want is one of those millions, or if you want to sign a deal, I'm prepared to take a share of the profits—say fifty percent!"

I try a different tactic. "And just where did you stumble across these famous missing pages from King's diaries? They just suddenly appear in a dream, did they?"

He shakes his head and refuses to be insulted. "Oh no, nothing dream-like or mysterious. My father was an aide to our old friend J. Edgar Hoover and as such was the FBI's go-to guy when they needed someone to clean up a mess.

"When informed that Mackenzie King is so upset about the idea of killing Stalin that he's discussing it with his dead mother and then writing it all down in his diary, Hoover flies into a rage. 'That damned stupid Canadian Prime Minister is going to start a bloody war,' he shouts to my father, 'kill the son of a bitch, or at the very least rip those pages out of his diary and warn him that if he utters one whisper about this—even to his dog—we'll blow his head off!' Or words to that effect."

He pauses to ask, "Do you want to hear the rest?"

I don't believe a word of it, but it's too good to stop now. "Sure!"

Thus encouraged, he continues. "And so my father arranged the removal of the incriminating material and delivered some kind of warning to King. Believe it or not, Hoover never asked for the pages—he probably didn't want to dirty his hands. I guess he thought they had simply been destroyed. My father, who died last year, kept them in a safety deposit box. I have the key to the box. Simple as that."

This is all so weird I find myself shaking my head. But after listening to those tapes and researching Gouzenko's story for the past year, I have to ask myself, "Is anything normal anymore?"

"So let me get this straight," I say, "if I give you a million dollars, you will provide documentation not only proving that the book

I have just finished is completely true, but will also reveal some kind of plot by the West to assassinate Joseph Stalin? Is that what you're saying here? By the way, I don't even know your name. If I write you a cheque for a million dollars, which by the way I'm not, but if I do, who would I make it out to?"

He waves a hand in a dismissive gesture. "We'll worry about that when the time comes. My name is not important. Do we have a deal?"

I still can't figure out whether this guy is completely nuts or if maybe he does have something that at the very least might provide some interesting dinner-table conversation, so I pump him with a few more questions.

"This plot to bump off Stalin. Who was going to pull the trigger or pop the poison into Uncle Joe's vodka? And, by the way, how did you find out that Gouzenko has been talking to me? Who told you I've been working on a book about it?"

He slowly rises to his feet. "I'm leaving now; I'll call you at your home tomorrow night at eight for your answer. All I will tell you now is that Beria was supposed to be the triggerman. And by the way, it was Beria who, eight years later, finally got around to doing the job and finished off Stalin with rat poison.*

If we strike a deal we'll rock the world with the facts including why it took Beria so long to get the job done. Tomorrow night—eight o'clock."

---

* **FACT:** Stalin died on March 5, 1953, under very suspicious circumstances. Beria boasted that he fed him warfarin, a rat poison that would have produced many of the symptoms Stalin is reputed to have exhibited prior to his death. Beria was killed by his political enemies in December of 1953.

I follow him as he walks out, bombarding him with more questions but he just shakes his head and disappears into a crowd of public servants just released from a nearby government building.

Back in my office, I phone the publisher and tell them to hold off printing my book for a couple days. "I may want to add a few pages." I tell them.

· · ·

As you can imagine, I'm waiting anxiously by the phone the next night, but the only call I get is from someone trying to sell me lawn care. "So I wasted the better part of an hour with a kook," I tell myself. "Oh well, not the first one I've run into and probably not the last."

I think no more of it until I arrive home late the next afternoon and my wife greets me with a strange look and a large brown envelope. "Someone put this in our mailbox while I was out shopping this afternoon," she says. "It wasn't addressed to anyone so I opened it. Tell me the truth, should we be worried?"

Inside is the front page from the morning's edition of the *Manassas Journal Messenger* newspaper. The main story is circled with red ink. My heart pounds as I read:

Police are still trying to identify the body of a middle-aged man found dead on the front lawn of a home on Palm Drive in upscale Oakton, Virginia last night.

While the cause of death is as yet undetermined, foul play is suspected. The body is that of a white male believed to be in his late fifties, approximately five feet ten inches in height, weighing about 200 pounds, balding with graying hair and wearing black slacks with a grey shirt. He carried no identification other than a small diary with the name King scrawled across the torn cover.

Police ask anyone with information relating to this situation to contact them…

Several phone numbers are listed, but I'm shaking so badly they don't register with me.

My wife is staring at me.

"Well," she says, "is it anything to worry about?"

I reply as honestly as I can.

"I don't know. I really don't know!"

Acknowledgements

I would like to thank Wendy O'Keefe and Gail Baird who have spent countless hours working with me on this project. A thank you as well to the ladies of the Wine and Read Book Club for their comments and suggestions and to my friend and lawyer Paul Niebergall, who provided the legal view of bringing dead people back to life. Thanks also for the keen proof-reading eyes of Danya Hernandez. And as always to my wife Deborah, thank you for your guidance, patience, understanding and occasional criticism, without which I would have difficulty getting out of bed in the morning, let alone find the energy to write books.

—Lowell Green

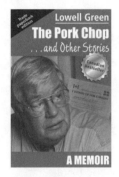